VEGAS

Stormy Souls MC Book 1

BY

Payton Hunter

Copyright © 2022 by Payton Hunter

Second e-book edition June 2022

Book design by
Joetherasakdhi
Editor: Darcie Fisher
PA Tammy Carney

ISBN print
978-1-7385414-1-6

www.paytonhunterauthor.com

ABOUT THE BOOK

This is the book I always wanted to write but never dared to. It is a pure work of fiction, featuring what I love most—badass bikes and the hot men to go with them!

It contains no cheating and a HEA, though there may be backstory elements stretching over several volumes.

All people, places, institutions, and businesses are a work of my imagination, and similarities to real life are coincidental and unintentional.

This is the second edition, fully re-edited and with new content added.

TRIGGER WARNING

This book includes scenes of physical violence, abuse, explicit sexual acts, and strong explicit language. It is not suitable for people under the age of 18 or people with triggers relating to any of the above.

ACKNOWLEDGMENTS

Thank you to my editor, Darcie Fisher. I would not have been able to do this without you.

Thank you to my family and friends for continuously supporting me. Thank you to my PA, Tammy Carney, for your hard work and unwavering support, and Tilya Eloff and Lola Wright for your encouragement.

Special thanks go to Kenty. You and your 44s have been an amazing support.

DEDICATION

This book is dedicated to my best friend, DB.

You have been inspirational and instrumental when throwing ideas around and keeping me on the right path.

CHARACTER LIST STORMY SOULS MC

Road Name	Rank	Name	Old Lady
Raven	President	James Saunders (Jamie)	
Rusty	Vice President	William Greenwood (Bill)	
Slender	Sergeant at Arms	David Brewer (Dave/ David)	
Pennywise	Enforcer	Noah Nixom	
Spen	Treasurer	Spencer Dalington	Debs
Dawg	Secretary	Pete Cooker	Caroline
Clusseaud	Road Captain / event planner		
Ferret	IT Guy		
Vegas	Member	Vincent Albright (Vince)	Ashley
Moggy	Member	Craig Parkers	
Sparks	Member	Jason White	Ally/ Rainbow
Ratchet	Member		
Zippy	Member		
Flakey	Member	Carl Staunton	
Dougal	Member		
Halfpint	Prospect		
Elijah	Prospect		
Greg	Prospect		
Mom	Club mother, mother to Pennywise,	Helen Nixom	

TABLE OF CONTENTS

About the book iii

TRIGGER WARNING iii

Acknowledgments iv

Dedication v

Character List Stormy Souls MC..vi

Prologue - Raven 1

-2- Ash 5

-3- Vegas...11

-4- Ash 17

-5- Vegas...30

-6- Ash 41

-7- Vegas...51

-8- Ash 64

-9- Vegas...78

-10- Ash 84

-11- Vegas...90

-12- Ash 99

-13- Vegas...107

-14- Ash 116

-15- Vegas 128

-16- Ash 135

-17- Vegas 146

-18- Ash 155

-19- Vegas 164

-20- Ash 174

-21- Vegas 184

-22- Ash 193

-23- Vegas 202

-24- Ash 211

-25- Vegas 222

-26- Vegas 232

-27- Ash 244

-28- Vegas 255

-29- Ash 265

-30- Ash 273

Epilogue 282

PROLOGUE - RAVEN

"Who dares?" I growl into my cell. I don't need this at five a.m., especially after only returning from a run at three. This better be good!

"Jamie, sorry to disturb you, but I have to be at work at six, and my car isn't starting." My sister's apologetic voice reaches me, half asleep. I sit up and rub my stubbled chin.

"Can't Nathan help?" I growl, and Ashley sighs.

"He didn't come home last night."

"I'll be there in ten minutes, Ash. Tell Nathan I'll kick his ass for this!"

"Thanks, Jamie, you're the best," Ash replies softly.

Here I am, Raven, President of the Stormy Souls MC and assumed tough nut, going soft for my little sister. I shove my feet in my boots since I didn't bother getting undressed before collapsing into bed a few hours ago, grab my cut and keys to one of the club's cages, and head out. I know she won't ride on the back of my bike. She hates everything to do with the club since her mom, my stepmother, drank herself to death, and our father ended up behind bars for the rest of his life.

Our father is a piece of shit, and I guess he will remain to be until he's six feet under. Hell, even then, he will still be remembered as a fucking bastard. The world will be a better place without Stone in it. First- and second-degree murder convictions saw him incarcerated ten years ago, eight years having been spent on death row in Nebraska. His shit almost cost me, my family. Ashley carries the scars of that day, but thank fuck, she made it out alive. She and Nathan are all that remains of my family. My blood family that is.

Stone, the founding President of the Stormy Souls, groomed me from a young age to follow in his footsteps. When I turned nineteen, I prospected for the club the hard way. The club was a true outlaw 1%er club back then. It was tough, and I don't remember the hazing fondly, but I did my year handling the shittiest jobs imaginable. My patch-in party was epic, not that I remember much of it, and every day since, I've worn my cut and displayed our patch proudly.

Under Stone, we were heavily involved in extortion, prostitution, and gun and drug running. Eventually, Stone turned crazed by greed, resulting in several members ending up in prison or dead and the club almost destroyed. He hadn't even stopped to save his own daughter. She'd have burnt to a crisp had she not run away that night with Nathan. The thought makes me shudder.

But a lot has changed since those days. I became VP under Stone two years before his arrest. After his arrest, the brothers voted me into the top spot, and I put my all into proving myself and changing the club for the better. Enough of our brothers' blood had been spilled.

Slowly, bit by bit, we turned the club around. Now, we're a thriving MC with several successful businesses bringing in good money, and although we're not rich, we no longer have to worry about RICO and the boys in blue. We own a bar, a custom bike garage, a security business, and a tattoo shop in the works.

When the club was started, they bought an old farm on the outskirts of Duluth, in sleepy Arnold, close to Mud Lake. It has a lot of surrounding land and outbuildings, including an old World War II underground bunker we've converted for our use. A large, two-story farmhouse with a full-sized cellar was renovated and now boasts rooms for the

2

members upstairs, a bar and common room, a large industrial kitchen, my office, and, of course, church.

The cellar has been converted into an underground garage with gates and an exit ramp. It serves as our bike, general storage, and a safe room, should we ever need one. The bar and common area are equipped with a giant screen TV, a pool table, sofas, tables, and chairs, as well as lots of free party space. And for our amusement, a pole for the bunnies to use.

The club officers have cabins on the property, each cabin usually shared by two officers. As the President, I have my own cabin. It's a similar size to the others, but I live on my own, so I've converted it into an apartment.

I yawn, rub my gritty eyes, and shake myself out of my tired thoughts as I pull into my sister's driveway. Ashley is standing outside waiting for me. Hopping out of the truck, I walk around and open the passenger door for her. Before I know what hits me, she throws her arms around me and whispers, "Sorry, Jamie. Thank you for coming to the rescue."

I close my arms around her and hug her tight.

"No problem, Ash. I'm always here for you," I grumble into her short black hair before gently pushing her into the truck and climbing in the driver's side. "I'll get one of the prospects to pick your car up, bring it to the garage, and let you know when it's done. I'll send one of the boys to pick you up tonight if it's not finished."

"You look tired. I'm so sorry to drag you out here," Ashley sighs. "Maybe it's time to look for a new car. I don't have a clue what's wrong with it. Any idea who will pick me up?" She looks at me expectantly.

"Likely Elijah or Greg. We're busy, so it'll fall deep into prospect territory." I glance at my sister, who looks as tired as me. "Is Nate being a problem?" I ask.

3

"No, not really. He's just a normal nineteen-year-old, doing his own thing. He stayed at a party last night. All above board, though." I bring the cage to a stop in front of her work, and she leans over to kiss my cheek. "Thanks for doing this, Jamie," she says.

"No problem, sis, any time." I grin at her before putting the truck in gear and head back home to my warm bed. I need a few extra hours of sleep to be able to face the world.

-2- ASH

I watch Jamie drive off and turn to look at my home for the next twelve hours. I love my job, but sometimes I wish I could do more for these kids. Shorter shifts are a close second on my wish list. Spending twelve hours with severely disabled children, going through autism tantrums and Down syndrome communication frustrations, drains me. My heart bleeds for them. Some haven't seen their birth parents in years, having been sent away and forgotten because they can't live up to their parents' expectations. It's heartbreaking.

Working at the residential home fulfills me. I've never regretted moving from waitressing to being a caregiver. I've looked after my little brother, Nathan, from age eight or nine and full-time since our mother died. God knows he struggled with her death and my father's violent nature. Professional help finally sorted him out, and he's now ready to leave for college. A bit later than most, but well on his way to a brighter future . . . without the club.

I'm so relieved he decided not to prospect for the club or get more involved in that life. He's experienced the impact of club life firsthand. I shudder as I push thoughts of the old days aside.

No need to think about that. Not now, not ever.

"Morning!"

5

I turn around and greet Sarah, my co-worker and friend. "Morning, Sarah. How can you be so cheerful at this godforsaken hour?"

"Easy. Leo was a good boy this morning, no tantrums. He's at Grandma's house for the weekend, so I'm child free." She grins at me, and I inwardly groan. It's Friday, so I know where this is going. "So, are you finally going to take me to the club party tomorrow? You've been promising for ages," Sarah states.

"Sarah, you know I don't like the club much, and yes, the parties are awesome, but I'm not feeling it. Can we make it another weekend?" I beg.

"Ashley, I've taken the weekend off and organized childcare for Leo, which you know is almost damn near impossible. So, if you pull out now, I will not only have to slap you but withhold Leo from you for the next five years, and wine club will also be closed to you." Sarah stomps past me up the stairs to the entrance, not looking back. She's pissed. The wine club closure is tough, but not seeing my man, Leo, Sarah's thirteen-year-old autistic son, is too much.

"Okay, okay, you win." I race after her up the steps, and she smiles as we walk in together. Evil woman, she knows precisely how to railroad me. I consider for a split second asking my manager to change my rotation and put me down for different shifts, but Sarah knows my schedule since we work on the same floor. She'd immediately suspect it was me who initiated the change, and that's just not a temper tantrum I can handle. Hence, left with no choice, club party it is.

At least I don't have to dress up or think much about what I'll wear. Jeans and a T-shirt will be appropriate. I ain't looking for anything or anyone, nor would any of the brothers give me a second look. I'm family, after all—the club princess. No one would touch me even if I wanted

6

them to. Raven would go berserk, and they all value their patch too much. No one goes against Raven's edicts.

Besides, I'm not exactly ready for a beauty pageant or anything. Don't get me wrong, I'm okay, but I'm not a stunner. I like my curves, boobs, and hips. They suit me, I think. Most men today prefer super skinny to naturally curvy, and the guys I know, especially the brothers in the MC, are no exception. At five-foot-ten, I'm well proportioned, but model material? Definitely not. I look after myself, take care of my skin, walk ten thousand steps daily, and meditate to maintain a healthy body and mind. I'm happy with myself, inside and outside. Whoever dislikes me doesn't have to look at me. That's my motto.

◊◊◊

Today, I'm working with Belle, a beautiful little blond girl with Down's syndrome. Her almond-shaped, bright green eyes sparkle when she sees me.

"Ash, Belle wuvs you," she screeches, toddling toward me. I catch her in my arms and swing her around. Her screeches hurt my ears, but her giggles warm my heart.

"Love you too, pumpkin." I lean down to kiss her cheek. "Let's get you dressed and ready for breakfast, huh?" I smile at her and swing her around. She nods vigorously, scrambling to get down, then runs ahead of me to her room. At six years old, she normally attends a special school the next town over, but today, we're having a day out.

The home's minibus will take us into Duluth, where we'll go shopping, get her a haircut, have lunch, and then the bus will pick us up after speech therapy at two-thirty this afternoon.

Belle doesn't get out much. Her parents never visit her. Four years ago, her parents signed her up, dropped her off, and haven't been seen since.

I wonder if Belle would even recognize them.

Belle needs help washing and brushing her teeth, so I make sure she manages. All goes swimmingly until we get to the clothes laid out for her.

"No," she shouts and stomps her foot. I roll my eyes.

"What would you like to wear, sweetie?" I ask calmly. She runs to the wardrobe, pulls out every item she can reach, looks at it, and throws it over her shoulder.

"This one!" Her triumphant voice comes out from the bottom of the wardrobe. She turns and holds up a Princess Elsa costume for me to see. I groan, but it's not worth arguing about clothes with Belle because she'll throw a never-ending tantrum and make us late for our appointments. So, reluctantly, I help Belle get dressed, and we enter the dining room for breakfast. Rice puffs and a Pop Tart are already laid out at the table for her. She wolfs down her breakfast and just finishes when the horn of the minibus marks its arrival.

"Come on, princess, let's have an adventure." I smile at her, her hand firmly in mine. Let the fun begin.

◊◊◊

I'm exhausted by the time six p.m. rolls around, having spent hours today trying to get Belle's haircut. The poor salon lady, I felt sorry for her. Belle was so fidgety that even I considered using a trimmer for a crew cut, and my patience is usually endless. This was followed by a tantrum because Belle wanted blue ketchup with her fries for lunch, which had customers leave the diner en-masse, lots of them turning their noses up at us. We can safely say we weren't the most popular customers today. I can giggle about it now, but admittedly, I felt a bit intimidated by the vicious glare from the lady at the next table.

Clothes shopping had to be abandoned. Belle was in no mood to try on anything except pirate costumes. I guess that's a project for my day off over the weekend. The mere thought makes me break out in a sweat, and I think I may have to smuggle the clothes into her wardrobe when she isn't looking.

Speech therapy went well, though. Belle has come along in leaps and bounds. She'll still have to attend for a while, but she's improving slowly.

On our return, she was so tired and overwrought that reasoning with her became impossible. She refused to eat her dinner and snacked on chips and an apple. Good luck to Eve, the night caregiver I handed her over to. I love those kids dearly, but a day like today takes it out of me. I'm desperate to get home, have a long hot bath and a glass of wine, and read my Kindle for a couple of hours before going to bed.

Sarah walks toward me as I see a club truck roll into the parking lot of the care home.

"Hey, missy, what time tomorrow? I'll pick you up." I grit my teeth. She's so chipper and looking forward to the party; I can't really make an excuse without hurting her.

"Seven-thirty will be fine. We can chat, have a drink, and get there before nine."

"Sure thing." She smiles at me, looks at the truck's occupant, and whistles. "Is that hottie going to be there?" Weird. I would have thought that the prospects are pretty young and well out of Sarah's age range. As I look closer at my driver for the night, a hot and cold feeling creeps over me. *Vegas!* Out of all the club members, it had to be Vegas. I still drown in shame when I think about our last accidental meeting.

Get over it already. That was two years ago. I give myself a stern talking to and shake my thoughts out of my mind. Before I can say anything else to Sarah, Vegas jumps out of the truck, stalks around to my side, and opens the door for me.

"Get in. I haven't got all night," he grouches, obviously as pleased to see me as I am to see him. I shrug my shoulders, climb up into the cabin, and roll my window down. Sarah stares open-mouthed at the exchange in front of her.

"Rude or what?" she grumbles, giving Vegas the stink eye. "I'll be at your place at seven-thirty, Ash; no worries, we'll take my car since it doesn't look as though yours is fixed." She waves at me and turns toward her car.

-3- VEGAS

"Ratchet, what the hell did you do with the torque wrench?" Man, it pisses me off when the tools are out of place. I need to finish this cylinder head rebuild so this beauty of a beast can move from the mechanical workshop to the custom build section. But right now, I want to punch Ratchet's pearly whites as he dangles the wrench in front of my face.

"Come and get it, big boy," he taunts.

Ratchet is the other mechanic at the bike shop, though he deals primarily with the custom builds. Sparks and Elijah, the prospect, are placing bets on how long it will take for Ratchet to be on the floor with my hands around his neck. Ratchet isn't tiny, matching my six-foot-four height, but I have the muscle mass over him and the speed of a Whippet. Plus, his age is against him— he's forty to my thirty-four.

"I'll give you a head start, grandpa."

I wipe my hands on my coveralls, which are tied at the waist, and charge after him. It only takes a few moments, and I have him pinned to the floor, the torque wrench by my feet,

11

laughing in his face. "You need to run faster, grandpa," I smirk at him while he struggles to catch his breath with my hands around his neck.

"All right, all right, I'll let you win this time," Ratchet croaks. I get up, offer him my hand, and pull him to his feet.

"Stop gawking, prospect. There's a floor to sweep and parts to de-grease." I growl at a grinning prospect.

Elijah, Eli for short, groans as he hands Sparks a twenty and gets back to work. He's a good kid. He's prospected for nine months and has more than proven his worth. When he first came and asked for a job, I gave him a chance, and he soon found he loved being around the brothers enough to prospect. That's how I came to be his sponsor.

A smack on the back of my head jolts me out of my thoughts.

"I don't pay you for daydreaming." Raven, the club President, glares at me. If I didn't know better, I'd say he's pissed.

"What's up, Prez? To what do I owe the honor of the almighty gift of your presence? Tired of riding your desk? Need a proper job?" I smirk.

"Actually, it's you who will get an extra job. I need you to pick Ashley up from work this evening. Her heap of a car ain't starting again, and I had to get up at five this morning to take her to work. Again! Greg is towing her car to the workshop in town, but they're busy, so it won't be done today," he tells me.

"Can't she use one of the cages?" I ask him. Wanting to do anything but pick her up.

"I'd let her, brother, but we don't have one to spare right now. Zippy has one to get supplies, Ratchet has one to get bike parts this afternoon, and the other is out of action. Only leaves one for you to pick Ashley up in. And I need it back by eight, so Rusty, Ferret, and

Slender can make the security assessment appointment the new bar in town asked for. Rusty's hip is flaring up, and he struggles to walk, never mind ride his trike."

"What time does she need picked up?" I don't let my irk show, but the last thing I want to do is spend time with Ashley in a cage . . . or time with Ashley, period.

"Thanks, Vegas. If you can get her at six, I'll owe you one." Raven throws the cage keys at me, which I catch with ease. "I'll take your bike back for you." I grab my keys and throw them over to him. Letting anyone else ride my baby gives me the creeps, but Raven is the Prez, so I can hardly say no.

It's telling that he asked me, not Rusty, the Vice President. Lately, their relationship seems a little strained. Rusty is of the old generation, having joined under Stone, and finds it hard to keep his nose clean. Figuratively as much as literally. As Raven's father's right-hand man, he supported Raven when he first took over. Although, he never *was* thrilled with the club getting out of extortion and running girls and drugs.

I never agreed with running girls. It's not something I'd want to get involved with. There are plenty of pimps out there, and we don't need to be added to the list. I believe women deserve their own choices and should never be handled unwillingly.

The club girls are different. They give their services freely, occupying the brothers in exchange for free room and board at the clubhouse. They're there because they want to be, not because they have no choice. Some aspire to become old ladies, but that rarely happens. No one wants an old lady who's been fucked by all his brothers.

There have been grumbles lately from the girls about Rusty that he's rough with them. Might keep my eye on him a little for now and maybe speak to Slender, our Sergeant at Arms, and Pennywise, our Enforcer, if more complaints come to light. They can approach the girls about it then.

I don't use the club girls. My tastes are too specific, and my needs are way too dark to inflict on the club girls. When the urge grabs me, I use my membership at Violets, a local members-only BDSM club, to cater to my needs. I don't date, and I prefer to keep my hook-ups private. It's best not to mix business and pleasure, in my opinion.

◊◊◊

It's five-thirty p.m. when I drop my tools and clean up. Just enough time to grab some food at Ally's, the club-owned diner ran by Sparks' old lady, Ally. They're high school sweethearts who have been inseparable for the past ten years or so. She runs a women-only MC—well, it's more of a party club, but nevertheless, it takes commitment. I have deep respect for Ally. She lives life true to her motto: If you can't beat them, join them. And whatever men can do, she can do better.

We call her 'Rainbow' because her hair color changes at least once a month to yet another wild and bright color. Carrying a few extra pounds doesn't take away from the beautiful person she is, inside and out. She and Sparks live over the diner, which means extra security for the diner and a short commute for Sparks, as it's only a block down from the workshop.

Ally is a whizz in the kitchen and the best manager we've ever had. We can count ourselves lucky to have her. Ally's is renowned for its great food and sassy service, and it's

14

always packed with customers. We have a reserved Souls booth, which other patrons never use, so finding a seat is easy. I walk in, throw Ally a grin, and take a seat. She saunters over.

"Hey, Vegas, what can I get you? The usual?" She asks me with a wink.

"Hi, Rainbow. I see it's sunshine yellow today." I point to her again changed hair color— a blinding bright yellow. Smirking at her, I pull my shades out and put them on, which earns me a slap on the back of my head, drawing a chuckle from me.

"Can I have the double stacked with fries and coffee, please, sweetheart?"

"For you, sure… Anything!" She smiles, giving me a middle finger wave, then turns and goes behind the counter to start my order. Ally has sass in spades, which is one reason we all love her so much. She takes no crap from anyone, gets straight to the point, and stands up for herself.

I look at my cell while waiting for my food. There's a message from Violets with an updated events calendar, but nothing else. My stomach growls as Ally brings the food. The smell is just amazing. She knows me so well that she even put some onion rings on my plate.

"Thanks, darlin'," I tell her as I dive in and groan with pleasure as the juices from the burger hit my taste buds.

My phone alarm goes off at five-fifty p.m. Just managing to finish my feast, I get up, grab my keys, and wave to Ally on the way out.

Here we go. One white knight in a black truck to the rescue of the club princess coming right up! Sarcasm is my middle name.

◊◊◊

I pull into the parking lot and see Ash waiting at the bottom of the stairs, chatting with another girl. Well, she's more woman than girl. I've not met her before, but she seems older than Ash. She's short and plump, and her long, curly red hair and fire-engine red glasses make her stand out even more. Not what I'd call subtle. She and Ash have their heads together, chatting.

Might as well get this over with. I jump out, walk to the passenger side, open her door, and growl. "Get in; I haven't got all night."

Red's mouth drops open as she shoots me an evil look. Ashley climbs in the truck, and I shut the door, returning to the driver's side. When Ashley rolls down the window, I hear Red saying, "Rude or what?"

I smirk. Was I rude? Sure, but that will keep conversation to a minimum. I stop listening, put the truck in reverse, and get the hell out of Dodge. I need to get her highness home, swap this cage for my bike, and ride home. Home, not the clubhouse, but my home.

-4- ASH

I'm fuming, despite a good night's sleep. Being furious makes it challenging to think of anything else. To calm down, I pour myself a cup of wakey juice—strong, black, with one sweetener—and sit at the kitchen island, taking deep, calming breaths.

To say the journey with Vegas yesterday took place in awkward silence is putting it mildly. I'd never been so glad to get out of a truck in my whole life. Who does Vegas think he is? Someone special?

Oh, you are so wrong, Mister! I hope his pompous ass blows out a tire, and he catches an STD from the club whores. Not at all over the top, Ashley, not at all!

My phone vibrates on the island. I pick it up and check. Sarah.

Sarah: How are you this beautiful morning?

Me: Fine!

Sarah: Liar, what's up?

Me: Nothing, I'm fine

Sarah: OOOOKAY then . . . Next question–what to wear tonight?

Me: Do we have to, Sarah? I'm really not feeling it.

Sarah: Oh yes, you party pooper, we have to! Remember, Leo privileges are at stake for you here!

Me: Alright, alright! Nothing too dressy. I'll be in jeans and a tee with my knee-high boots.

Sarah: So nothing too dressy? I'll see what I can come up with. Anything I need to know?

Me: I'll give you a bit of background on etiquette before we go. The dos and don'ts.

I switch my screen and ringer off and start cleaning. This is my regular thing to do on a weekend off—I do a deep clean. Nathan is back this afternoon to pack his stuff for college. He's getting everything ready to leave tomorrow morning. Jamie is taking him to settle him in, so it will not be a late night for me tonight since I'll have to be up in the morning by seven.

Jamie turns up at eight to load up the truck. The house is smelling lovely since I have finished all the housework; I decide to go for a walk.

I'd love to walk at Lake Mud, one of my favorite places, but not having a car; the local park will have to do. I meander around the green space, watching children play soccer on the grass, lost in my thoughts.

◊◊◊

Two years earlier . . .

I wish this shift was over. My feet are hurting, and Violet's is crowded for a Friday evening. I need to find another job. Way too many weirdos here. I don't get why people get such a kick out of being dominated, being led around on a leash, calling someone 'Master,' or getting strapped to what looks like an oversized railway crossing sign. And this is just what goes on in plain sight of the bar. What was I thinking? Let's hope the caregiver job at the disabled children's home comes through after my interview on Monday. I can't wait to get out of here.

18

Oh my god, is that Vegas walking toward me? No, no, no, no, no! Raven will go mad if he finds out I'm working in a BDSM club, even if it is only behind the bar and waitressing. Shit, I need to hide! Letting the other bar staff know I'm taking my break, I run for the staff room. He won't be able to see me there. What the hell? Vegas? In Violets? I thought he was getting serviced by the club girls.

After thirty minutes, I need to get back behind the bar. I cautiously peek into the bar area and can't see Vegas. Maybe he left? My relief escapes as a sigh. Safe for now.

I serve some customers at the end of the bar with a smile. When I turn around, a pair of steely gray eyes bore into mine. My knees turn to jelly. "A Maker's Mark, please. And open a tab."

That was not a drink order; that was a command. Who does he think he is? More to the point, why, oh why, does it send a tingle down my spine and cause my panties to dampen? Why do I want to reply with a demure 'yes, Sir'? My thoughts are racing as I fix his whiskey and put it in front of him, and I can feel my cheeks burn.

"Ashley, what are you doing here? This isn't a place for you." *Unbelievable!*

"And what, pray tell, Vegas, is the place for me? Let me guess, sitting at home, twiddling my thumbs, maybe doing a bit of light quilting? I got news for you—rent doesn't pay itself. Us normal people have to work for our money. We don't get club accommodations." *My chest is heaving with barely constrained anger.* "Did you get permission from your Prez to be out on your own?" *I spit out at him.*

"Whoa, whoa, chica, keep your hair on. I was just saying this doesn't seem like your kind of entertainment. And did you ask my Prez what he thought about you working here?" *Vegas smirks at me, winks, and then turns his back to me, surveying the main room in front of him.*

He looks good in tight black jeans and a black button-down shirt, the top three buttons undone, showing his tattooed skin. I can't help but stare at his butt. It looks fantastic and makes me want to inspect what's happening in the front. His Viking features and dirty blond hair tied in a top knot do things for me that shouldn't be allowed.

He checks his phone and looks toward the door. A beautiful redhead in a red corset walks straight toward him, and I can see his posture change. He stands straighter, his body tightens as he turns toward her, and I can see that all smirking has left him. He looks stern. The beautiful woman falls to her knees in front of him, her palms on her thighs.

"Good evening, Master; I hope I didn't keep you waiting."

"Did I give you permission to speak, pet?" he growls at the woman, who dutifully lowers her eyes.

"No, Sir, I'm sorry."

"Your absolute obedience is required," he adds sharply.

As he leads her to the main room, I watch in astonishment. I had no idea Vegas is a member, nor did I have any clue that he's a Dom with a submissive. He blindfolds her and begins to flog her slowly as he ties her to the cross. He stops and leans in, talking to her, and she nods and replies, then he steps back and uses the flogger harder.

I turn around, half embarrassed, half turned on. I'd never thought this kind of thing could excite me. But then, I have zero experience since my V-card is still firmly in my pocket. Raven would have his nose in my business if I attempted to rid myself of it. Not that there hasn't been interest from men but raising Nathan and looking after myself is hard work. Raven offered to pay for Nathan and me, but the last thing I want is to accept money from a club that I hate, the club that landed my father on death row and my mother in an early grave.

My father going down, wrecked her. She started drinking and was probably on something as well. She lost her way, made dumb decisions, and left me holding Nathan. I have no time for fooling around, dating, or giving my V-card away. I work for our livelihood, stay away from the club as much as possible, and relish my independence. In a few years, Nathan will have finished school and started college; then, I can live a little.

As I turn around again to face patrons at the bar, my eye finds Vegas. He's looking straight at me with his mouth on her, his eyes locked on mine, and a slight smirk appears on his face. My breath comes faster, and I feel flush. I can't do this with him here. I turn to my co-worker.

"Jane, I'm not feeling well. I need to go home. I think I'm coming down with something."

"Sure, Ash, no problem. The biggest rush is over anyway, so I can manage. Let me know when you get home. I'll worry otherwise."

"Okay, Jane, see you tomorrow."

"See how you feel, Ash. I'll ask Suzie if she can cover for you. So call in tomorrow at lunchtime and let me know, okay?" I nod, turn to grab my jacket, and leave. I jump in my old Honda Civic, praying it will start and not let me down.

As I park in front of the house and walk up to the door, my ears are assaulted by Nathan blasting Nirvana through the stereo to a point where the windows are rattling. Taking a deep, calming breath, I exhale slowly, walk through the door, kick off my shoes, and go straight into the front room, which, as usual, sits abandoned. Nathan must be in his room. Dog tired and wound up, I turn down the stereo and get ready for bed, trying to push thoughts of that sexy biker out of my mind.

A little girl shrieking with laughter breaks my musings and pulls me back to reality. I was so absorbed in my thoughts that I didn't even realize I sat on a bench and was staring into space. Better get back home if I'm gonna fit in a relaxing bath before Sarah turns up. I jog back to the house and find Nathan packing in his room. There are boxes upon boxes in the hallway, ready to be picked up in the morning.

It'll be strange not having Nathan around every day. He's been accepted at the University of Minnesota to study computer science, systems analysis, and criminology, of all things. His dream is to work as a forensic computer specialist, though I'm not sure what that entails. It's all a bit too technical for me. As long as he's happy, that's all that matters.

I knock on his door. "Nate, I'm gonna take a bath. I'm taking Sarah to the clubhouse for the party tonight. Do you want to come along?"

"No way! I have too much to do. James will be here early, and you know what he's like if I keep him waiting. You have fun, sis. Don't do anything I wouldn't do," he says, chuckling. He refuses to call Raven by his road name. To Nathan, he'll always be his big brother, James.

◊◊◊

Hearing Sarah's classic Beetle turn into the drive, I open the front door for her. Seven-thirty on the dot. If nothing else, she's punctual. I watch her get out of the antiquity, and my jaw drops. Did she not get the memo about casual dress? A tight red dress shows off her voluptuous figure, and she's piled her hair into a messy bun high on her head, errand tendrils of her red locks

22

framing her face. She looks stunning. And those shoes! Six-inch, red suede Manolos . . . in a biker clubhouse! Staring at her in shock, I inwardly groan, imagining all the bikers with their tongues hanging out. And here, I thought we could stay unnoticed. Suddenly, I feel woefully underdressed. I feel like a fish out of water in my tight black jeans, knee-high low-heeled black leather boots, and Rolling Stones cold shoulder T-shirt.

"Wow, I feel overdressed," mutters Sarah while taking me in.

"I told you, it's not dressy. We're talking about bikers here, loud rock music, beer, and whiskey. Come in; coffee's ready in the pot." Sarah takes her shoes off by the door, plops herself on one of the oversized couches, and sighs happily.

"This thing is so comfortable."

"Thanks, that's why I bought them." I grin, handing Sarah her cup.

"Okay, so what gives? You'll have to prep me. I've never been to a biker party." Sarah leans forward, waiting for me to give her the lowdown.

"Okay, so, for starters, all the family members bring a food contribution to the Saturday parties. I prepared a large salad, bought a couple of pies at Ally's, and made a humongous amount of garlic bread. There'll be a BBQ with all the food outside in a gazebo. Everyone just helps themselves."

"Who cooks all the food?" Sarah gives me a quizzical look.

"The old ladies will be Ally, Debs, and Helen, Pennywise's mother, who everyone calls 'Mom' since she's like a mother to all the guys. Sometimes visitors bring food, too. If Auntie Ellen and her husband, Laffo, are there, she'll bring rolls or something like that to go with the BBQ since Laffo delivers bread for a living when he's not partying. The club bunnies are supposed to, but we're all better off if they don't. Food isn't their strong point. Last time, Ebony made prawn salad, and lots of people got sick," I grimace as I recall that horrific scene.

"Club bunnies? What on Earth is that? I thought of rabbits, pets, but I presume that's not the case."

I'm laughing so hard that I cough. Pets . . . that's a hilarious thought!

"Oh god, I can't breathe," I manage between bouts of laughter. "Club bunnies are girls who live at the clubhouse. They . . . shall we say service . . . the guys, take care of their physical needs, and for that, they get free room and board. Before you ask, they're there voluntarily. Some would like to bag an old man, but that rarely happens. Others just like the sex and the variety. They all have their own reasons for being there." Sarah looks at me, red-cheeked and embarrassed.

"Are you trying to tell me they get laid by bikers for a living?" I snicker at her and continue.

"Yes, that's exactly what it means. That's what club bunnies do. A lot of the guys are single and real man whores. They call them 'club pussy'. But saying that, the ones with old ladies treat women, especially theirs, with a huge amount of respect."

Sarah wrinkles her nose. "How old do you have to be to be an old lady, and how old are the old men? Is there anyone under fifty? Sounds like a league of old folks. I work as a caregiver, but not for the elderly," she grumbles, laughing even harder after I'd just calmed myself.

"An old lady is the biker term for a committed girlfriend. Being an old lady is like being married in the citizen world. Bikers are picky and don't claim someone as their old lady unless they're one hundred percent sure they've found the one to spend the rest of their lives with. It's an honor to be an old lady. Those men are no angels, far from it, but when they love, they love hard, fast, and true. They can be crazy protective of their old ladies and families."

"Well, Ash, that doesn't sound so scary then." Sarah giggles.

"When we get there, let me introduce you to the old ladies first, Sarah, and we stick with them. That makes it clear to everyone where we belong and will keep unwanted attention at bay. Of course, you can talk to anyone, but remember, these guys can be rough around the edges. I'll introduce you to some of the nicer ones. Just stick with the old ladies and me, and you'll be fine," I reassure her.

"Don't you dare leave me alone. Can I borrow some jeans and a T-shirt, please?" she begs.

"Sorry, hon, no time to get changed, and you're a different size than me. Your backside is bigger and your legs shorter, so my jeans won't fit." I shoot her an amused glance. "Come on, kiddo, let's do this. Grab the salad bowl for me, and I'll grab the pies and the garlic bread. Let's go, let's go!" I usher her first into the kitchen to grab everything and then out the door. We struggle to fit everything in the backseat of her Beetle, but at last, we're on the road. I turn the radio on to drown out Sarah's incessant chatter on the way. She's nervous, and I would rather be anywhere else but here.

◊◊◊

We pull in fifteen minutes later; the parking lot is so full it's almost bursting, so we park by the gate near the bikes. Half-pint and Eli, two of the prospects, are on gate duty tonight. I clear the spot with them, and Eli offers a hand with taking the food out of the car and to the gazebo near the BBQ. I'm grateful for his help, as Sarah, in her six-inch heels, will struggle walking on the rough ground outside. She totters after us, swearing when her heels get stuck in the grass. Eli and I exchange a smirk, and I roll my eyes.

"She won't wear those shoes again. Lesson learned; I think." I grin at Eli, and he nods and chuckles in response.

"Good to see you, Ashley. You haven't been around much lately. How's work?"

"Busy, busy, Eli. How's prospecting? Any closer to finishing yet?" I tease. He groans, puts the salad and pie he was carrying on the table, and mock salutes me before making his way back to the gate. I look behind me and see Sarah has nearly caught up. More than one pair of eyes follows her progress. Dougal and Sparks are busy with the BBQ, but as soon as they spot me, they come over and wrap me in bear hugs.

"Ash, so good to see you. Where have you been? My heart's broken; I missed you so much," Sparks banters.

"Leave her alone. She's *my* princess," says Dougal as he mock-headlocks Sparks.

"You just wait 'til I tell Ally you hit on me. Your life won't be worth living," I tease him.

"Oh, no, please don't." He coughs. "I like my balls where they are, thank you very much." I smile at the two wackos, then I turn and introduce Sarah, who's staring at us open-mouthed.

"Sparks, Dougal, this is Sarah, my friend from work. Sarah, these two idiots are Dougal and Sparks."

"Welcome to the crazy, Sarah," Dougal greets her.

Sparks sends a pleading look at her. "Please don't tell on my flirting, or I'll have to sleep on the couch again," he begs, causing Sarah to giggle.

26

"I like these two," she states, pointing at them, less nervous now.

"Are you hitting on my sister? Do I need to give them a beating, princess?" Raven snuck up on us with no one noticing, and I'm sure he was a ninja in a former life. I throw myself at him.

"Hey, big bro, so good to see you. Handsome as always. They've been behaving themselves. No beating needed. *Yet.*" I smile up at him. I love my big brother. He single-handedly turned this club around and got them out of all the illegal stuff they were doing while Mom was alive and before Dad went to prison.

"Is Nathan all packed up?" he asks.

"Yup, he was just finishing up when I left the house. There are boxes everywhere. Do you think he'll be alright?" I have to ask because it's bothering me that Nathan will be away from home, even if it isn't too far away.

"Ash, stop worrying. He's almost a grown-up and can look after himself. He'll be fine." Raven gives me a tight squeeze. I know he's right. "Hey, Sarah, nice to see you." He and Sarah had met before when Raven picked me up from work. She gives him a little wave, just watching the interactions between all of us. We've all known each other for most of our lives, so the banter is second nature.

I watch Rusty approach, limping on his crutches. He's seedy, brash, and deeply unpleasant, and he's given me the creeps for years. He's a dodgy character, but he's Raven's VP, so I stay out of his way and have nothing to do with him.

"Come on, let's go, Sarah. I need a drink." Linking my arm with hers, we walk toward the clubhouse, and I nod to Rusty on my way past. He just ignores me, which is fine.

Inside, the room is busting at the seams. I see Auntie Ellen and Laffo on the dance floor amongst a throng of other people and spot Ally and Debs at a table in a quieter corner. I pull a couple of chairs over and plop down, and Sarah follows my example.

"Hello, ladies." I grin at them. Ally hugs me across the table, and so does Debs.

"Who's your friend?" Ally questions.

"This, ladies, is Sarah, my friend and partner in crime at work. It's her first club party, so be nice," I tease them. "Sarah, this yellow-haired ray of sunshine here is Ally, Sparks' old lady. You met him by the BBQ. This here is Debs, Spen's old lady. I haven't seen him yet, so I'll introduce you to him later."

"I hope Sparks behaved, or do I need to make him sleep on the couch again?" Ally asks with a twinkle in her eye.

"No, he was well behaved, I promise." Sarah winks at Ally. "Oh my god, how do you survive with all this hot man meat around you?" Sarah asks with slightly glazed-over eyes.

Debs giggles and fills her in. "Years of practice builds some immunity, and hey, we can enjoy the view, even if we can't touch."

"Anyone want something from the bar?" I stand to make my way over.

"Let's do shots!" Ally shouts excitedly.

"Tequila!" adds Sarah.

"And aspirin," Debs states with resignation on her face.

The bar is mad busy as I wait to be served. Poor Greg is trying to keep up but is failing miserably. Just then, I spot Mom and Vegas arriving to help Greg. I'm hoping Vegas serves on the other side and am in luck when Mom spots me and comes over.

"Hey, Ash, long time no see. How are you, sweetheart?"

"Hi, Mom, I'm fine, thanks. Nervous about Nathan leaving for college tomorrow but fine otherwise. We need to get together and go for lunch to catch up." She nods in agreement.

"What can I get you, hon?" I give my order, and in no time, a tray with three tequila shots and a Coke is in front of me. One of us has to be the designated driver because there is no way I'm staying here.

"Hello, my lovelies, so good to see you." An excited Caroline comes rushing over, hugging Ally and the rest of us. Ally does the honors of introducing Sarah.

"Caroline, this is Sarah, Ashley's friend. Sarah, this is Caroline, Dawg's old lady. They only recently joined us. Dawg is Nomad but has been here for three months now. Looks like he may be growing attached to this group of reprobates." Ally laughs, and Caroline nods vigorously.

"I think he wants to catch Raven tonight to see if there's a chance of patching in." She smiles and bounces excitedly in her seat.

"Well, if you're staying, do you want to join me and the girls? The Wild Pixies would be glad to have you. I know you ride more than you use a car." Ally winks. "It's not like a male MC. We go to rallies, have fun, ride out together, are there for each other, and, if need be, protect each other."

"That sounds great, Ally. I'm in, providing we can stay."

Caroline is a lovely person and a fab fit for the Wild Pixies. She told me she and Dawg go to many rallies whenever possible, and they ride on their own bike every day. She *will* ride on the back of Dawg's bike for Souls Rides MC rides or functions and when required but prefers to be her own woman. It wouldn't surprise me if she loved her custom Sportster more than Dawg. I smirk to myself. She's good people, and I like her.

29

-5- VEGAS

The clubhouse is crammed with people. They spill out into the front yard, where picnic tables are scattered around, lit fire pits, and a BBQ farther down. Most of our members mill around, apart from the prospects who man the bar and gate. I raise my hand to greet three of the hang-around Rod, Laffo, and Auntie Ellen, standing by the BBQ. Laffo is in deep conversation with Dougal, Sparks, and Ferret, while Helen is chatting with Ally. Their cackling drifts over on the light breeze. It's good to see they're enjoying themselves. Laffo and Auntie Ellen are close friends. He's chairman of one of the local party clubs and attends every rally or event possible with Auntie Ellen as his tried-and-true sidekick.

Raven appears next to me and slaps my back.

"Church at ten in the morning, sharp!" I nod and put my arm around Ebony, who has sidled up to me.

"You look as though you could do with a distraction," she says as she eagerly smiles at me, running her hand over my arm.

"Not tonight, sugar. Maybe next time. Go find another brother to help." I hug her quickly and place a quick kiss on her cheek. She's a good girl and not as pushy as some of the other bunnies. Her dark skin is flawless; she has ample tits and ass and a sunny, friendly disposition.

Cute and nice are always a bonus. I smile, watching her meandering up to Flakey, who looks like he could do with a pick-me-up.

Rusty makes his way over to me.

"What do you need, VP?" He never approaches me unless he wants something.

"Help in the bar, Vegas. One of the staff hasn't turned up, and they're close to rioting in there." He sounds panicked.

"Okay, I'll see if I can persuade Mom to give me a hand, too." I turn on my heel and jog toward the clubhouse. I'll do anything not to have to deal with his ass. I know he's my brother and VP, but I never got along with him. He's a smarmy bastard and way too much into the old days and Stone for my liking.

The heat and noise hit me as I make my way to the bar. I stride past the bar and walk into the kitchen, where Mom is usually found. Mom is Pennywise's mother, and she's been an integral part of the Souls family for what feels like forever. Her old man got killed in a shootout under Stone's reign, and now we look after her as much as she looks after us. She's the club's momma, always helping, cooking our meals, monitoring the bunnies, and ensuring the place is shipshape. She reigns with love but also an iron fist. I, for one, never want to get on her bad side.

f

I find her just out the back door, smoking her roll-up. No one's allowed to smoke in the kitchen. Mom's number one rule, and she reigns supreme, so no one would dare go against her. Her tongue can be razor-sharp.

"What are you after, you handsome devil?" Her eyes twinkle with mirth.

"Rusty ordered me to bar duty. One of the bar staff didn't turn up, and the prospect can't cope on his own. Would you be willing to help with the bar?" I put my most pleading look on my face. I'm not beyond begging.

"Sure, son, we'll have it shipshape in twenty minutes between us." Ha, she obviously hasn't seen the state of the bar.

"I bet you we won't. I reckon it'll take us more like forty minutes." She can't resist a bet, so I throw it out there.

"Okay, you're on! You're on dish duty the entire week if we clear it in twenty, and I'll give you twenty dollars if it takes longer than thirty minutes to clear the bar." I look away, hiding a smirk while we make our way to the bar. It didn't pass my notice that she paled slightly when she saw the lines of rowdy folks shouting for beers. We get to work, and the crowd gets calmer with every beer handed out. Crisis averted.

"Thanks, man," Greg mumbles. "I was losing my shit."

"No thanks needed. We'll be alright," I reassure him. Greg is one of the newer prospects, still finding his feet a bit. He seems like a nice guy and hasn't messed up majorly yet. The brothers like him, and he looks to be good prospect material.

Thirty-five minutes later, with a twenty begrudgingly slapped in my hand, the crowds have thinned, and I can take a breather. I can hear the roaring laughter from the old ladies' table all the way over here. I saw Ash when we went behind the bar. Man, she's hot in those jeans and knee-high boots, and she has curves in all the right places. She has no idea how hot she is, which is a beautiful thing.

I'm flooded with memories of her with fewer clothes on, and my cock is at half-mast instantly. *Fuck.* She's the Prez's sister, and Raven would kill me if I made a move. I know she hates the club. She wouldn't look at me twice, but right now, I find it difficult to ignore my body's reaction. I blame it on the overuse of my hand lately and no visits to Violets.

I'm about to turn and walk over to Pennywise, my best friend of many years, and often partner in crime when it comes to pranking the brothers, when Red, Ash's co-worker, waves at me and toddles up to the bar. She's clearly had one too many.

"Hey, rude dude, I remember you from the parking lot. Four tequilas, a Coke, and water, please." She smiles while swaying gently, holding onto the bar for support. I ignore the snide comment and pour her drinks as Dougal comes up next to her.

"Vegas," he shouts over the noise, lifting two fingers to indicate he wants two beers, so I slide them over to him. Just at that exact moment, Red loses her balance and topples over. I'm too far away and can't stop her, but Dougal drops his beers and catches her at the last second.

"Whoa there, pretty mama. Throw yourself at me like that, and people will start talking." He winks at her, and I attempt to hide my grin. She flushes bright red and starts stuttering.

"Err, thanks . . . I think. Err, hi, I'm Sarah and . . . I'm a *little* drunk. S-sorry to have ruined your beers. Let me get you new ones."

"No need, pretty mama, all in a day's work. Always happy to assist a lady." Dougal ramps up the flirt. I swear he'd bat his eyelashes right about now if he was a chick. Good man because who can blame him?

"Hey, brother, who's this pretty chick? Is she yours?" asks Rusty, who's quite loaded. I turn and roll my eyes. "Can I buy you a drink?" he smarms. Dougal places himself between Rusty and Red, who I now know is named Sarah.

"The lady is talking to me. Go annoy someone else." Dougal smiles, but it doesn't reach his eyes, and his tone is steel. Sarah steps around Dougal.

33

"Hi, I'm Sarah, Ashley's friend. Pleased to meet you. And who are you?"

"Oh, are you with Ashley?" He smiles at Sarah, but I don't like his tone. It sounds seedy and winds me up.

"Rusty Darling. I'm the Vice President of these rejects." He puffs out his chest, then turns to me. "A vodka for me and whatever she's having," he orders, nodding toward Sarah. I catch Dougal leaning into her, quietly talking to her and switching glances between her and Rusty. Her smile falters for a moment; then, she nods tightly at Doug.

"There you go, sweetheart." Rusty hands her the freshly poured tequila and flashes his brightest smile at her. Creepy, if you ask me. Sarah thanks him and turns to go with her tray in both hands.

"Here, let me." Dougal takes the tray and steps aside to let her walk past. At that moment, I spot Rusty taking his crutch and lifting Sarah's dress up to her waist.

"Really?" I hiss at him. "Was that necessary? If she tells anyone, your ass is toast, and I'll be the one who'll kick it."

"Let me tell you something, *brother*. I'm the VP. You will *not* disrespect me like that again, or I'll have to bring it up in church and put your loyalty up for discussion." His face is red with anger, and beads of sweat are pearling on his forehead. He pushes his finger in my face, and I really want to snap it off. What a piece of shit! I feel Mom's hand on my arm.

"Vegas, can you come over and give me a hand a second?" She gestures for me to follow her. I'm seething. At the other end of the bar, she collars me. "He's not worth it, boy. He's always been a slimy, self-absorbed prick. Over the years, he's gotten worse. I know you want to smash his face in, but don't give him that satisfaction. He'll take it to the table; you know he

34

will. He isn't worth your trouble, son." She smiles and pats my cheek. "Now, go on and spend your winnings. We're fine here now."

I return her warm smile and meander over to Dougal, who is now sitting with Dawg. Dawg glances at me, my stormy mood obvious.

"Someone needs to put that fucker down." He scowls, looking me straight in the eye, giving me a chin lift. Dawg is a Nomad, but he's been with us for three months. He's an excellent brother, and I'm hoping he'll stay.

"Man, I tried to warn her. He's a brother and the VP but mostly a cunt. Good thing she was too drunk to notice," Dougal spits out, his voice dripping with venom.

This is not how things are done here. We respect women—well, most of us do, Rusty aside. We protect and treat them well. None of us would ever lay a hand on one nor make unwanted advances. We're rough and tough around the edges, but we don't take what isn't willingly given. For bikers, we have a moral code.

I keep my eye on Rusty as he wobbles over to the old ladies' table. It's too far away to make out what he says, but I can see the way he sneers at Ashley, which makes my blood boil. He whispers something to Sarah, and I've never seen a woman—especially a drunk one—jump out of her chair so fast in my entire life. Before Rusty can react, she slaps him across his face, leaving a red handprint.

"You dirty old bastard," she screeches at him. The club goes silent, and all eyes turn to the old ladies' table. Dawg, Sparks, and Spen make their way over. "If you're fucking ass ever touches me again, I swear I'll put a bullet in your fucked up leg before I slice your dick off," she yells. The pussycat has claws and a roar. I secretly try not to laugh.

"What the fuck is going on?" A pissed-off Raven steps in the middle of the action.

"This swine here," Sarah starts, pointing at Rusty, "only made sure everyone knows what my underwear looks like. He's a freaking pervert." Sarah is vibrating with fury as Ashley stands and grabs her arm.

"Come on, Sarah, let's go," she mutters, keeping her eyes downcast and leading Sarah outside. I can't help but feel uneasy, but I'm in no position to get involved.

"VP, my office, now!" Prez is furious. He waves at Slender, our Sergeant at Arms, and all three disappear into the office.

Giving Dawg and Dougal a chin lift, I grab my keys, walk outside, and cock my leg over my bike. I let her roar and ride home, my mind still on that incident and how Rusty sneered at Ashley.

◊◊◊

Pressing the button as I come up the drive, the gate to my house and garage door both open automatically. I ride into the garage, turn off the engine, and activate the button that brings the door rattling down. I get off my bike and pat her tank. I love this girl. Sleek and powerful, the guys and me built her in our shop. Entirely black and chrome, she's got the club insignia airbrushed on both sides of the tank. I stick my helmet on the bench. Strictly speaking, I don't have to wear one, and on scorching days, I often wear just a wraparound, but I usually value my head more than anything. I look around at my collection of bikes. My big tourer is in its space, waiting to be used for long runs, and my dirt bike really needs a good run out. My F-450 is parked next to them. Why have so many rides? Because I can. Having choices is my prerogative.

I open the door to the main house and switch off the garage lights, making my way to the front door to disarm my beeping alarm. When I bought this house with the money my gran left me, I saw it as an investment. Now, it's my peaceful haven. The club doesn't know much about my place. They know I have a place of my own but not where it is or what it looks like. I like to keep my private affairs private.

Kicking my boots off by the door, I hang my cut on its hanger with my jacket and move to the kitchen. There are beers in the fridge, and after tonight, I need one. I walk through the archway separating the kitchen from the large, open living area. Throwing myself onto the leather sofa facing the large screen TV that hangs over the fireplace, I flick through channels with the remote.

Covering my eyes with my arm, I only half-listen to whatever is playing. My thoughts keep going back to Ashley and Sarah. I admire how Sarah handled herself tonight. That woman has spunk. Ashley, however, worries me. She looked uncomfortable and intimidated. I could feel the anxiety radiating off her in waves. Why is Rusty causing that reaction? Yes, he's an asshole, but I can't imagine why she's so scared of him. She hunched her shoulders, making herself look small whenever he's around. It's not the first time I've noticed. Maybe I should ask if she's alright.

Why am I even thinking about her? Why do I suddenly feel so protective of her? She's my Prez's kid sister, and he'd kill me if I got too close. Annoyed with myself, I take a long pull of my beer. As I close my eyes, I picture her in tight jeans and high boots, that t-shirt showing off her tits. My cock throbs at the thought. I sigh and release my throbbing hard-on. It needs relief.

I picture Ash undressing for me, her t-shirt first, showing off her flawless skin. Her bra follows, and I can hardly resist putting my mouth on those pebbled buds. My hand grips my cock tight and slowly strokes up and down. I can feel the pre-cum oozing from the head. I need her mouth laving it, blowing my mind. Popping her button, I peel her out of her jeans and boots. She stands in front of me in just a black lacy thong, which drives me crazy. She smiles at me.

"Come and get it, handsome." I can't believe she said that. In a swift move, I sit on the bed, pull her over my knee, and rub the round globes of her ass. She gasps, and I can feel her heat and smell her arousal. She likes this. I lift my hand and land a swift smack on each cheek, and she groans in pleasure. I can see her skin flushing, and I hiss, speeding up my strokes, feeling the pressure build at the bottom of my spine and my balls tightening.

Throwing Ash on the bed, I spread her milky thighs. I can't wait to taste her. My tongue runs from one end of her entrance to the other. She tastes amazing. I flick her hard nub with my tongue, and she's writhing on the bed. I suck her clit into my mouth, my finger deep inside her, and I can feel her tightening. She comes screaming my name. My balls pull up tight, and I explode into my hand, panting. Grabbing a tissue from the box on the table, I clean myself up, no less frustrated than before. These hand jobs just don't do it anymore. I need more. However, that little fantasy I just had was amazing.

I finish my beer, trying to shake my thoughts back into shape and not think about her. It'll never happen. She's too good for me. I'm rough and hard around the edges and have dark sexual tastes. Ashley would run away from me in a heartbeat, just like she did when she saw me with Olivia. Olivia was my long-time sub; we'd played together for a few years, but then she wanted more to make it a more permanent and mainstream relationship. Olivia was a great sub,

38

but I had no interest in anything more, so we parted ways over a year ago. Since then, I haven't bothered with another sub.

I play at Violet's when I'm invited, but I act as a room monitor when I'm there, ensuring everyone playing is safe. I was shocked to find Ashley working behind the bar at Violet's' She looked flustered and embarrassed but sexy in her short black lace dress. She made me hard then, so I played harder with Olivia, but my thoughts were on Ash. I must be mad or have a death wish or something. I've thought about her for as long as I can remember, but I know better than to show those thoughts in front of my brothers. I'll be a dead man walking if I do.

◊◊◊

It's late, and church starts at ten in the morning. Yawning, I make my way to my ensuite bathroom, take a quick shower, and go to bed. I set my alarm for eight. That's plenty of time to get ready and get there before the meeting starts.

I sit up in bed with a start around one a.m. My phone is flashing, and when I open it, I have had three missed calls. As I'm checking who they're from, it goes off again. 'Prez' flashes on the display.

"Yeah," I growl.

"For fuck's sake, what took you so long?" Prez sounds agitated. "Get your ass to the hospital, now! I'll catch you at the entrance."

Jumping out of bed, I throw on my clothes and chuck on my boots; I put on my jacket, cut, and make my way to the garage. I'm on the bike and out of the garage in less than five minutes, reaching the hospital in record time. Raven is waiting by the main door.

"At last," he grumbles. "Flakey is in the emergency room. They're working on him."

"What happened?" I'm stunned. He looked okay earlier when he took Ebony upstairs. As we walk into the waiting area, Raven catches me up on what happened. Sarah and Ashley are sitting there looking very pale with the old ladies. The whole club is here to support Flakey. Everyone but Rusty.

-6- ASH

Coming out today proved to be a great idea. I needed this more than I realized. A good laugh and catching up with the old ladies is just what the doctor ordered. Ally is a hoot. She's had the entire table roaring with stories from rallies with her club and from the bakery. Caroline fits right in. They've attended many of the same rallies, and it's a miracle they haven't run into each other before.

Sarah looks happy, if a little glassy-eyed, but that's what five tequilas do to you. She's in her element, joining the conversation and laughing. Her anxiety about her age and looks are forgotten. She outwardly seems brash and loud sometimes, but in reality, she's hiding her insecurities. I know she's worried about her age and about going through the change. Menopause frightens her. She suffers from hot flushes at work, needing to go outside or stand by an open window. There was the initial panic when her period didn't show up, and she thought she was pregnant. And the mood swings. She feels old and crusty most of the time and battles with her mortality.

Then there's Leo, her beautiful teenage boy who she's been a single mother to since he was born. He's autistic, and it took until two years ago to get him diagnosed. Before that, he was merely labeled a naughty, disruptive child whom teachers couldn't cope with. He'd been

41

expelled several times from different schools. She brought Leo to work two years ago after he'd been expelled yet again. Our manager pulled strings to get him the proper assessment he needed, and life has improved for them ever since he was properly diagnosed. Leo is now getting the help he needs, going to a special school where he has all the support necessary, and our boss accepted him into the day center. He's thriving in his new environment. He'll never be like other children, but he is making friends and better able to make sense of his surroundings.

It's been tough on Sarah. Being at home with Leo and working is pretty much all she does if you don't count our weekly get-together. Playing with Leo comes easy to me. Sarah and I watch a movie at her place and usually seek comfort in a large tub of Ben and Jerry's and a bottle of wine. That's why I don't mind being the designated driver and letting her have fun. She deserves this.

I don't feel comfortable drinking here, anyway—too many eyes on me. Jamie frequently looks over and grins at me. Rusty looks too, but he sneers.

I caught Vegas looking over several times with an unreadable look on his face, making me very self-conscious. Every time my eyes wander over to the bar, his eyes bore into mine. The heat in them makes my entire body tingle.

I don't have a clue as to why I react so much to the way he looks at me. Maybe it should scare or repulse me. After all, I had seen him in action years ago. I turn my eyes to Sarah, who is currently singing along with AC/DC's "*Dirty Deeds*," and I'm amazed at how good she is. She knows it word for word and has a crazy good voice.

"Wow," Ally silently mouths in my direction. Caroline's mouth is hanging open in surprise; Debs claps her hands, hollering in support. Ally wolf-whistles, and so do some of the members. I catch Dougal eyeing Sarah from the doorway as he makes his way over to the bar.

The song ends with more clapping and wolf whistles. Sarah stands, takes a mock bow to the room, and shouts, "Tequila!"

It's wonderful to see her relaxed, having fun, and meeting new people like this. She sways slightly as she stands, and it's clear she's happily drunk. "Alright, girls, I'll get them. It's my turn."

I watch her tottering, swaying slightly as she makes her way to the bar. From the other side of the room, I notice Rusty leering at her; his eyes firmly focused on her tits. Sarah is well endowed in the boob department. His expression gives me the creeps, and I shudder. Ally follows my eyes.

"God, he's a creep. I know he's a brother, but he needs put in his place," she mumbles loud enough for Debs and me to hear.

"Tell me about it," says Debs. "Spen hates him and has forbidden me to wear skirts or dresses to the clubhouse."

"He's right. Sparks won't let me wear dresses either, not that I often do unless it's a wedding, but Rusty has a reputation amongst the members. Not sure why Raven does nothing, it probably has something to do with the perv being old school, going back to the time of the dinosaurs." Ally doesn't mention Stone's name since she knows how much that affects me, but it's who she meant.

"He's been VP for a long time and has supported Raven when he took over the reins. He's like the foul stench mold—lingering so long, you just can't get rid of it." Ally's observation is very accurate.

Sparks would never talk club business with her, as she doesn't talk club business with him where the Pixies are concerned. Over the years, it's caused friction, yet I believe she has a

43

very valid point here. I hate that animal. We have ancient history that no one else is aware of, not even Jamie. Rusty threatened me, and I'm not the forgiving type, but I stay out of his way as much as possible.

"Oh, my god," Ally whispers. "Did you just see that?" I look at her, puzzled. I see Sarah tottering over to us with Dougal following her. He's carrying her tray for her, a grim look on his face. Sarah is smiling. "He just did it again to Sarah. I'm going over there and knock his teeth out!" Ally is furious, fuming.

Turning to look at the bar, I notice Rusty and Vegas glaring at each other. Then Mom pulls Vegas away to the other end of the bar, and I release a relieved breath. A fight isn't what I need to see. Sarah retakes her seat, still laughing.

"Don't," Dougal grates at Ally, who is standing now. "Sit down, leave it alone. I'll take it to church," he growls at her. Ally nods and sits, and the table goes quiet.

"Come on, what's up? Someone die or something?" Sarah giggles. "I thought we were here to have fun. Oh man, this is great; we have to do this again in town. Let's exchange numbers, and we'll have a girls' night out." She grins around the table. Numbers exchanged, and we return to talking, but Ally and I exchange worried glances. Once Rusty sets his sights on something, he's like a dog with a bone and won't let it go.

Our worries are confirmed when he appears next to Sarah, crutches in hand, and whispers something in her ear. I can only make out the word 'lace,' and the music drowns the rest out. Sarah nearly topples the table over when she jumps up.

Before he can react, she wallops him right across his face, her red handprint in stark contrast to his pasty skin.

"You dirty old bastard," she screeches at him. The club goes silent, and all eyes turn to our table, with Dawg, Sparks, and Spen making their way over to us, standing close to Ally, Debs, and Caroline.

"If you're fucking ass ever touches me again, I swear I'll put a bullet in your fucked up leg before I slice your dick off," Sarah screams.

"What the fuck is going on?" My pissed-off brother steps between Sarah and Rusty, facing Sarah.

"This swine here," she points at Rusty, "made sure everyone knows what my underwear looks like. He's a freaking pervert." Sarah is vibrating with fury. Jamie turns to look at Rusty.

"VP, my office! *NOW!*" He storms off to his office, and Rusty follows him but not before he glares at me. Jamie waves Slender over, indicating for him to follow, and they all disappear into the office. Sarah is heaving with fury, her eyes blazing.

"Someone spit out what happened," she says, suddenly sounding very sober. Ally looks at me and sighs.

"When you turned around at the bar, he lifted your skirt with his crutch to your waist." she cannot look Sarah in the eye as she's telling her. Sarah turns to Dougal, who is still standing there.

"And *you* . . . you didn't do a thing to stop him." She's seething. "Nice one. Thanks for the carry of the tray. You can fuck off now and annoy someone else." Dougal gives her a hard stare, clearly wanting to say something but thinking better of it. He turns and walks back to the bar, shaking his head.

I stand and take Sarah's arm. Best to get out of here now that we've had enough drama for one night. Why can't anything ever just go like clockwork?

45

"Come on, Sarah, let's go," I mutter in the now silent room, leading her outside. She follows me out but then pulls me to stop.

"No! I refuse to let that asshole spoil my night. I was having a good time, and I like the other girls. If I leave now, he wins, and I'm not having that," she argues. I sigh, knowing when I'm beaten.

"Let's take a little walk around the back to cool off." She nods at my suggestion, and we start walking to the back of the property, where the cabins are and sit on the grass at the back of the clubhouse. Breathing deeply to try to calm down, I understand why she doesn't want to leave, but that glare from Rusty really unsettled me, and right now, I wish I was anywhere else but here.

I can still hear his voice inside my head and see the vile gleam in his eyes, even after all these years. *'Keep your mouth shut, or your smile won't be as pretty anymore.'*

The cool night air calms us, but my unsettled feeling remains. After ten minutes, I look at Sarah and ask, "Ready to go back inside?"

Sarah stands and nods, holding out her hand and pulling me up. We return to the table, which is now much quieter. The mood in the room seems subdued. The club girls are nowhere to be seen, Dawg and Dougal are standing at the bar talking, and the music is much quieter now. I don't see Vegas. Maybe he's in the kitchen. But why do I even care?

"Sorry, Sarah, I should have told you as soon as you got back to the table, but I didn't want to upset you." Ally smiles apologetically.

"He does that with every woman. That's why Spen doesn't allow me to wear skirts or dresses at club events anymore," Debs chimes in.

"What a dick. He needs a be beat down or tossed out," Caroline states, looking angry. "That would not have been tolerated anywhere else we've been, never mind the founding charter."

Sarah looks around, shrugging her shoulders. "Let's not give him the power to ruin our night. I refuse to do that. Others have tried and failed to intimidate me, and he's no different. Come on, whose turn to get rounds is it?" She grins at all of us.

Caroline smirks. "I'll get it. I need to check in with my old man at the bar anyway." We watch her saunter over and wrap her arms around Dawg from behind. He turns, wraps her in his arms, and places a loving kiss on her head. She kisses him full-on, and, Jesus, those two emit some heat. We're all watching, fanning ourselves.

"I need a cold shower now." Sarah laughs, and we all start giggling, the earlier drama forgotten.

"Yup, these men are hot, hot, hot. Lava hot in bed, for sure." Ally throws a cheeky grin toward us all.

"Go on, *do* tell, is Sparks average? Or packing?" Debs asks, giggling.

"I'll give you his measurements if you give me Spen's." Ally playfully slaps Deb's shoulder. "But then you'd only be jealous."

I groan and roll my eyes. The booze is clearly talking, and by the looks of Dawg and Caroline, it will make some clothes fall off any minute now. Seeing them so obviously in love and lust is nice, and it warms my jaded heart.

A piercing scream rips me out of my thoughts, and every head whips toward where the noise is coming from. Ebony is on the stairs, tears streaming down her face.

47

"Help! Help! Flakey collapsed, and he's bleeding everywhere!" The door to the office opens, and Slender and Jamie burst out. I look at Sarah, and we nod at each other. Sarah takes her shoes off, sprints to the stairs, and I follow her close behind her. Being trained in First Aid through work, if we can help, we will. Sarah shouts at Ebony to lead the way, and we run after her.

She opens Flakey's door, where he's sprawled out on the floor unconscious, blood everywhere. He retches, and more blood bubbles out of his mouth. On instinct, Sarah and I jump in and turn him on his side so he doesn't choke. Sarah feels for a pulse.

"His heart is beating way too fast, and his breathing is too rapid." She looks at me, and I turn to Jamie.

"Call 9-1-1! *Now!*" I order, and Slender makes the call as Jamie tries to find out what happened.

All Ebony repeats over and over is that Flakey was fucking her from behind, then he suddenly stopped, threw up blood, and collapsed on the floor. That's when she ran to us for help. Sarah and I are watching Flakey closely, but there's nothing else we can do. At last, the ambulance arrives, and the paramedics load him onto a stretcher and carry him out to the vehicle. The guys all get on their bikes, and Sarah and I follow the ambulance to the Emergency Room in her car.

Almost the entire club has turned out. Relieved to see that Rusty is absent, I don't question why, just count myself lucky. Worried about Flakey, I blame myself for not noticing him being sick. He seemed tired earlier but perked right up when Ebony gave him her attention. Flakey is one of the quieter guys, liked by all, and always willing to help anyone and everyone.

Everyone is on edge, me included, so I stand, walk to the coffee machine, and begin to grab coffee for everyone. Sarah, Ally, and Debs join me to help carry it all.

The wait seems endless, and the guys are pacing back and forth. All eyes turn to the ER door as it opens, and a nurse approaches.

"James Saunders?" Jamie steps forward. "Mr. Staunton is awake now, and the doctor will see you in a minute." A sigh of relief goes around the club. So, we wait some more.

The doctor steps into the waiting room. "Mr. Saunders?"

"Raven. No one calls me by my given name."

"Well, I had to go from the next of kin information, and Mr. Staunton listed you as his next of kin."

Ally leans toward me and whispers, "Doesn't he have family? Someone we should notify?"

"No, there isn't anyone," I whisper back, shrugging my shoulders.

The doc continues talking to Jamie. "He lost a lot of blood. We're giving him a transfusion right now. We need to run more tests to find out the reasons for the bleeding. It could be a stomach ulcer, or it could be something else. We're keeping him here, anyway. Could you have his personal things brought in?"

My brother nods. "Of course. When can we see him?"

"We're just helping him clean up. When we are done, you can see him for a few minutes. He'll be on the floor tomorrow. The front desk will tell you where he's moved to and the visiting hours."

An audible sigh of relief and the sound of the brothers backslapping each other travels through the waiting area. People slowly disperse until only Jamie, Vegas, Sarah, and I are left.

"Vegas, you stay here in case he needs anything. I'll let the doc know." Vegas nods and gets comfortable on the seats in the waiting room. He looks tired and runs his hands over his stubbled chin. The stubble suits him, adding to the handsome features of his face. His eyes catch mine, and a little smirk plays around his lips—the lips I want on mine so badly.

Oh my god, where did that come from? I shake my head at myself in disgust. *Ashley Saunders, stop this right now. He's not for you. The man is a member of the club. He's bad news, and Raven would kill both of us. It can't happen.* My thoughts ran away from me for a second. Sarah yawns. We're exhausted now that the adrenalin rush has worn off.

"Raven, you can go in and see him now," a nurse calls out, but I grab his arm.

"I'll see him tomorrow. I'm heading out, so have someone drop his stuff by my house. I'll relieve Vegas. I'll be here about nine in the morning. I know you have church." He nods gratefully.

"Get yourself home, sis. Thanks for everything you and Sarah did tonight. The club owes you."

"Nonsense," Sarah pipes up, "we did what we could, and we would've done the same for anyone. You don't owe us a thing." I nod in total agreement. We make our way out of the waiting area as Jamie walks in to see Flakey. Vegas nods as we leave, but I can feel his eyes burning a hole in the back of my head. The sense of him watching me is intense.

-7- VEGAS

I stare at the clock in the waiting room, and the hands don't seem to move. At three a.m., I have a long night ahead of me. Raven left a few minutes ago, and I'm waiting for someone to come and get me once they've found a bed on a floor for Flakey.

Raven said he's still having his transfusion and looks pasty but has been joking, meaning he's out of danger.

Constant thoughts run through my mind. Have I missed something? I speak to the guy every day and didn't notice anything wrong. He looked tired and struggled more with some jobs, but I thought he was just having lots of late nights at the bar, which is his primary job. Karen, the manager, is not known for pulling her weight, but she deals with the business side of Stormy's, so we keep her on. Why didn't I ask my brother if he was okay? I presumed he'd tell me on his own.

Pacing back and forth, I'm trying to make sense of the evening, but to no avail. I need a smoke despite having given them up a few weeks ago. I stumble through the reception area to my bike and rummage through the saddlebag. Right at the bottom is the half-empty, crumpled pack with a lighter to boot. Lighting up, I take a draw and inhale deeply, feeling the instant hit and dizzy spell from the nicotine rush. Sitting sideways on my bike stops me from falling over.

Maybe this wasn't such a great idea.

I make my way back inside. Gonna check if I can see numb nuts yet.

A nurse is waiting for me as I return to the waiting room. They moved him to the hematology floor or something like that. Shit, I don't know all these medical terms.

The Nurse gives me directions, and I make my way to the elevator. It's empty at this ungodly hour, thank fuck. Last thing I need is to be stared at. I get to the correct floor, open the door to the room, and there he is, in his own room. A hot nurse is taking his vitals, and the dirty bastard is flirting with her.

"Well, darlin', what do you expect? My heart rate is bound to be up, as is something else." He smirks, pointing at the tent under his sheets. "I think I need a bed bath."

"Do you now? I guess I can oblige." She smiles sweetly and hits the call buzzer, and as the door opens, she turns to the orderly entering. "Jason, this gentleman requires a bed bath. Could you find me a wire brush and disinfectant, please? I believe he needs a thorough cleaning." Roaring with laughter, I watch Flakey blanch, and his tent swiftly disassembles.

"I can't breathe." I'm bent over, coughing with laughter. "I like you, darlin'," I choke out, and she holds out her hand for me to shake.

"Chloe. I'm this clown's nurse for the duration of his stay. He's caused me overtime already, so I'm going to disappear. But if he gets rowdy again, just ring the buzzer and ask for Jason. The wire brush and soap will be ready and waiting." She grins at me, looks at numb nuts, shakes her head, and leaves. She sticks her head back through the door and throws over her shoulder, "Behave, will ya? I'll be back at three this afternoon for my late shift. I'm sure you'll have blood tests and scans in the morning. See you around three."

"Man, what crawled up her ass and died?" Flakey moans. "Seriously? Wire brush, Disinfectant? She's an evil bitch. I hate doctors, nurses, and hospitals. Spring me out of here, brother, I beg you. I'm fine now that I'm topped off." I shake my head, smirking. "Not a chance, brother. You made quite a mess of your room and nearly put Ebony in an early grave. What the hell happened?"

He looks puzzled. "I wish I knew, brother. One minute, I was giving it hard to Ebony, watching my cock disappear in her cunt. The next thing I know, I wake up seeing a bright light, thinking, 'That's it. I fucked myself to death and died a happy man, ready to go to hell.' But to my disgust, a doc shoved a needle in my arm, and the red stuff started running into me. As if I don't have enough of that in me already. What a waste."

I cough. "Man, from what Ebony said, you pulled out, turned, threw up a load of blood, and passed out cold. She came down, screaming bloody murder. Ash and Sarah ran up, monitored you, and made sure you didn't croak. You were puking so much blood, man; it was scary. You had us worried there for a moment. And you can't remember anything?"

"Nope. Last thing I remember is having my cock buried deep in Ebony. Oh shit, who took off the condom?" His face is a picture of horror.

"I hate to tell you this, brother, but Ash and Sarah got to you first and had you in their hands when we got there. No sight of a condom."

"Jesus fucking Christ, they were handling me? They played with my junk when I was out? I can't believe it. My junk touched three chicks last night, and I can only vaguely remember one of them." He groans while I try my hardest not to laugh.

53

"Get to sleep, man. I'll stay here in this chair, so shut the fuck up, close your eyes, and let me get some Z's before I smother you with a pillow." I'm still chuckling.

"Ha, I'll tell Chloe, and you'll be on the receiving end of her wire brush. Kiss my ass and die, asshole," he grumbles but closes his eyes, and within moments, all I can hear is snoring. Man, I need some earplugs.

◊◊◊

During the night, I'm regularly woken by nurses seeing to Flakes. Right now, he's being true to his name; he's flaked the hell out. Luckily, he didn't wake up when his vitals were taken. I did, though, and I'm ripping the head off the next person who comes in. It's only six a.m., and no chance of any more sleep in this noisy shithole. Man, I won't be able to smell anything but disinfectant for weeks. I hate these places.

I must have dozed off, though, because the next thing I know, Flakes is taunting me.

"Hello, sleeping beauty. Wakey, wakey, rise, and shine. I need a piss." I jump wide awake.

"Do I look like your orderly?" I growl. "Press the God damn button, princess, or wet the bed. I ain't helping you piss, and I'm not touching that shriveled dick of yours."

"Nice to know you're a helpful brother." Flakes smirks, batting his damn eyelashes at me.

"Listen, punk, if you weren't in that bed and connected to cables, probably a battery charger they nicked from the workshop, I'd polish your teeth with my fist right now." I try hard to sound pissed but struggle not to smirk.

I'm glad he's back to his mouthy self and feeling better. The door opens, and a nurse and an orderly walk in, washbasin and towels in hand.

"On that note, I'm out of here."

"No, Vegas, brother, don't leave me with them. Wire brushing is not on my agenda today," Flakey pleads. I give him a one finger wave and make my way to the cafeteria, needing some chow and java.

The food is better than I expected, but the coffee is the equivalent of three-day-old dishwater. I can't get myself to swallow this shit. Water from the cooler it is. I get back to the room and a sulking Flakey.

"They made me whizz in a bottle. While they stood there and watched." He's not happy, that's for sure, requiring me to slam my lips together to stop laughing. The door opens, and in strolls Ashley. I look at my watch. Damn, it's eight. I need to go home, shower, and get to church.

"Morning." Ashley smiles sweetly, and my dick suddenly wants to wave hello. I nod and tell myself it's best to get out of here. "Gotta run, bro. I'll get one of the brothers to pop in with your phone after church."

"Yeah, no sweat. I owe you one, bro." I wave at Flakey, head out the door, and down to my bike.

◊◊◊

Unable to reign in my dick, it got a bit of hand action in the shower. Raven would put a bullet between my eyes if he knew I was jacking off to thoughts of his sister. If I were Raven, I'd

55

shoot me too. As far as the brothers are concerned, they believe me to be a hit it and quit it kinda guy. Mostly, I don't hit in the first place, and when I do, I do so in Violet's with consenting like-minded women. Ashley would run a mile in high heels away from me, screaming if she knew what I preferred in the sack, and Raven would have me in the bunker for sure.

Shaking my head to dislodge the thoughts, I put a pot of life juice on. It should be illegal to sell that shit they try to pass off as coffee at the hospital. I can smell the freshly brewed aroma in my rarely used kitchen. I don't cook, so the only appliances I use are the stainless-steel microwave and the dishwasher for my mugs. Pizza comes in boxes for a reason, so you don't have dirty plates. It's nine-thirty, so I have just enough time for my java, and then I have to get my ass in gear.

I arrive at the clubhouse just in time, make my way straight into church, and take my allocated seat. We have church weekly, and it's mandatory to attend unless you're half dead, in the hospital, can't ride, or in jail. If any excuses are accepted, those are the only ones that might work, and that's a big IF.

I look around. Raven is at the head of the table, with Rusty to his right and Slender to his left. Next to Slender is Pennywise, then Ferret. On the other side of Rusty is Spen, the Treasurer, and Secretary. No one has stepped forward to become Secretary, so Spen does both at the moment. Then there's Clusseaud, the Road Captain, one of the old guards. He held the VP patch for a while but didn't agree with a lot of what Stone did. Instead of leaving, he stepped down and was semi-retired. He can be a grumpy old fucker, but the rides he maps out and organizes go off without a hitch. His experience shows.

The others at the table are Moggy, Ratchet, me, Sparks, and Zippy, then Flakey—whose chair is empty as he has a valid excuse—Dougal, and another couple of empty chairs between him and Ferret. Ferret is our IT guy. There's not much he can't do with a laptop and the rest of his setup. He's also responsible for background checks on prospects and anyone who comes in close contact with the MC. Prospects and Nomads are not invited to church unless it's a special occasion and they're required. Some clubs let Nomads sit in church, but we don't.

There are three prospects at the moment. Halfpint is closest to patching in. Eli, who is not far behind him, and Greg, who's relatively new to us. Our prospects are precisely that, for twelve to eighteen months. Then they get either voted in, can be given an extension—not that this ever happened—or we vote them out. If you're not in after twenty-four months, you're out and blacklisted from prospecting for the Souls.

"Right, fellas, let's get this show on the road," Raven bellows into the room. Silence quickly falls around the table. "Okay, we have a few items on the agenda today. Business side to start with. Spen, the floor is yours."

Spen shuffles his papers about. "Nothing unusual. The bike shop, Stormy Souls Customs, is pulling in good profits. The security business is booming, with Lightning Security having grown significantly in the past six months. I'll give the floor to Slender in a moment to update everyone on progress. Ally's is doing great as always. Profits are up against last month. I'm concerned, though, about the bar. Stormy's seems to be slow lately. Unfortunately, Flakey isn't here to give us his thoughts, but the profits have been down three months in a row. It's something we need to investigate. Maybe it needs a remodel? There are admittedly nicer places to get a beer in town." A few nods go around the table, and Raven looks deep in thought at that announcement. Spen continues.

"Zippy, have you looked for a building for that tattoo shop yet?"

"I've had a look around, and there are a couple of places that might work. I'll get you the details after the meeting." Spen nods at Zippy.

"All subs are up to date, no fines, and we have a healthy bank balance. Healthy enough to invest some of our earnings, to keep it growing." At last, the boring portion of the meeting is done with.

"The bar not doing well doesn't sit right with me." Raven looks thoughtful. "I'll have a word with Flakey when I see him later tonight, see what his thoughts are." Agreement is nodded all around the table.

"Settle down," Raven commands over the murmuring brothers, and silence once more resumes. "There are a few other important things. First, I want to put it to the table that Dawg has approached the officers and me about patching in. I'm more than happy to have him. He's a good brother, but I need a unanimous vote on this. Does anyone have anything they would like to say on the matter before we vote?" Dougal is the only one.

"He's a great guy. I find him trustworthy and very loyal. His old lady fits in well. I think he'd be an asset, especially with his security experience."

"Right, let's get to it then. I'll start the vote with a sound aye."

Rusty echoes, "Aye," as do all the other brothers around the table.

"You got the rocker?" Raven's eyes land on Spen.

"Sure." He grins and hands the rocker to Raven.

"Better call him then." Slender nods and gets his phone out.

"Dawg, we need you at the clubhouse. Now, man. Shit is going down," he says and hangs up, an evil smile on his face.

"Okay, while we wait, let me make sure we're all very clear on how we act toward our women and guests at parties. There will be no skirt lifting, no intimidation, and no unwanted attention. This is unacceptable. We treat our family members with respect here. Any more complaints about this behavior, brothers, and there will be dire consequences. I'll kick the next brother's nuts myself and then hand him over to Slender and Pennywise. Do I make myself clear?" Raven is pissed off and wants it to be known. We all give him a chin lift. "I also think we ought to thank Sarah and Ashley for what they did for Flakey until the paramedics arrived," Raven adds.

"What do you want me to do? Send flowers or some shit like that?" Spen asks with a raised eyebrow.

"Nope," Raven says, popping his 'p' decisively. "I reckon we'll take up a collection and ask Ally to get them some spa voucher or something like that. That'd be more their style." Ferret gets up, goes into the bar, and gets a pint glass, putting it on the table and stuffing a twenty in. We each open our wallets and stick what we can in the jar.

"Get the rest out of club funds if needed," Raven tells Spen, who nods and takes notes. We all hear the loud rumble of Dawg's Harley. He bursts through the clubhouse door, gun in hand, ready to protect the brothers. We all smile. Looks like we made the right decision.

"What the fuck," he mutters and holsters his gun.

"Dawg, how good of you to join us," Raven shouts.

"What's on fire? Who do I need to kill?" Dawg shouts across the room.

"Get your damn ass in here before I fine you for being late," Raven breaks into a wide grin. "Welcome aboard, brother!" Dawg smiles from ear to ear, then slaps each brother on the back around the table.

"Thanks, brothers, you won't regret it. Looks like I'm finally home." He takes a seat in one of the empty chairs next to Pennywise.

"Patch-in party!" Everyone is shouting and getting boisterous.

"Shut your mugs!" Raven hollers. "Let's get this finished. Then we can party."

"Clusseaud, where are we with the planning for the Restless Slayers rally?" Clusseaud stands and hands out copies of a roadmap and a copy of the rally site.

"Okay, the route is planned. As you can see, the site is tent camping only. No campervans or RVs." Everyone joins the chuckle going around the table. "Prospects will drive the van as a support vehicle, with all our gear and spares. They'll act as sweeper crew as well. Make sure your bikes are shipshape. I don't want to see a recovery truck with one of ours. Ya, hear me?" Clusseaud has a real bee in his bonnet about keeping on top of our bikes. Rightly so, it keeps us safe and reduces spills to a minimum. Road rash is not a pretty sight, and that's if you get off lightly after a spill. I'm in no mood to be scraped off the tarmac, so my bike is in tiptop condition.

"You can see the site there. I marked our space, which is adequate for all our tents and gear. We'll park the van at the side, with access to beers and water for coffee in the morning. Prospects are on food duty, fetching and carrying, and security of our space when we're making the rounds or at the stage. There's a great line-up this year. And for either the brave or idiots, there's rock karaoke." Snorts of laughter erupt.

"We set off at lunchtime, three weeks on Thursday, to get us to site for that evening. We'll have spotlights and a generator in the van to make setting up in the dark easier. All gear must be at the clubhouse the Wednesday evening before to be loaded up. Tents are here; you just need to pack your personal stuff and whatever else you feel you need. No, club bunnies do *not* count as a mattress. Members, old ladies, and invited guests only. We leave at one p.m. sharp. Make sure the businesses are covered; this is a mandatory run." Clusseaud finishes through the sniggers and teases in the room.

"Great stuff, Clusseaud, thanks." Raven nods in his direction. "Okay, now the long-awaited update from Slender and Pennywise." Pennywise sits up straighter.

"Okay, so Lightning Security is doing really well. We have several new contracts. The club in town we looked at a few days ago wants to go ahead. It's a full security install, including cameras and systems. That'll make good dough. We need to expand on the security personnel side as well. We have more inquiries about bodyguards and a general supply of door staff. I want to ask Dawg, are all your certifications up to date? You got your concealed carry and all that jazz?"

"Yup, sure have. Do you need me?"

"We sure could use you, Dawg, unless you want to work somewhere else."

"No, I'm happy with security, Slender."

"Okay, see me tomorrow morning, and I'll fill you in on what's going on and set up a schedule for you. Pennywise will sort you out with ID and everything else you need." Dawg nods.

"Any other business?" Raven looks ready to stand.

"Yes, I need help. I can't do the two roles," Spen pipes up. "I'm doing the books for the clubs and the businesses as well as the roll of Secretary. With the businesses growing, it's a full-time job. I nominate Dawg to become Secretary. I know he did well with it in his old chapter."

Dawg groans as if in pain. "Oh, please, no, not again!"

Raven snorts and asks, "Anyone second?"

"I do," Rusty responds, smirking.

"Okay, I need an eighty percent vote on this. All in favor, say aye." The 'ayes' go around the table, and there are only two nays, one from Dougal, who knows Dawg hates the job, and one from Dawg himself.

"Successful vote. Dawg, do you accept?"

"Not like I can say no, can I?" Dawg grouses, and Spen shoves over the records and smirks.

"You can record your vote now. Thank fuck that's off my hands," he gleams, rubbing his hands. That finishes the meeting. Dawg suggests that as everyone starts to leave that we move his patch-in party to the rally, which all brothers are more than happy with. Everyone heads out to the bar to find a bunny or head home if they live off-site. Sparks gives me a wave and chin lift before he kicks down and opens the throttle.

Raven catches me on my way out. "Hey, Vegas, hang back for a moment and come to my office." Oh shit, what have I done now? I'm wracking my brain to try to come up with whatever I'm going to get my ass chewed out for, but I'm failing.

"Close the door." Raven looks beat. "Is there a problem between you and Rusty?" he asks. I'm confused.

"Why are you asking? I don't like how he treats the women, club family or not. It makes me mad, and I see red. If he isn't being a shithead, I have no big issues." I look Raven straight in the eye as he rubs his stubbled chin.

"What went on yesterday is unacceptable, and Slender is dealing with it. Just do me a favor and don't start anything with Rusty. Try to stay out of his way."

"Yeah, boss, no problem there," I smirk at Raven. "Look, Prez, if you need something, just say the word, and I'll help if I can." Raven opens his desk and brings out a bottle of Maker's Mark and two glasses. Passing one measure to me, he leans back in his chair.

"I'm worried about Flakey. I hope they get to the bottom of what's going on with him soon. How was he last night?" Unsure of what to say, I decide to go with the truth.

"He looks like shit, been tired all the time for a while now, but he hasn't asked for help. I don't think Karen is pulling her weight. Make sure you ask him about that. I know a guy, the hanger-on, Neil. He's been around for years. He doesn't want to join the club, but he's loyal. I know he managed a cocktail bar in Reno before moving this way. He might want a job at the bar to bolster the staffing," I suggest.

"That could work. Let me get with Ferret, get a background check done, and speak to Neil. He's a good guy. I like him. Did Flakes say anything to you? How long has he been feeling off? I feel guilty for not noticing."

"I asked myself that same question yesterday, Prez, and he never complained or mentioned anything. Hopefully, the doctors will put him right. If the nurse doesn't get him first with her wire brush." Raven throws his head back, roaring with laughter.

"Do I want to know what he did to annoy the nurse?"

"Nope." I pop my 'p' and wink at Raven.

"Okay, Vegas, get gone. I'm gonna shoot by the hospital before I go home and get some shut-eye. Took Nathan to college this morning at godforsaken o'clock. Can you arrange a schedule for hospital visits next week?"

"Sure." I nod in his direction and make my way to my bike

-8- ASH

"Morning," Sarah groans. "My head feels as though a marching band is playing lambada in it, but very bad and very loud." She squeezes her eyes shut, and a pained look crosses her face. Sarah stayed over last night after the party since she was pretty drunk and didn't want to go home. We returned after one in the morning, and she was in no state to go home. So instead, we finished the open bottle of wine from the fridge, and Sarah slept on my sofa. She snored like a freight train and slept through Raven, turning up at six this morning to take Nathan to college and drop off Flakey's bag. She also missed their laughter at her mumbling in her sleep something like 'don't crack the eggs, you fool.' She's blissfully unaware. I hand her two painkillers and a glass of water.

"Take that; it'll help." She gratefully grimaces at me but takes my offerings.

"No hair of the dog then?" She asks with a sigh. "Can I borrow your shades? Turn off the sun; it's evil." I can't help the chuckle that escapes.

"What time do you have to pick Leo up?"

"I don't. My parents will drop him off at three this afternoon. Oh my god, did I dream what happened last night? That decrepit asshole hitting on me, lifting my skirt, and then the guy upstairs bleeding? Did we hightail it to the hospital? It's all vague today."

"Yup, it all happened. Do you remember us putting him on his side or not wanting to leave when I offered to take us home? I think Dougal took a liking to you until you ripped into him." I wink at Sarah, who has the grace to look slightly embarrassed.

"Oh god, I didn't read him the riot act, did I? Dougal, I mean?"

"Yup, sister, you did, but not as much as you ripped Rusty a new asshole and offered to shoot him." Sarah's mortified, shocked look makes me crease up laughing.

I fall onto the other sofa, laughing my ass off, trying to tell her what happened last night. She sits there, her hands in front of her face, peeping through the fingers, bright red and embarrassed.

"You had a dirty potty mouth last night." God, I love winding her up. She's so funny when embarrassed.

"I'm never setting foot in that place again," she groans while I desperately try to keep my laughter in check.

"Can I use your car to do some running around?"

"Sure. It's not as if I'm in any fit state to drive," she says.

"Right." I get up and grab my purse, keys, and Flakey's bag. "I'm off to the hospital now to get this stuff dropped off and relieve Vegas. Raven won't be back here after dropping Nate off. He'll go straight to the clubhouse. You have the house to yourself; make the most of it. Go take a nap in my bed and drink plenty of water before you do. You'll feel better. I'll be back at lunchtime. Gotta hit the stores and get some groceries after the hospital." Ignoring her groan, I walk to the door, waving over my shoulder.

◊◊◊

65

After finding Carl's room and slowly opening the door without knocking, I see Vegas— hot as ever, giving my ovaries a workout—standing by the bed, listening to Flakey moan.

His shoulders are shaking slightly. Flakey looks terrible. Pale and pasty, not sure how else to describe it other than he looks like death warmed over. Not wanting to be caught sneaking, I open the door fully and breeze in with a smile.

"Morning." I beam at them, trying to hide my shock at Flakey's appearance. Vegas gives me a weird look, his eyes traveling over my body, leaving me suddenly feeling naked. *Don't flush, don't flush!* It shouldn't be the problem as all the blood suddenly disappeared into my nether region. I drop Flakey's bag on the chair while Vegas says his goodbyes and stalks out the door. I try not to turn to watch him leave.

"Right, sugar pie, you've got me for the next few hours to keep you company. Anything you want?"

"Na, darlin', I'm fine for now. You don't have to stay, girl, I'm honestly fine" just then, the door opens, and nurse walks in.

"Time for your blood tests, and afterward you're booked for a scan. So, it'll be a while before you're back." She apologetically smiles at me. I shrug my shoulder.

"No problem. I'll do my shopping quick and then come back. That okay with you, Flakes?"

"Whatever," he grumbles. I take that as a yes, help the nurse transfer him into a wheelchair and walk out with them.

◊◊◊

66

The whole way to the grocery store, I battle with my concern about Flakey. He doesn't look good. I feel like an ass. I've known him for years and years. He's a good guy, but I let my dislike of the club blind me to the fact that most of them are good people. That has to stop. They are my family, after all. The club isn't the same as it was with Stone in charge. As if by telepathy, my phone rings. The display shows the Tecumseh State Correctional Institution. My heart sinks. I know who that is. I pull over to the side of the road and turn the engine off.

"Hello?"

"Hello, darlin', how are you?" My father's voice sounds cheery, as though nothing is wrong.

"Hi, Dad," I bristle at calling him that, but I can't do with a lecture today. "How are you? Everything okay? It's all good here. Nathan left for college this morning. Raven took him and helped get him settled."

"I'm okay, sweetheart, just the same as always. How's Flakey?" I don't know why it still shocks me that he knows everything going on almost immediately. You'd think it would be difficult to get the information where he is, but apparently not.

"He's okay, I think. I went to see him a little while ago, and they were taking him for tests, so I left, but I'll go back later to keep him company for a bit." No point making something up; he obviously has informants. Swallowing hard, I find that I have nothing to say to him. Every time we talk, it brings back sour memories and reminds me that he's in the joint for a reason, never to come out again. Speaking to him unsettles me.

"I tried to call Raven, but he didn't pick up," he complains.

"He was probably driving or getting ready for church." I don't know why I feel like I have to apologize for Raven. I feel stupid for it but can't help it.

"Ashley," he says, his tone serious, "I'd love to see you next visit." I knew it was coming. I haven't seen him in years. Every time I went, it depressed me so much that I spent days in tears, feeling sorry for myself. Not him, never him, but for myself. So, I stopped going.

"I'll try," I find myself half-whispering.

"Please do. I haven't seen my daughter in years. I know you're angry and upset with me, but I'm your father. I miss you and the boys." It sounds more like a command than a plea, making me bristle. The days he could command me are long over. They died out when Mom did.

"I said I'll try," I grate out between clenched teeth. "Sorry, gotta go." I hang up the phone while he's still trying to talk. I can't deal with this shit.

To be honest, I'm furious and hurt. It bubbles away deep inside of me. The way he treated Mom, the beatings dished out, the constant presence of violence, drugs, and guns. I hate him for what he turned our lives into. And there are days I hope someone will soon set the date to rid the world of his filthy mug forever. Then I immediately feel guilty.

Luckily, Nebraska is quite a ways away. Over six hundred miles and around nine hours if you're driving. That gives me a good excuse. With a busy job, I can't afford to take a few days off to make the journey. He knows I'd never accepted money from the club, so it's a great excuse.

Sitting there for another few minutes, calming down, I realize I need to speak to Raven later. He needs to know that Stone knows everything going on with the club and its members. Taking a deep breath, I put the car in drive and pull back onto the road. I need to calm the hell down before I do anything else.

Without planning to, I find myself in front of Ally's. I park and walk into the empty diner. Ally looks at me and, without saying a word, brings me a cup of coffee. She sits down opposite me in a booth.

"Hey, girl, what's up? You look as though you've seen a ghost this morning." Her concerned gaze takes me in, and I laugh sarcastically.

"If only it had been a ghost."

"Oh," Ally looks down at her intertwined fingers on the table, "it's *that* day. Sunday call day, huh?"

"I shouldn't let it get to me, but he does it every damn time," I fume. "He even knows Flakey is in hospital." Ally looks at me, her eyes wide with surprise.

"Wow, looks like someone is snitching, or he has excellent connections in there. I know exactly what you need right now."

She gets up, goes behind the counter, and comes back holding a large plate full of cupcakes with rude decorations and two large pieces of chocolate cake. She looks at the wall clock, shrugs, turns the open sign to closed, and locks the door. I laugh at her— she knows me so well. Inspecting the cupcakes, they put a silly grin on my face.

"I hope Sparks didn't model for the penis decorations," I joke, and Ally claps.

"Why didn't *I* think of that? But I would need bigger cupcakes then, more like a tray." She sniggers. "So, sister, spill. Auntie Ally will make it all better."

Gearing up, I pour my hate and anger onto Ally's lovely table. It'll need a double disinfectant wipe before I'm finished spewing poison. When Ally hands me a pack of tissues, I notice tears streaming down my face. Shit, I promised myself *no more tears* years ago, yet here I am, bawling again and word vomiting all over Ally. She doesn't stop me or asks questions. She's just there, listening and radiating warmth.

"Ash, if you don't want to see him, don't. Don't make yourself do something you have difficulties coping with. He's where he is by his own doing. He doesn't deserve nor need your empathy. The only one who deserves empathy here is you. You owe it to yourself to put your mental health first. If it doesn't make you happy, stay away from it. You are a choice, not an option, and he chose his fate with no regard for you, Nathan, or even Raven. You don't want to see him? Don't. I'm sure Raven understands, even if Stone doesn't. In my humble opinion, Stone was and is a complete narcissistic asshat. My god, he has psychopathic tendencies. Stay away if you can. I'm willing to bet he's putting pressure on you for his own purposes. In fact, I'm so sure I'd forsake tequila for an entire month if I'm wrong." That statement has me sniveling and grinning at the same time. Ally could never go a month without her favorite tequila. She loves the stuff too much. But she's right, and deep down, I know it.

"So, what else is on your mind? I know this isn't all. Come and tell Auntie Ally where it hurts. Dr. Ally is in the house."

"Err, everything else is fine, really." I try to sound convincing, but even I can hear my bravado sounds as fake as Ally's hair dye looks.

"Look, honey, you don't have to tell me anything. Know that I'm always here for you. No questions asked, no judgment, and no fucks given whether others may think it'll make you look bad. I've known you for a long time, watched you suffer, become a strong woman, and brought up your brother all alone. You don't have to suffer alone, Ash. I'm here for you and will keep whatever it is to myself. I swear on my bike and Sparks' man parts." That has me giggling.

I take a bite out of my chocolate cake. Wow, the flavor explodes in my mouth, and I groan with pleasure.

"Oh my god, this is orgasmic."

"Did I tell you how sad you are, girlfriend?" Ally shoots me an alarmed look. "You need a man. Now then, who can I hook you up with?"

She looks off into the distance, and I can practically hear the cogs in her brain turning. I have got to get her off this train of thought. No good will come from it.

"B.O.B. is doing a great job, thank you very much. He doesn't leave dirty socks around, mugs in the sink, or oily footprints on the carpet. And he doesn't want his dinner cooked or hogs the remote."

"What you need is a hook-up, sister—a hook-up with the feel-good factor, delivered by a sexy hunk. Okay, let's get our thinking caps on here. Who would qualify?" She taps her nails against her teeth, deep in thought. "Any hot men at your work?" She looks at me curiously.

"Nope, none," I reply.

"Hmm, slim pickings around here unless you count the brothers. They are all quite nice on the eyes. Well, maybe with one or two exceptions. Ugh, when I think about Rusty or Spen, that is just . . . no . . . just no!" She shudders visibly, and I giggle.

Oh my god, Spen? He's lardy, six-foot-two has a mountain of a beer gut, and greasy hair—well, the three odd strands he has left of it. His glasses are milk bottle bottoms and make his eyes look huge, he's walked with a stick since he crashed a couple of years ago, and he still thinks he's God's gift to women. How Debs puts up with him, I don't know. She needs a medal.

71

When Ally mentioned Rusty, a chill crept up my spine, and I was instantly agitated. Memories I don't want to remember are assaulting me, and I can feel my breathing speed up. My vision blurs, my chest hurts, and then I feel myself start to shake. I'm lost.

"Ashley! Ashley!" I hear Ally calling from far away, like through a long tunnel. "Ashley, what's wrong? Breathe, Ashley, breathe!" she screams at me. "Ashley, for fuck's sake, breathe!"

That makes my eyes connect with hers. "Breathe," she repeats. "Follow my breathing. In through the nose, out the mouth. In through the nose, out the mouth. Yes, that's it, in through the nose, out the mouth. Good girl. I'm here with you. Everything is okay."

After five minutes, my breathing returns to normal, and my vision clears. Ally hands me a glass of ice water. My mouth is as dry as the Sahara Desert. She looks at me, her brows drawn together in concern.

"What the fuck, Ashley? You just had a full-blown panic attack. In my café. What the flaming hellfire is wrong? And don't tell me you're fine because that doesn't wash with me after that performance. I'm your friend, and I love you like a sister, so tell me what the hell is going on."

Oh my god, oh my god, what now? I can't tell her everything. I just can't. I look at her and press my lips together in defiance.

"Look, Ashley, *something* is going on, and I'm *not* taking no for an answer. You either talk to me, or I'll speak to Raven and see if he can get it out of you." Ally is angry and looks hurt.

"No, please, Ally. Please, please, please, don't tell Jamie." I'm all but begging on my knees. If he finds out, he'll go berserk.

"You better get talking then, missy, before I lose my last bit of patience and drag you to the clubhouse," Ally hisses.

I take a deep, calming breath and look around, my eyes flitting everywhere and anywhere except Ally's face. How do I even start this conversation?

"Ally, I'll tell you, but you must swear not to talk to any brothers about it, not even Jason. Swear, or I'll never speak to you again if you let me down." I look at her, and she locks her eyes on mine. They are full of searching, trying to dissect my thoughts, which are racing around in my head in pure chaos. "I need you to swear, Ally." She nods, waiting for me to start. I take a deep breath, let it out on a sigh, and begin.

"You know my mother died when I was young, right? You know she drank herself to death?" Ally says nothing, patiently waiting for me to continue. "I was about ten. The school bus dropped me off, and I couldn't wait to see Mom, so I ran all the way to the house. I was excited because I got an A on a test and couldn't wait to show her." I swallow hard. "The door was open, so I walked right in. I could hear noises from the kitchen, so I ran in, and there they were; Mom bent over the sink, and Rusty fucking her with all he had. They didn't even notice me for a while. It wasn't until they finished that they looked to the side."

Ally's eyes go bigger and bigger during my confession, then she gets a look of disgust on her face. She takes a breath, but I raise my hand. I'm not done yet. Now that I've started, I might as well get it all out.

"I was frightened and confused and couldn't understand what I saw. My mother's jeans around her ankles, and Rusty's were around his knees. It made no sense to me whatsoever. He pulled out, waved his dick around, slapped my mom on the ass, and said, 'Bitch, you're still a great ride. Next time, we might have to invite Ashley in.' My mom gasped in shock, noticing me

73

standing there, looking confused." My eyes are burning with tears again, so I blink and swallow hard to stop them from falling. Ally's mouth is hanging open, and the horrified look on her face speaks volumes. "He pulled his jeans up, grabbed me by the arm, and dragged me outside.

"He said, 'You can never tell your father what you just saw. Keep your mouth shut, or I'll shut it for you. I'll slit your throat and put you in a ditch where no one ever finds you.' I never told a soul. My mom died a week later. I know everyone was told she drank herself to death, but I found the autopsy report a few years ago. Accidental overdose and extremely high levels of alcohol. I never knew my mother to take drugs, and I overheard Stone saying once she never touched drugs at all." I stop to take a breather.

"My gut feeling now is that Rusty got her hooked on something that killed her in the end. I'm not saying he went out to kill her, but I think he had a part to play in her death. Whenever he sees me, he sneers at me or reminds me to keep my mouth shut. I want to throw up. I feel so sick if he's anywhere in sight."

I gulp in a breath and wait for Ally's reaction. For a long time, she says nothing. Then, she stands and paces the diner, making me even more nervous. Ally is not one to keep her opinion to herself. She disappears behind the counter, gets two shot glasses, and fills them with tequila.

"Here, drink this. We both need it." Her face looks grim. "I don't know what to say, and that's gotta be a first." She sighs. "Ashley, I'm so sorry you had to go through that, and alone too. That must have been hellish. You were so young, had so much pressure. My heart is crying for you right now. But my brain is so mad." She continues to pace. "I want to rip his head off and shit in his mouth. That slimy bastard! I don't know what to be madder about, how he treated you, or why he went there in the first place. No wonder he didn't want Stone or Raven to find out. He was the VP, for fuck's sake, and still is the VP. That dickhead has a lot to answer for. Bad enough, he took a brother's old lady and wife, but his President's? And to threaten you? I'm so furious; I want to shoot the bastard myself." She rants on.

"Ally, stop," I shout at her. "You cannot say anything to anyone. Not Rusty, not Sparks, and sure as hell, not Jamie. I suspect what you said about tattling is right, and if anyone tattles to Stone, it would be Rusty. We can't even tell Stone because he wouldn't believe it. Rusty would deny it, and I could not cope with the drama. I told you because you made me and because I trust you. Don't make me regret my decision," I plead with her. Ally has never looked at me more questioningly and seriously.

"Ashley, Raven has to know. If it were my club and my family, I would want to know, and I would get mighty pissed if I found out someone I trusted knew all along and said nothing."

"I know," I nod, "that's why I kept silent for so long. I don't want Jamie hurting, and I sure don't want him to be the next one in prison for dealing with that slime bag. I need Jamie. I can't lose him too. Not now, not ever." My eyes are burning with tears.

"I knew he was and always has been a cockroach, but this? I didn't expect this." Ally groans. "Now I get why you are always so jumpy around him, why you always went the other way when he appears, even if that means leaving. How can I help?"

"You can't, Ally; no one can. I'll carry on as is and stay out of his way. The only thing you can do is not ask me anymore about it. Promise you'll keep my secret."

"I swear, no one will hear it from me." Ally looks at me. I can see she's not happy and conflicted, but I trust she will keep my secret safe. At least for now. I'll deal with everything as I go along. The door opens, and Sparks steps in.

75

"Hear what from you?" I look at Ally in complete panic mode. My breath starts coming in pants, and Ally puts her hand on mine, squeezing it gently.

"Damn it, Sparks, now we have to swear you to secrecy too." My panic rises to an epic proportion.

"What's going on?" Sparks quizzes, waggling his eyebrows.

"We were talking about Ashley's secret crush if you must know, and you came in too early. She hasn't told me who it is yet," Ally exclaims, winking at me, and I let out a slow breath of relief. Oh, thank God.

"I know who it is anyway," jokes Sparks, pointing his finger at me. "She hasn't stopped making moon eyes at Vegas for weeks." He exaggerates wildly, but I can feel myself flushing beet red.

"Oh . . . my . . . God!" Ally shouts and laughs. "It's true, isn't it? It's Vegas! Don't even try to lie to me. The color of your face says it all. No one flushes like that if the person in question isn't at least at the top of the rub bank material list."

"What can I say? No woman under fifty can be immune to that pantie melting smile." I mock pout, batting my eyelashes at Ally. If you can't beat them, join them. "And those man buns, in those jeans, that's enough to make my knees wobble." I fan myself with my hand. "That man is hot stuff!" Sparks is howling with laughter, and Ally looks at me like I have a screw loose.

"Eww, disgusting," Sparks grunts out, still laughing

"I swear, I'll keep your secret. I don't want to get a broken nose. My beautiful smeller means a lot to me, you know." He can hardly get the words out through his chortling and snorting.

Secretly proud of my ingenious save, I get out of the booth. "Right, kids, I have to go.

Have to get back to the hospital and then home to let Sarah have her car back."

"Yours will be ready tomorrow. I have it on good authority." Sparks winks at me. Ally

unlocks the door, and I step out into the street, letting out a breath I didn't know I was holding.

-9- VEGAS

After my little *chat* with Raven, I'm just too beat to ride home. I go upstairs to my room, unlock the door, and stop dead in my tracks. A very naked Tequila is spreadeagled on my bed.

"Hello, big boy, at last, come and play with me, sugar," she invites me in her husky voice. I sigh. This is not what I need. The club sluts are getting a little brazen, and Tequila couldn't take my kind of kink. I'm definitely not in a vanilla mood today.

"Not today, sweets. Go and play with the other brothers. Got stuff to do, sleep to catch up on." She throws me a pleading look, but I just hold open the door. "Get out, Tequila. Come on, move," I tell her in a sterner tone.

"Don't be like that, Vegas. I haven't sucked your cock in ages. I just want a taste to relieve your stress," she pushes.

"I won't repeat myself. Get out! Now!" I growl at her, stand up straighter, and let my Dom out. Hand on my hip, my eyes shutter from all emotions. "I'll give you five seconds to get the fuck out of my room. You'll regret crossing me, Tequila. You're a slut, and one I don't want in my bed. Your pussy isn't magic, just another club pussy. Now, get the fuck out!" I watch her scramble off the bed, grab her clothes, and storm off into the hall.

"You are such a dick, Vegas," she screeched.

78

"Yup," I shout after her, "and don't you forget it!" Smirking to myself, I close the door. Mission accomplished. I'm not keen on club bunnies at the best of times, refusing to put my dick where everyone else's has been. Tequila has made the rounds of the brothers for years now. I wonder if she was here when Stone was in charge? The years have not been kind to her. Peroxide blonde bleached hair, wrinkles around the eyes, and wrinkly, large, pored hands show her age; no boob job can fix that. She wears skirts narrower than my belt, and to say her tops are almost nonexistent is putting it mildly. She looks and sounds . . . lived in.

I don't discriminate against age, but I *do* have standards. If all that isn't reason enough to stay clear, she's also Rusty's go-to slut. That's a red flag for me, and no way in the world would I hit that. I've been a bit of a man whore in the past. I've used club bunnies and strangers from the bar in town. But since I have specific tastes, it went nowhere. One night is all they get from me, and I make that clear from the outset. The only time I make an exception is if I have a mutual agreement with a sub, which only happens at Violet's. Hasn't happened for a long time now, must be a year or so. I got my dick wet with a stranger in the meantime but feel the urge to get to Violets soon. My needs are building, and I need some release. That might chase Ashley's face out of my mind. I sigh, sit down at my desk, and start on the hospital visitation schedule for Flakey. I pick up my phone and dial Ferret.

"Hi, Ferret. Raven asked me to do a schedule for Flakey's hospital visits. Could you let me have the staff shift patterns for the next week, so I can work around them?"

"Sure, Vegas, anything else you need?"

"No, thanks, brother, that is all. I'll email you a copy when I'm done, so you know who's at the hospital and how long."

"That's cool. Don't rush; just shoot it over when you're done. No worries," Ferret replies and ends the call.

After getting the information from Ferret, it takes me a couple of hours to do the schedule. I send it back and ask him to send it to everyone. God knows everyone loves a good, long group message on a smartphone. I decide to get a couple of hours' sleep and relieve Raven. Not a lot to do on a Sunday. Most who have families are home with them, Sunday lunch and all that. Not my thing. The shop is closed on Sundays, so there is no work to do there. I yawn and stretch out on my bed, setting my alarm for two hours.

I groan when the alarm sounds. It feels as though I only drifted off only minutes ago. I go to the bathroom, relieve myself and sit my ass on the edge of the bed. I find the group message from Ferret, true to his word and efficient as always. Ferret's a great brother. Things he can do with a computer are unreal. He's a real wizard in his field and there aren't a lot of things he can't hack into or know a backdoor to. He also does all our security checks, makes sure our conceal and carry permits are up to date and runs the security business with Slender and Pennywise. Lightning Security is making a name for itself in the industry. I can't help but smirk.

We'll all turn law-abiding folks yet. I chuckle at the thought. Yes, we're running our businesses legit, but angels we are not. We get our hands dirty if need be.

After grabbing some food, I'm on my way to the hospital. My phone vibrates in my jeans, making me pull over. I have a missed call from Pennywise.

"Hey, what's on fire?" I ask as I return his call.

"Nothing's on fire, bro. Keep your hair on. Just wanted to know if you wanted to grab a few beers tonight, thought about going to Stormy's, to check out what's going on. I don't like what came up in church." Pen sounds uneasy, and I can't blame him.

"Sure, Pen, what time? I'm on my way to see Flakey. Meet you after that?" I offer.

"Sounds good. Make it eight?"

"Sure, meet you at eight at the bar." I hang up and am back on my way. I might even have time to catch up with Raven about what Flakey had to say.

As I open the door, Nurse Chloe is just leaving. She's obviously on a late shift. She gives me a slightly evil grin as she walks out. Do I want to know? I think I'll pass. That woman has devious written all over herself. Raven is sitting on a chair, trying hard not to laugh. Flakey looks pissed and grumbles under his breath something about evil women and where she can stick her bedside manner. I try not to snort.

"Hey man, Flakester, how's it hanging?" I ask with a grin. Raven bursts out laughing

"Apparently not much longer if he doesn't behave himself. She feels he may need something more than soap, or rather less sausage with his eggs." Raven is coughing and hardly able to breathe with his laughter, as he waves his hand to zipper area, showing just what the excellent nurse had meant, by making the universal sign for scissors with his hands.

"Oh, Flakester, will you ever learn?" I mock sigh at him. "Do I need to give you some more flirting lessons?" I bat my eyes at him.

"Fuck off, asshole. If you were a true brother, you'd tie her up and keep her away from me. That evil witch!" We both look up as Raven bolts upright in his chair.

"You can't tie medical staff up for dealing with your sorry ass," he gripes. I shoot him an inquiring look.

"Go home, Raven, and get some sleep. I've got this. I'm keeping our little boo boo man company. Pen and I are meeting for a beer later. So go home, rest, and do your Prez shit. Take it easy, man," I tell him calmly. He works too hard and today has been rough. "I've done the

81

schedule, and Ferret has sent it out. Flakey is covered. If you need anything, just let me know, okay?" I sincerely hope he takes my offer.

"Okay, I can see when I'm not wanted," Raven jokes. "Flakey, behave and stop propositioning the nurses. It won't improve the sponge baths." Someone comes in with Flakey's meal, so I walk out with Raven.

"I'll be back when you're done eaten, bro. Just grabbing a coffee in the cafeteria," I throw over my shoulder.

"Did he say anything?" I ask Raven as I close Flakey's door, and Raven sighs.

"Let's take a walk, get some java first," he says. We make our way outside, coffee take-out cups in hand, and find a quiet spot.

"He mentioned Karen not pulling her weight. She makes out like she's the bigwig, but Flakey does all the running and some of the office work, too. He said it made him more tired than usual, but the doctors aren't sure what's up yet. He's waiting for more tests tomorrow." He looks at me, rubbing the back of his neck, tense with a concerned look in his eyes. "I can't help it, Vegas, but I have a bad feeling about this." I nod in Raven's direction. Something is not right here.

"Pennywise and I are going to pay Stormy's and Karen a visit tonight. We'll have a few beers and watch what is going on. Speak discreetly to some regulars." I offer.

"Thanks, that would be great. When can you get hold of Neil? We really need another barman," Raven states.

"I can call him tonight and feel him out. Just have to get Ferret to do an in-depth security check on him, and I reckon he'll be able to hit the deck running, so to speak."

"Thanks, Vegas, I appreciate it." He looks beat. If the circles under his eyes get any worse, he'll pass for a panda.

"We've got this, Raven. Go home and rest, get some sleep. Anything urgent and we'll call you. But you know we can handle this. So, take your own advice and get gone," I tell him jokingly. It earns me a stern look, a nod, and a back slap for a goodbye. Raven turns on his heel and walks to his bike. I wait until he's pulled out into the traffic, then make my way back up to annoy Flakey.

-10- ASH

An hour after leaving Ally's, I regained enough control to make my way back to the hospital. As I quietly open Flakey's door, the doctor is with him.

"I'm afraid it's not good news. Looking at your blood results and your scan, it looks like advanced acute myeloid leukemia. We're still waiting for the results of the lumbar puncture, but I'm pretty sure it will confirm the diagnosis." I stop dead in my tracks and gasp. I don't think they realized I was there. Now, they turn their heads, and I feel like a deer in the headlights.

"How long have you been standing there?" asks Flakey, looking very pale and angry.

"Long enough," I squeak out, having to clear my throat. "Sorry, long enough that I heard what the doctor said."

"Shit," shouts Flakey, punching the bed with his fists. "Damn it, Ashley, you're such a bloody creeper. It's not enough that I have to deal with this shitshow, now you know and the whole club will know."

84

"Are you trying to say I can't keep my mouth shut?" Fuming, I round on Flakey. "Carl, you're being an asshole. Being sick does not give you the right to speak to me like that. I get you're facing horrendous possibilities, and that sucks, but why the hell do you think I would tell anyone? A, it's not my story to tell, and B, you'll need confirmation first. I knew you could be weird sometimes, but I never had you down for being such an asswipe." I turn, walk out of the door, and slam it as hard as I can. Let the windows rattle, see if I care.

I'm stomping down the corridor and hear Carl shouting. "Ashley, come back. I'm sorry." Well, he can take his sorry and stick it where the sun doesn't shine. I'm not having that.

I stomp to the car, and as I sit in the driver's seat, the gravity of it all hits me. Oh my god, leukemia, advanced stage. Jesus jumping Jehoshaphat, tears overwhelm me and I sob uncontrollably. The big C is not a diagnosis anyone wants or needs, but advanced leukemia? That means it's . . . I'm trying not to think of the word, hopeless. There has got to be something they can do, surely. Maybe the diagnosis is wrong? Maybe the lumbar puncture results will come up clear? I know I'm clutching at straws, but hell, I've known Carl for a heck of a long time. We used to be best friends when I was growing up, and I classify him as family.

I root through Sarah's glove box for a tissue. I shudder and gulp in some air, trying to calm myself. *I'm such a bitch!* How could I leave him like this? I get back out of the car and make my way back to his room. I knock and don't wait for permission to enter. Carl is in his bed, his arm across his face, his shoulders shaking but not with laughter. I race over to the bed and throw myself at him, hugging him tight.

"I'm so sorry, Carl. I was such a bitch to you. I'm so, so sorry." I sob against him. He looks at me with a tear-stained face.

"Me too, Ash, me too. I didn't mean that."

"I know." We are both sobbing, trying to make sense of this craziness. It takes a long time for the tears to stop welling up.

"I've been in a lot of pain," Carl murmurs, his voice still wobbly, "and it's been going on for months. Never thought anything of it. I worked extra shifts at Stormy's, saving up for a deposit on a house, wanting to settle down." His eyes are empty as they sweep the room. "I've been so exhausted that I struggled to get my leg over my bike for runs. My concentration shows lapses, which had me nearly spilling a few times. I thought it was just being overworked. My arms and legs were aching badly lately, and I had lots of nose bleeds, which I put down to high blood pressure from work stress." He sighs, and his attempt at laughter is entirely without humor. "I should have gone to the doctor sooner and not have been such a pussy."

"Carl, stop. You can't blame yourself. It's not something you brought on yourself. You could not possibly have suspected this," I tell him firmly.

"Well, darlin', it looks like karma got me in the end. All the shitty and nasty things I've done in the past have finally come to bite me in the ass. I always wanted to go out on my bike, not like a sick person, slowly suffering to death. This was not the plan."

"Carl, stop it. Nothing is certain yet. There will be treatments, and you're a fighter, a scrapper, so fight like you never have before in your life. Stick your middle finger up at the devil. You're not ready to join him yet, so don't sound like you are."

"Who says I won't go up to see the big man? Might get to the pearly gates yet." He smirks at me. I raise both eyebrows and roll my eyes.

"Really? That's what you reckon?" I smile wryly.

"The irony is not lost on me." He lets out a sarcastic chuckle.

"Carl, is there anything you need? Anyone I should call, family maybe? Just let me know ,and I'll make it happen."

"No, doll face, thank you. I have everything I need for now. There is one thing I have to ask of you, though. Keep this between you and me. Don't tell *anyone*. Not the brothers, not Raven, not *anyone*. I need to get my head around this first; then I'll tell them if and when I'm ready. Can you do that for me?" I look at him, feeling deep sadness and a pinch of panic rising. How can I keep this a secret from Raven? His brother is likely fighting for his life. He'll want to know, and he's going to be extremely mad when he finds out that I kept this from him. I look into Carl's pleading eyes and sigh.

"Yes, okay, I won't tell a soul. But promise me you'll call when you need to talk. I'll come and visit you regularly too. Don't forget Carl; I'm here for you. You are my brother, too." Carl swallows, and I can see his eyes tearing up again.

"Thanks, little sis; you don't know how much this means." I kiss him on the forehead and turn to leave. Just as I do, Jamie walks in. We exchange a swift hug as I struggle to look him in the eye. I hope Carl tells him, and soon. I'm not sure how long I can keep this bombshell of a secret. Taking a deep, grounding breath, I smile at the men and walk out.

◊◊◊

"Where the hell have you been?" Sarah screeches at me, her voice vibrating with anger. "I blew up your phone all afternoon. Have you seen the time?" she grates out between gritted teeth. I check my phone, which I had put on silent at Ally's, and there are fifteen missed calls and several text messages. They're frantic at first, getting more and more pissed as time goes on.

87

Sarah: Where are you? Are you okay? XX

Sarah: Don't forget I have to pick Leo up at three. Please don't be late. XX

Sarah: Are you okay? Please answer me. I'm trying to call you. X

Sarah: Ash, where are you? It is nearly three. X

Sarah: WTF Ash, I'm gonna be late for Leo. Get your ass back here now!

Sarah: Ashley Saunders, formerly known as my best friend, I'm so pissed at you! Where the fuck are you? You better be in a life-or-death situation. That is your only acceptable excuse!

Sarah: Ashley, you are officially no longer my best friend!!!!

I hunch my shoulders. It is four-thirty in the afternoon. She should have been home for Leo at three. "I'm so sorry, Sarah," I stutter, my eyes filling with tears.

Oh, please let today's emotional rollercoaster be over already, I plead, sending up a quick prayer.

"I'll make it up to you. Please don't be mad. I'm so sorry. Sarah, I lost track of time," I whisper, feeling like the greatest asshole in the universe. Poor Leo, I hope his grandma isn't hopping mad. She hates anyone who is not punctual. It's her pet peeve, and she can be a bitch at times. The disappointment in my best friend's eyes cuts me to the core.

"Whatever," she grunts, then she turns and walks out, keys in hand. I drop onto the sofa, put my head in my hands, and sob.

A couple of hours and a large Ben and Jerry's helping later, I take a hot shower. I'm such a crap friend. First, I didn't spot Carl feeling bad, then I let Sarah down, and third, I didn't warn her about Rusty. I attempt to wash the lousy feeling down the drain, but that is only partially helping. I take a deep, fortifying breath.

I'm strong, I'm a good person, I'm worthy, I'm loved. I'm strong, I'm a good person, I'm worthy, I'm loved. I repeat that mantra several times, in time with my breathing, while the warm water cascading down my body comforts me. If ever there was a time for mindfulness, this is it.

After half an hour, I feel calm enough—and shriveled like a prune—to get out of my steamy bathroom, get dried and dressed, and face the music. I fucked up big time. Now, it's time to do some serious groveling. Sitting on my bed, I dial Sarah's number. It goes straight to voicemail. I try again with the same outcome, but I leave a message this time.

"Hi, Sarah. I'm so sorry I was late. I know you're mad at me, and you have every reason to be. I got held up at Ally's, and then Carl really needed me. I'm so, so sorry. Please call me when you get this. I want to make it up to you and Leo," I plead with her. All I can do now is wait and be ready for her full-on rant. I deserve it.

-11- VEGAS

As I open the door to Stormy's, I wrinkle my nose in disgust as the smell of old beer, stale air, and sweaty body odor assaults my nose. I've not been in a long time, and now I remember why. Has it always been this bad? My eyes adjust to the dim lights, and I can make out the dirty, sticky carpet and unloved interior. Man, this place is going to the dogs. I'm ashamed to know it's ours. As I walk to the bar, the room is only partially filled with patrons. It's Sunday, but I would have expected more customers. The beer is cheap, after all. Pen is waiting for me, beer in his hand. Karen polishes glasses behind the bar and greets me with a smile.

Taking in the rest of the patrons, I notice Dawg, his old lady, Dougal, Ally, and Sparks sitting at a table. As usual, Dawg is making an ass out of himself, much to the girls' amusement. One arm is around his old lady, the other is around Ally, and he's sniffing Ally's ear. The women are howling with laughter while Dougal is sitting on Sparks, who is a second from jumping over the table to rip Dawg off his woman. Caroline is nearly falling off her chair, laughing her ass off. Looking at Pennywise, I shrug my shoulders and turn toward Karen.

"Beer, please." I place my order and within seconds, a cold long neck is in my hand. Karen knows not to give me the tap. "Who's working with you tonight?" I ask with a raised eyebrow.

"No one. I'm on my own this afternoon since Flakey is flaking in his cozy bed," she snips back. I don't like how she puts him down and seems to feel put out.

"Well, we pay you well enough to work, and it's not as if it's a full house," Pen replies, shooting me a warning look. He knows me well enough to feel the tension radiating off me.

"Can't rely on anyone nowadays. Not like he's breaking his back when he graces us with his presence. Slacker," she mumbles as she turns and walks to the other end of the bar.

"What the fuck?" I hiss to Pen, my temper rising. I'd have no qualms about beating her into shape if she wasn't a woman. But as she is a woman, and an employee, so that's not an option.

"Calm down, bro. I don't like it any more than you do, but if we want to find out what the fuck is going on, we need to keep calm and not tip her off. Got me?" Pen shoots me a warning look.

"I'll behave, but the way she talks about a brother, a sick one at that, pisses me the hell off," I grate out.

"She's getting too big for her heels; I'll give you that," Pen states before grabbing his beer and making his way over to Dawg, with me following. Distance is the safest for now. "Dawg, you old bastard, are you enjoying your wind-up games?" Pen chortles. Dawg looks at Pen with a lolling tongue and panting like a dog in heat.

"Oh god, stop. I think I just peed a little." Caroline is bent over, laughing, coughing, and spluttering. She slaps Dawg around the back of his head. "Stop it, you idiot. Sparks is literally sparking over there." That has all of us chuckling . . . well, apart from Sparks, who's ready to go fire-spitting dragon on Dawg's ass. Ally, evil as always, smiles sweetly at Sparks and shrugs her shoulders innocently.

"What can I say? I'm adorable. He's an easy target but loves my bacon pancakes too much to lose his shit." She grins at Sparks. "Come on, big boy, let's go home, and you can show me just how much you want to spank me right now." She giggles, but Sparks' face promises retribution.

"You won't be laughing when we get home, and don't bank on being able to sit for a while," he grates, a flare of heat and amusement in his eyes. Ally fans herself with her hand.

"Ladies and gents, see ya some other time. Places to be, the beast to tame, and all that—" She can't finish her sentence, shrieking as Sparks picks her up and throws her over his shoulder, stomping outside.

"Man, what happened to this place?" Dawg raises an eyebrow in question. "I see the old hag is still here." He looks in Karen's direction, another one who sees right through her. We watch her failed attempts to flirt with a patron who looks angry and agitated. She looks at us, and we slowly make our way back to the bar, standing behind the guy who's now shouting.

"If I wanted piss, I'd drink out the toilet. You call this watered-down shit beer?" he roars at her, and Pennywise taps him on the shoulder.

"Problem man, can I help you?" He looks the small, irritating suit up and down.

"Not talking to you, biker boy. I'm talking to the wench behind the bar who's selling me shit beer for inflated prices," he growls at Pen. Oh boy, wrong move. He turns around and sees *biker boys* surrounding him, proudly flying our cuts and colors.

"Calm down, man." Pennywise looks him straight in the eye. "Wouldn't want your cheap suit to get wrinkled and dirty in the parking lot now, would we?" He smiles a slightly evil grin at the suit. It looks as though he wants to get up and start something he won't be able to finish but thinks better of it. He throws a ten on the bar, but Pen picks it up and stuffs it in the man's top jacket pocket. "On the house, now get gone," he orders. Dougal mock bows and shows him to the door.

"Is it always like this?" Pen asks Karen, and she smirks.

"Sure hasn't gotten better since the last order to decrease the beer content on the taps." We all look at each other, stunned. Where the hell is this coming from? It sure wasn't a church decision. She answers the question we are all thinking about but haven't had time to ask out loud. "Rusty passed orders from Raven, who never shows up now, by the way. Rusty is collecting the earnings every Sunday night and deposits them Monday mornings, so I don't have to go out of my way to go to town."

Pennywise bites his tongue, nearly drawing blood. His jaw is set like stone. As Dougal returns from escorting the earlier gentleman outside, Karen pipes up.

"Are one of you able to relieve me for half an hour? I need my break and a visit to the ladies." Dougal nods and gets behind the bar.

"Keep an eye on her, brother," Pen quietly tells Dougal, who gives him a nod and chin lift.

"Best take my old lady home," Dawg states and returns to the table, pulling Caroline out of her chair. Pen and I sit at the table they just vacated.

"Any idea what that was about?" I ask with my eyebrows raised to the hairline.

"No, but it can't be good," mutters Pen. I look Pen in the eye and know he shares my suspicion and dislike of our VP. We're also aware that we're treading very dangerous territory, so steer the conversation into safer waters, discussing our bikes and watching the bar where Karen is notably absent. It's getting busier now, and I spot Dougal having several conversations with the increasing stream of customers. I also note that he's mainly serving bottled beer.

"That's a hell of a long break," grumbles Pen. We've been sitting here for over an hour and a half with no trace of Karen returning. Pen gets up and walks over to Dougal, talking to him before he disappears through the 'Staff Only' door, looking for Karen and taking a closer look behind the scenes. I look around, bored out of my skull. The jukebox springs to life, '*Ladies Love Country Boys*' blaring. Oh god, who the hell likes this? It's torture! I want to pull my brain out through my ears.

The dark-haired chick leaning over the jukebox and tapping her foot makes me brighten up. What an ass she's got in those painted-on jeans. They show off her curves in just the right way. I smile as my dick becomes alert, wanting to play with that ass.

Then the beauty turns around, looks me straight in the eye, and winks at me. My mouth drops open right before I splutter and cough my beer all over the place. Oh, hell to the no! What the hell is she doing here?

Ashley walks to the bar, sits on a stool, and flirts her ass off with Dougal, who gets Captain Morgan out and pours a generous helping into her glass before filling it with Coke. That must have been at least a triple. He winks at her, and I feel my teeth set on edge. What the ever-loving fuck is Ashley doing here? Alone, at that? I watch her from a distance as she finishes her first drink, and then Dougal quickly refills her glass.

I watch her intently as she moves to the beat of '*Heart-Shaped Box*' roaring through the speakers. This is a bit more like my jam. She looks lost in the music and unaware of her surroundings, which becomes immediately evident as two guys nearly knock her off her stool, and one of them tries to grope her luscious ass. In less than a second, I'm up, my chair falling over behind me and stalking my way to the bar in long strides. I arrive just in time to hear Ashley say, "Hey, I said no. Take your hand off my ass or lose it."

94

"You heard the lady," I growl out behind her. Her eyes shoot to me in surprise.

"Meet my boyfriends, Dougal and Vegas. They don't like sharing with anyone else, do you, boys?" Ashley winks first at Dougal and then beams a blinding smile at me.

"That's right, princess," I growl. "Who do I need to kill? Let me have your names for the tombstones, I beg you." The two football player types turn around to face me, spot my Stormy Souls cut, and raise their hands apologetically.

"Sorry, man, we don't want trouble. Didn't realize she's one of yours." I take a long, hard look at these two.

"Once is an accident; twice is a beatdown. Don't let me catch you doing it again." I take Ashley's hand and drag her over to the table, shoving her into a chair.

"Thanks for the save, Vegas," she says with a grateful look.

"So, now I'm your boyfriend? And joint with Dougal?" I can't help the disbelief in my voice. She throws her head back and laughs. Her laugh is music to my ears and makes me smile. Not sure why, but I wish I could keep that laughter coming.

"Yeah, sorry about that. I couldn't think of anything else on the fly." She giggles, and my lousy mood goes out the window.

"What has you coming in here and drowning in rum?" Curiosity must clearly show on my face. She stares at her feet.

She sighs. "Would you believe I said it's been a bad day?"

"Hmm, let's see, after last night at the clubhouse, I might just make an exception for your little white lie there." I wink at her, and her smile returns.

"Oh, biker boy, did you just wink at me?" She bats her eyelashes playfully at me, and I can't help but smile.

95

"Sure, princess, why are you asking? Are you objecting, or is there something wrong with your eyesight?" I tease her. She looks me up and down, her eyes lingering on my chest and waistband just a bit longer than appropriate, has my cock stirring. *Down boy!*

"Nothing wrong with my eyes, cowboy, just making sure I'm sitting with misery guts Vegas and he's cracking jokes." Her eyes are alight with humor and something else. Is that want I can see staring back at me?

"Talking about eyes, princess," I shoot back, "mine are up here." I point to my eyes and watch as a pink flush creeps over her cheeks. *Yes, girl, busted.* "So, come on, flower, spill. What's got you coming here and drinking your troubles away?" I tease her. A deep sigh leaves her, and her eyes cloud over. I sit up straighter.

"I messed up, Vegas. Really messed up." She sighs and looks at her hands. "I *did* have a bad day. I went and talked to Ally and then went to see Carl." She looks at me with bone-deep sadness in her eyes, and I want to kill who or what put it there. I wanna slay her dragons. *Wait, where did that come from?* She takes a deep breath and continues. "In the end, I took Sarah's car back to her very late. Her mom was looking after her son, Leo. He's autistic and needs a lot of extra care, but he is the most special person under the sun." She smiles, lost in thought. "Now Sarah is seriously pissed at me. Her mom doesn't enjoy looking after Leo overnight, never mind her being unable to drop him off and him being picked up an hour and a half late." Guilt is written all over her face. I reach for her hand over the table.

"I'm sorry, princess. Sounds like a bad day indeed." She looks at me, and a small smile plays around her luscious lips.

"Thanks for listening. She's my best friend, and I adore Leo. Having her understandably mad at me I find upsetting. She won't answer my calls or texts. I can only hope she calms down

96

after sleeping on it." I suddenly feel this need to pull her into me and comfort her. This is all kinds of wrong. I drop her hand as I see Dougal coming up from the bar with another beer for me and what I guess is rum and Coke for Ashley. Karen is behind the bar, looking extremely pissed, and Pennywise looks as though he's giving her a speech.

Dougal puts the Coke in front of Ashley and bats my hand away from the beer.

"Get your own," he mutters. "Do I look like your waiter? I heard your last one quit though, being overworked and underpaid," he grumbles. Ashley giggles and I roll my eyes, but I love that happy sound coming from her. She doesn't laugh enough. Always serious, always with both feet firmly planted on the ground. She's had a lot on her plate, raising Nathan and putting up with Stone's shit. I know she struggles with the club and stays far away from it if she can. That's why I'm so surprised to see her here. I watch Pennywise strutting over with a forced smile.

"Breaks are sorted now. You won't need to cover again tonight, Doug," Pen says with a smile that doesn't reach his eyes. The rest of the night passes with the four of us sitting, Ashley drinking, and the riders switching from beer to Coke. Ash sways as she gets up to go to the ladies' room.

"Wow, she's loaded," mumbles Pen. "Sorry, guys, I'll need to head out now. I need to catch Raven tonight and let him know about the shitshow going on here." Pen gets up ,and fist bumps Dougal and me.

"I'm with you, man. I got some things to report from the patrons, too," Dougal replies. "Are you coming?" They both look at me expectantly, but I shake my head.

97

"I'll stay and make sure Ashley gets home okay. She must have walked because her car is still in the shop. Can't let her walk home loaded on her own," I reply. My brothers nod and turn to leave.

-12- ASH

What the hell am I doing? It was a *stupid* idea to go to Stormy's to drown my sorrows. I so should have known better. And to flirt with Vegas? *'Danger, danger,'* the tiny voice in my head screams at me, and I can literally hear a siren going off in the background. But hell, I have the same right to be at Stormy's drinking as anyone else. To hell with it.

The room is spinning slightly, and I have to hold on to the table to steady myself as I get up to visit the powder room. Oops! I snort to myself. Well done, madam, flirting with the lava hot guy *and* not being able to hold my liquor. Great idea. Still giggling at myself, I wobble my way to the toilet. After doing my business, I splash cold water on my face. Good thing I wear little makeup. I feel slightly less buzzed and decide to put my shitty day aside. Fuck it; some fun and laughter are sorely needed. I'm amazed that Vegas has a sense of humor as well as having a hot bod!

As I return to the table, it's only me and Vegas left. Everyone else has chickened out.

"I take it the others were lightweights?" I ask. Vegas nods with a smirk, one that I would like to wipe off his face in all the best ways. *Hold on, missy, you can't go there! Behave!* Pep

99

talk over. "Your eyes are a weird color, and they change with the light." I look directly into his steely gray eyes, mesmerized, like a deer in the headlights. I can't look away from them. He leans forward and looks into mine. There's heat in his eyes has my cheeks flaming. This is so bad.

"What color are they, then?" he teases me.

"Well, err . . ." I stutter and can feel my cheeks heating to boiling point. "Hypnotic steel?" *Oh my god, Ashley, what are you doing? You're poking the bear, and not well either, like a first-grader with her first crush. Please, ground, open up, and swallow me. Right the hell now, if you please.*

"Was that supposed to be a pickup line? If it was, let me tell you, it sucks, and you need practice." He laughs at me, and his eyes twinkle with mischief.

"I'd have to go to the gym a few times before trying to pick you up, biker boy. You and your ego are a little on the large side," I volley back.

"Hey, are you trying to say I'm fat? Let me tell you, this is six foot two of darn good-looking muscle here!" he pats his chest in mock outrage. I can't help it and burst out laughing.

He watches me with that strange smile playing around his lips. Those lips I really would like to take charge of mine right now. We sit there quietly, just looking at each other, and the atmosphere around us is charged with a sizzle that shouldn't be there. I watch as he shifts in his seat. My mouth is dry, and my body tingles. All the blood seems to have rushed to below my waist. Suddenly he stands, takes my hand, and drags me to the dance floor by the jukebox. I stumble along behind him, a little off balance. The rum hit me harder than I thought. I watch him drop some money in the jukebox and choose a song.

No sooner does the music start as I find myself drawn tight to him, to the sounds of *'Knocking on Heaven's Door.'* I love that song, and it makes me forget that I shouldn't be dancing with Vegas and give myself to the music and enjoy the feel of his hard, hot body touching mine in all the right ways. His hand on my ass pulls me closer. My heart is racing, and my breathing speeds up. Leaning my head on his shoulder feels like the most natural thing to do. Even though I am of average height, he still towers over me with his height and bulk. I feel surrounded by his warmth and strength and relax into his hold. Who would have thought? That man has moves! Moves that make my panties dampen more and more. It is impossible not to notice that I affect him. His hardness pressed into my front, and his hand rubs up and down my back. I hear a rumble coming from him and realize that he's quietly singing along. As I look up, his eyes capture mine, and it feels as though the world stills around us, as though only he and I exist as he sings the words. Like he's singing them only for me. With that beautiful baritone singing voice.

His eyes have me spellbound; mine are fixed on his lips. I can't stand it anymore I reach up, pull his head down to mine, place a gentle, chaste kiss on his lips, and feel him tense for a few seconds. As I try to pull back, he pulls me closer and takes over the kiss.

Nothing chaste about it now. My heart hammers in my chest as he kisses me hard licks my lips with his tongue until I open to him. Our tongues warring, heat surging, the kiss turns hungry. My hands grip his hair and pull him closer. I can hear him groan deep in his throat. My panties are soaked. I cannot let go of his mouth. It teases and works mine in the best of ways.

Loud wolf whistles and shouts of "Get a room!" make us return to reality with a bump. *'Oh my god, as I look around, I can see it was Karen who wolf-whistled at us, smirking. This can't be happening!'* Thoughts are racing through my head. I must be insane! If Raven finds out, he will not be happy! And Vegas will bear the brunt of his ire! I need to get out and away from here, pronto. I can feel panic rising and my hearing going dull.

"Ashley!" Vegas' loud voice breaks through the fog. "Breathe… slowly, in through your nose, out of your mouth." He leads me outside and helps me gain control.

"Do you get like this often?" He sends me a questioning look.

"No, not at all. Not sure what happened there!" *'Liar, liar, pants on fire!'* I can't look him in the eyes. "Okay… I won't ask again." He replies, and it is obvious that he sees through my bullshit. I'm a terrible liar.

"I'm sorry, I shouldn't have kissed you," I stutter, looking at him apologetically.

"Hey, stop that. It takes two, you know. I could have stopped you but didn't, despite knowing you're drunk. I took advantage, and am sorry, Ashley, my control ought to be better than this," Vegas growls at me.

"We shouldn't be doing this," I whisper.

"I know, and that's why I'm taking you home now and then myself straight to the clubhouse to bed before I do something we'll both regret." I look at him, stunned.

"You can't want me, Vegas. I mean, you're you, and I'm just little ole me," my voice is full of disbelief.

"Ash, stop. Stop that right now. Of course, I want you, in case you haven't noticed. You're beautiful, witty, intelligent . . . It takes all my self-discipline not to bend you over my bike right now and fuck you senseless. But I know you would regret it in the morning when the alcohol wears off and neither of us could face Raven. So, don't talk like that again. Now, get your ass over to my bike, so I can take you home." I can see him warring with himself while speaking to me, but his loyalty to Raven wins out as it should. My rational side agrees with him, but that small part of me wants his body to make good on what he promised. It must be the alcohol. I nod, and we walk over to the bike, my hand in his, telling myself it's because I'm buzzed, and he wants to keep me safe.

But I wish that hand holding mine was running over every inch of my body. I shake myself out of my trance and grab the helmet he holds out to me. He makes sure it's fastened, and I swing my leg over the bike to sit behind him, leaning in close, wrapping my arms around him, my hands linking on his hard abs. He shifts in his seat before the engine roars to life. The deep rumble of his Rocker goes right through me, puts a smile on my face, and does nothing to cool my panties down.

He pulls out of the parking lot and onto the street. I hold on tight and whoop with joy as he opens her up a bit, and we are gaining speed. I can feel his body shake with laughter. Clearly, I wasn't as discreet in my joy as I'd hoped. I cringe. We go past my house, but I don't care, loving the freedom, the wind in my hair. It feels like nothing else. For the first time in a long time, I don't have to be a sister, care support worker, responsible, or sensible. I can be unadulteratedly me. Plain and simple me. I can breathe and have not felt so free in a long time. Peace settles around me, and I'm almost sad when Vegas turns around after a while and finds his way back to town. As we stop outside my house, I feel carefree and happy. I get off, hand him the helmet, and smile at him.

"Thank you, Vegas. I didn't realize how much I needed that and missed riding." I quietly smile at him. Leaning forward, I press my lips gently to his. "Thank you." I turn and walk to the door. I know his eyes are following me, so I sway my butt. Silly? Sure. Fun? Absolutely. As I unlock the door and turn the lights on, a smile plays on my face as I turn to look at him. He's there, smirking, and with a wink, he starts the Rocker and takes off down the road toward the clubhouse. I watch until he's out of sight and then close the door with a happy sigh.

The silence screams at me as I walk into the empty house. I flop onto the sofa and turn on the TV, but I'm not focused on what's going on with the news. My thoughts are still in an uproar about a blonde, gray-eyed hunk I shouldn't want. He's everything I thought I hated—a loud-mouthed, hard-faced, alpha biker surrounded by club culture, loyalty, and 'club business.'

God, how I hate those two words and more so being treated like property. I watched my mom turn from a loving, trusting person to an anxiety-ridden wreck, seeking comfort in the depths of a bottle or several bottles. She drank herself to death before I reached ten years old and Nathan was only two. It wasn't long after I had discovered her secret affair with Rusty. I had to grow up quickly.

I hate what the club was then. Of course, club business was kept from me, but you didn't need to be Einstein to realize that they were up to the neck in criminal activities. Mom, Pennywise's mother, helped bring Nathan and me up to a certain extent. Pennywise was a couple of years older than me and in a different year in school. Jamie was nineteen and already deeply involved with the club as a fully-patched member. Things only started changing after that fateful day when the Stormy Souls got into a shootout. Several members were killed, Pennywise's father among them, and Stone, my father, ended up in prison. Jamie took over the club and slowly changed it. I know they run their businesses legit now, but I just can't see past what once was.

I sigh, turn off the TV, and get ready for bed. When I wake in the morning, I feel as though I haven't slept a wink. My dreams were plagued by that tall man with blonde hair, steel-gray eyes, and the wanting, burning need he left me with.

"That's all I need," I mutter to myself, "being hot and ready like a hormone-struck teenager on a Monday morning with no hope in hell of a release. Discipline, Ashley, get your mind out of the gutter and your backside in the shower." Luckily for me, I'm on a late shift.

After my shower, I grab some breakfast and sit at the kitchen bar, slowly eating my cereal and hoping that with the next cup of coffee, my pounding headache will subside. I hear engines rumbling up to the house and go to open the door. Sparks jumps out of my car and hands me the keys.

"Here ya go, Ash, all fixed. She'll be good for a while now." He grins, turns, and walks to the SUV parked behind my car. Knowing that my car is already paid for and the club won't accept me paying them back, I call the local pizza shop and order some pizzas, fully loaded with all the trimmings, to feed six. It's the least I can do.

A sigh escapes me as I grab my phone, hoping to find a message from Sarah. I have fifteen messages but none from Sarah.

9:45 p.m. Nathan: Hi sis, just wanted to let you know I'm all settled. Can you lend me a twenty? Need to buy a book. Thanks, you're a star!

Typical Nathan.

10:30 p.m. Dougal: Hey Ashley, would you let me have Sarah's number please? I need to speak to her about something, club business. Thanks, hon.

Club business? What does Sarah have to do with club business? I'll have to ask her first. I won't give her number out without her permission.

Me: Hey Doug, I'm sorry, I can't give her number out without asking. I'll see her at work and talk to her. I'll text you the number if she okays it later.

1:00 a.m. Vegas: Are you awake?

1:05 a.m. Vegas: I enjoyed sitting and talking with you. It was good to see you laugh.

1:15 a.m. Vegas: Not talking to me?

1:30 a.m. Vegas: Night night, beautiful, sweet dreams xxx

6:30 a.m. Jamie: Sis, hope you're okay, heard you were getting razzed. No Tabletop dancing ;) Have a great day!

There's more from Vegas, all of which I delete, red-cheeked. I can only presume he got drunk after getting back. He doesn't usually text me at all . . . ever. I wonder how much Jamie knows. The thought of him finding out about my alcohol-driven escapade—yes, that's what I'm telling myself—does not fill me with excitement.

7:00 a.m. Carl: Hey honey, can you pop in and see me later? Can you bring me some toothpaste and mouthwash please? I'll transfer you some money into your account if you let me have the details.

Me: Sure, not a problem. Will be with you in a couple of hours before I go to work. Behave yourself and leave the nurses alone :) See you soon.

-13- VEGAS

Pen returns from the back with Karen in tow. She's unceremoniously dropped behind the bar, and Dougal and Pen return to the table, none of them impressed. Doug is in a foul mood and eager to get off. Ash just wobbled over to the ladies.

"Man, she's loaded," states Pen. "I got to head out in a sec and have a word with Raven. Can you call Neil? As in now?" I nod and start dialing.

"Yes, fucker, what can I do for you?" Neil jokes as he answers the phone.

"Hey, asshole, I heard you're looking for a job?" I ask, smiling. I've known Neil for many years, and I like him. He's good people.

"Good news travels fast, I see." His sarcastic voice hits me. "Yeah, man, I could do with a job just about now. What have you got in mind?"

"Well, since you're asking, how about some bar work to start with? Stormy's is really short. You got Raven's number; call him; he'll tell you about pay and insurance," I tell him.

107

"Man, that would be great," Neil replies. "I'd be grateful and can help with whatever crops up. Used to be a bar manager, so I know the score. To be honest, right about now, I'd clean clubhouse toilets. The missus left and cleaned out my accounts, so I'm broke."

"Sorry to hear that, Neil. When can you start?" I ask him.

"Tomorrow, if you need me." I think for a moment and look at Pen, who looks at me seriously. I mouth 'tomorrow', and Pen nods.

"Neil, that would be great. Just give Raven a call in the morning and sort out what needs sorting. I know Ferret will need to speak to you, too."

"Sure thing, man, no problem. And Vegas, thanks for thinking of me. Honestly, I owe you."

"It's all good, Neil. Just call Raven. Have a great night, man. Catch you later." With that, I end the call. "I'll stay and make sure she gets home safe," I tell Pen and Doug, who nod at me, then turns to leave to go to the clubhouse and speak with Raven. My watch shows it's ten p.m. Losing myself to my thoughts; I admit that I enjoyed tonight more than I thought I would. It was great talking with Ashley and learning a bit more about her. I feel like making her laugh is one of my greatest achievements. Then again, hearing her laugh has my dick standing to attention. I had to readjust myself several times discreetly. The smell of her perfume invaded my nostrils, and I'll be damned if it didn't make me harder. I know I shouldn't react to her, but hey, I'm only human. That woman does things to me. And even though I know nothing can happen between us, my dick has not gotten the memo. Clearly.

Her lips are full and lush and begging to be kissed. Just one taste . . . down, boy! I can't think about how good they would look wrapped around my cock.... damn it, I can feel my dick throbbing. She's my kryptonite and turns me into a horny, wet-dreaming teenager. I want to dig my hands into her short dark hair, push her down in front of me, and . . . oh shit, no, no, no, where did that come from?

"I take it the others were lightweights?"

Ashley has returned, and I nod with a smirk. If only she knew what my filthy mind had just conjured up. Thank God she has zero telepathic skills.

"Your eyes are a weird color. They change with the light." She looks directly into my eyes, holding them captive. I lean forward and stare into her green ones. My dick needs readjusting again, and if I could, I would try to live out my earlier thoughts right here. My hunger must show, as she's blushing a sexy pink.

"What color are they, then?" I tease her. "Well, err . . ." she stutters and flushes a deeper shade of pink. "Hypnotic steel?" Ashley that is so cute.

"Was that supposed to be a pickup line? If it was, let me tell you, it sucks, and you need practice." I laugh at her. It's great to see her blush. I'm enjoying this.

"I'd have to go to the gym a few times before trying to pick you up, biker boy. You and your ego are a little on the large side," she volleys back.

"Hey, are you trying to say I'm fat? Let me tell you, this is six foot two of darn good-looking muscle here!" I pat my chest with intent and pretend I'm outraged. She looks at me for a second and bursts out laughing. Full-on belly laugh, Christ, she's sexy when she laughs. It draws my attention to her lips again, sorely tempting me to kiss the shit out of her. It takes all my willpower not to get up and drag her onto my lap.

We sit there quietly, just looking at each other. The air is charged around us with a sizzle that shouldn't be there. I can see my hunger reflected in her eyes, making me hard as steel right now and shift in my seat. Fuck it; I have to move. This is killing me. I inwardly groan, stand, take her hand and drag her to the dance floor by the jukebox.

She stumbles along behind me. Trying to keep up with my long strides, a lot off balance, and I imagine I took her by surprise. I'm not usually the dancing type, but I need to feel her next to me and closer than across a table. She's driving me nuts. I drop some money in the jukebox and choose a few songs. I smirk at my cunning plan.

As the first notes of *"Knocking on Heaven's Door"* drift through the speakers, I pull her to me, holding her tight. She looks at me with fire in her eyes, and her soft body touches mine just the right way. We're close, but it's not close enough. Raven pops into my mind, and I know I'm going to hell, but I don't care. Ashley feels too good, as though her body is made to fit mine perfectly.

I run my hand down to the curve of her ass and pull her tighter, rubbing the globe in my palm. She melts into me and drops her head onto my shoulder. I can feel her heart racing against my chest. Swinging her around, I pull her back into me. Yeah, I can move to the rhythm, and I smile at the surprised but needy look she gives me. She's fully aware of how hard she makes me, clearly able to feel my hard length pressing into her, and she pushes back into me. The atmosphere is crackling with an electric charge. I quietly groan. This is killing me, and I don't know how long I can keep control.

To take my mind off my unbelievably hard cock, I sing along quietly to the music. I know this song word for word—it was my Nan's favorite. Ashley lifts her head and looks up at me, her eyes capturing mine, and for a moment, I lose sense of our surroundings. I continue singing the song to her as though only she and I exist in this room. My eyes shift from hers to her mouth, and I try to control the inner beast commanding me to kiss her, throw her over my

110

shoulder, take her home, and fuck her senseless. She surprises me by reaching up, pulling my head down to hers, and placing a gentle, chaste kiss on my lips. God, her lips are so soft and warm. I'm overwhelmed for a moment and can feel her pulling back. *Oh, to hell with it.* I can't hold on any longer, so I pull her closer and take over the kiss. There's nothing chaste about it now as I deepen it.

I tease her lips, then my mouth ravishes her, and my tongue plays with hers until she opens to me completely, and our tongues are warring. She gives as good as she gets, and the kiss turns hungry. Gripping my hair in her hands, she pulls me closer. So much passion emanates from her, and I can smell her arousal mixing with her perfume. It's the headiest scent I have ever encountered. I groan into her mouth as her tongue toys with mine.

Loud wolf whistles and shouts of "Get a room!" make us come back to reality with a bump. *Shit! What did I do?* I almost lost control and in the middle of a bar. Not just any bar, Stormy's, where everyone can see and report back to Raven about what they saw. We were providing entertainment in the worst possible place. When Karen smirks at us, I know it was she who whistled. *Shit, shit, shit!* I can almost guarantee this is going to get back to Raven. Knowing I'm a dead man walking, I watch Ashley closely. She's gone very pale and is panting, her eyes flitting around, seemingly not seeing. She looks as though she's going into a full-blown panic attack. I know what they look like because I've witnessed Ferret at his worst when his PTSD is triggered.

"Ashley?" I almost shout at her to break through. "Breathe . . . slowly, in through your nose, out your mouth." I lead her, ensuring she breathes with me until she calms down and can maintain her rhythm.

"Do you get like this often?" I ask.

"No, not at all. Not sure what happened there," she answers, looking at her feet. She's a terrible liar, but I don't push her on it. I'll be there if she needs to talk, but I won't force her.

"Okay . . . I won't ask again," I tell her.

"I-I'm sorry. I sh-shouldn't have kissed you," she stutters.

"Hey, stop that. It takes two, you know. I could have stopped you, but I didn't, despite knowing you're drunk. I took advantage, and for that, I'm sorry, Ashley. My control ought to be better than that." I growl at her, angry with myself.

"We shouldn't be doing this," she whispers.

"I know, and that's why I'm taking you home now and then taking myself straight to the clubhouse to bed before I do something we'll both regret," I tell her. She looks at me in utter shock and bewilderment.

"You can't want me, Vegas. I mean, you're you, and I'm just little ole me."

"Ash, stop. Stop that right now. Of course, I want you, in case you haven't noticed. You're beautiful, witty, intelligent . . . why wouldn't I want you? It takes all my self-discipline not to bend you over my bike right now and fuck you senseless. But I know you would regret it in the morning when the alcohol wears off and neither of us could face Raven. So, don't talk like that again. Now, get your ass over to my bike, so I can take you home."

Honestly, I would like to do nothing more than fuck her into next week, but it would mean certain death by Raven's hand. My loyalty must be to my Prez, not my protesting dick. Is that regret in her eyes? She nods, and we walk over to the bike, my hand holding hers. I tell myself it's to keep her steady, but in reality, I just want to hold on to the feel of her skin a little longer. I pass her my spare helmet and hold out my hand to help her get on. Once I'm settled on the bike, my jeans sitting uncomfortably tight, making me shift in my seat, I sigh as she links her hands and rests them on my abs. This is going to be one hell of an uncomfortable ride. I start the Rocker, my pride and joy. No woman has ever ridden with me. I firmly believe that only one woman will ever sit on the back of my bike, and that will be *my* woman. But this is an emergency. At least, that's what I keep telling myself, consciously ignoring the option of calling the prospects to take her home.

The deep rumble of the engine makes me smile every time. I love the sound and the vibrations. Pulling out of the parking lot and onto the street, Ashley holds on tight, and I can hear her whoop with joy even over the engine as I open the throttle and we pick up speed. I can't help but laugh. She sounds like a kid on Christmas. I see her house coming up but fuck it, it's a beautiful night, and she's enjoying herself. To be honest, so am I. Riding helps me blow the cobwebs away.

After about half an hour, I make my way back into town. I love the feeling of her tight on my back, her lush tits pushing into me. But my dick can't take much more. If I don't ride back now, I might just make good on what I said earlier. Pulling up outside Ashley's house, I half expect Raven to be waiting for me, gun pointing at my head, but all is quiet. Ashley gets off and hands me the spare lid, throwing a huge smile at me.

"Thank you, Vegas. I didn't realize how much I needed this and missed riding." She leans forward and places a chaste kiss on my lips. "Thank you," she throws over her shoulder as she turns and walks to the door. I watch her swaying ass along the path. Mesmerized, I wait for her to unlock, switch the lights on, and lock the door from the inside. She shoots me a knowing smile when she turns to me before she steps in. I smirk and wink at her, start the bike, and take off down the road.

113

No sooner have I parked outside the clubhouse than Raven steps out the door. My semi hard-on instantly deflates, looking at his pissed off face. *Any last words, Vegas?* I think to myself. I'm sure that news travels fast, and Karen is a spiteful bitch. I guess my hunch was correct, and she phoned Raven the minute we were lip locked. I'm screwed!

"Vegas, office, now!" Raven thunders. I take a deep breath and follow him inside, ready to accept my fate. At best, I'll get a beat down; at worst I'll have my patches stripped. Panicked, my heartbeat must be about two hundred beats per minute. I'm such an ass!

Raven points to the seat in front of his desk.

"Karen phoned me earlier," he squeezes out between gritted teeth. I know this is it, sitting here shaking in my boots, and my sphincter is working overtime. Taking a deep breath, I wait for the explosion. He looks at me, and his eyes can only be described as evil.

"Not enough that you were lip-locked with my sister, making a display of yourselves, and trust me, I'm pissed, but we'll come to that later. I'll beat ten tons of shit out of you. But more maddening, she tells me that Rusty has told her to water down the drinks, and apparently, I couldn't organize a fist fuck in a glove factory." He's seething. I don't think I have ever seen him so crazy mad as he's right now.

"Who the fuck does that prick think he is? How dare my VP bad mouth me? I spoke to Dougal and Slender already. They confirmed it. Now, what did you find out?" he asks while pacing back and forth behind his desk.

114

"Same as the others, boss. She said Rusty told her to water down the beer and that he comes and gets the deposit to take to the bank. I thought that was strange. If anything, I would have thought Spen does that since he does the books." I shoot him a questioning look. Raven doesn't say a word but gets out a glass and a bottle of Maker's Mark, pouring himself a large helping. He chugs it down in two swallows.

"Neil rang tonight. Ferret is doing a background check as we speak, and I'm meeting him tomorrow at the bar to introduce him to Karen. I'll also inform her that her management skills are no longer needed. She can work shifts behind the bar, but she'll have no access to the cellar, deliveries, or books anymore," Raven growls out.

Raven walks around the desk and stands in front of me. In anticipation, I stand and take a step backward. Lightning quick, Raven's hand shoots out and grabs hold of my cut, and he forces me against the wall. His other fist connects with my face. I can taste blood and know he split my lip. I don't move or try to defend myself as he rearranges my face. I'm sure my nose is broken, and my right eye is swelling shut, but I take what he's giving me. I deserve it.

"That's for hitting on my sister," he screams at me. "You know she's been through some shit the last few years, and you know she hates MC life. You know all of this, and yet you make a move? On my sister? Are you just plain stupid, or do you have a death wish? You're a brilliant brother, and I love you like one, but right now, you overstepped the line by a country mile, and I'm fucked if I let you get away with it. My sister is off-limits. To you and anyone else from the Club. Got me?" I nod at his agitated, angry, teeth-grinding face, trying to look him in the eye to show him sincerity. "Don't make me kill you, Vegas. You hurt her, and I'll kill you, slowly and painfully. Do we understand each other?"

"Yes, Prez, understood. Crystal clear.

-14- ASH

How did I think that double rum and cokes were a good idea? Ever? My head is pounding like a road crew is using a pneumatic drill right between my eyes. God, I hate hangovers. That's why I rarely drink. Must have had about three pints of water and two Ibuprofen, but it is not letting up. At least the queasiness lessened after breakfast. I hope my shift's gonna be a quiet one, or else I might not survive. I sigh as I park outside the hospital. On my Carl supply trip, I got him his toothpaste, some sweets, fruit, and the newest American Iron magazine. That should entertain him for a while.

I make my way to his room, and as I open the door, I spot Elijah and Greg slouching in chairs in the corner, playing games on their phones. Carl is sleeping. I tiptoe over to him, give the other two a small finger wave, and lean over Carl to kiss his cheek. He opens his eyes slowly.

"Hey princess, how are you?" he sounds tired.

"I'm fine, lazy bum. What are you up to? Other than annoying the staff and lazing about in bed?" I ask with a lighthearted wink I don't feel.

"Oh, you know, keeping everyone on their toes." His smile does not reach his eyes. I turn to Elijah and Greg.

116

"Hey boys, I have an hour to spare, so why don't you go get some food and coffee? Bring me one back while you're at it. I'll keep an eye on this one." I put my sunniest smile on, winking at them.

"Thanks, Ashley, that would be great. We've been here since six am, so we could do with a break." groans Eli as he stretches his long legs. They both nod at us as they make their way out the door.

"So," I say to Carl, looking him in the eye, "how are you? Don't even try to fool me." I haven't asked about his tests.

"I feel like I have been run over by a dump truck, honey. Had my tests this morning, fuck that hurt, and afterward I felt so tired like I'd gone ten rounds with Ali." I grip his hand and squeeze it, just letting him know I'm here for him, sending him a bit of strength.

"When will you get the results?" I quietly ask.

"Should be sometime today or tomorrow, the doctor said." He sighs. "Ashley, please, I don't want anyone to know just yet. Even if it is bad news, there is nothing anyone can do to make me better. Not the brothers, anyway. I don't want to cause worry and upset them unless it is absolutely necessary," he pleads with me. This whole keeping secrets doesn't sit well with me. But I nod, as I feel I must respect his wishes. It is his story to tell, not mine.

"So, come on, give me the dirt. Greg mentioned you went to Stormy's and got drunk?" Carl smirks at me. Oh my god, news travels fast. Have they got nothing else to gossip about?

"Just a little, Carl. I was only tipsy, not full-out blind drunk. I had a falling out with Sarah and got frustrated. So, I went to Stormy's. Karen was her usual pleasant self, *not*. Just sat with Penny, Dougal, and Vegas, and then Vegas saw me home." He looks at me and starts grinning.

117

"Ash, your flush is equal to Pinocchio's nose. There's more to this, isn't there?" He smirks.

Oh, what the hell? I might as well tell him the whole sorry saga. He's too astute to be happy with half-truths. I pull up a chair and spill my guts, telling him about my fight with Sarah, my night out, and yes, about the kiss, the ride home, the messages, everything.

When I'm finished, I lay my head on the side of his bed and wait. I can't look him in the eye. I'm so embarrassed. The full gravity of the situation with Vegas just hit me. Not being able to shake his image out of my head since last night hasn't helped the situation. And that scares me. I don't usually feel a connection with anyone from the male species. Carl is the exception, as he feels like my brother from another mother. I don't look at him in that way.

Carl is quiet and just listens. I'm anxiously waiting for a reaction and shuffle nervously in my seat.

"Well, shit, you got yourself in a right old mess there," he says, looking at me with sympathy. I'd hate to think of it as pity. "Where Sarah is concerned—" He stops mid-sentence as the door opens and a nurse comes in with a blood pressure monitor and other paraphernalia. She smiles at me and introduces herself.

"Hi, I'm Chloe, this misery guts' nurse." I return the smile.

"I'm Ashley, his sister, not by blood but by choice. Is he giving you trouble, Chloe?" I wink at her.

"Nothing I can't handle," she grins, "but his pickup lines are the worst." She laughs at him. I cover my mouth with my hand to suppress a laugh. Suddenly, Carl looks very grumpy.

"She's immune to my charms, Ash. I don't even get an extra pudding out of that woman. She's as mean as they come," he whines.

"Do I need to call the orderly? Or will you let me take your temperature this time around?" Chloe asks him with an innocent smile.

"You tried four hours ago, and the answer is still no," he grumps.

"Carl, stop being so stubborn, or I'll get the orderly myself to hold you down." I mock growl at him, trying hard to hide my amusement. He sighs defeatedly.

"Okay, okay, just get on with it." His mood has improved none, and his petulant stares are not making it easier to contain my laughter.

"Okay then," Chloe says with a wink in my direction, "roll over and pull your pants down. I'll just get the KY jelly." She waves an under-the-tongue thermometer at him.

At that point, I have to turn and look out of the window. My shoulders are shaking with muffled laughter that I try to disguise with a cough.

"I'll give you two some privacy." I can't help the small snort that escapes.

"No way, no how are you getting anywhere near my perky ass with that thing." Carl is almost screeching. "If you think you're coming anywhere near me with that, you can fuck right off."

"Aw, but dear, you offered to show me your enormous balls yesterday. Now that I want to see them, you're clenching. I'm so disappointed," Chloe mocks him mercilessly.

"Oh, Carl, you didn't. I'm so disappointed with you. I thought we'd agreed you'd stop exposing yourself. We've been on about this since you were fourteen. I'd thought you'd gotten over it." I use my best acting skills, turn to face Carl and Chloe, and shake my head at him with sad doggy eyes.

"What the hell?" Carl shouts. Chloe, by this time, is bent over laughing, hardly able to breathe, and I finally collapse, roaring with laughter.

119

"Relax," Chloe chuckles, "your pert little hindy is all safe. Now, open your mouth and let me take your damn temperature." She winks at him. He points his finger first at me, giving me an evil look that tells me, you just wait, I'll get you back for that, then at Chloe, and like the petulant child we drove him to be, he opens his mouth, then closes it around the thermometer.

"Not fair," he yammers, which does nothing to stop us from giggling. Chloe completes the rest of her tasks, takes his blood pressure, and charts everything. She turns to me.

"If he weren't such a big baby, he'd be a nice guy, I reckon." She smirks.

"Yup, that's Carl for you. Why do you think he's called Flakey?" I chuckle.

"They couldn't get away with 'baby'?" Chloe asks with mischief in her eyes. I choke down my giggles.

"Something like that." She finally takes the thermometer.

"A little elevated, but you'll live. I'll bring your meds in a minute and get your antibiotic drip going." She nods at Carl thoughtfully.

"Did they tell you the results can take twenty-four to forty-eight hours to come through?" Carl nods. "On that note, can you please roll onto your side so I can check the dressing and wound?" Carl turns over, huffing. "Now, look, I know you're nervous, and this is a shitty situation for you," Chloe says as she inspects his back with gentle hands and changes the dressing, "but all joking aside, if there's anything on your mind and you need to talk, I've got broad shoulders, Carl, and I'm always here to listen. I might not be able to change the situation, but I can be here for you as a listening ear. Sometimes offloading is the best medicine." Chloe's tone has been as gentle and empathetic as her hands have been. I can't see Carl's face, but I notice him taking a deep breath.

"Thanks, Chloe, I appreciate it, but I'm okay for now."

His voice sounds hoarse and rough, so we know he's not fine.

"Okay, I'm finished. I'll see you again in four hours then." Chloe winks as she steps back and waits for Carl to turn back over.

"Don't hurry on my account," he scoffs at her. His tone is sarcastic, but his eyes show gratefulness to Chloe, that I can appreciate, and I'm sure she does too. She turns toward me.

"I like you, Ashley, you're funny," she grins at me. "Do you want to meet up for coffee? Carl told me you work in care for disabled children?" I nod.

"Yes, I do indeed. I'm a care worker, and yes, I would love to meet for coffee if we are both off," I reply. She scribbles something onto the pad she produced out of her uniform pocket.

"Here's my number. Give me a call or text later, and we can arrange something."

"Sure." I nod. Carl looks from one to the other, slaps his forehead, and groans.

"God help us." We both giggle, and Chloe leaves, closing the door quietly.

"She's nice," I tell Carl.

"I'm not sure whether I'd agree," he grumbles. "She has it out for me." I shake my head at him.

"And your grumpy moods and inappropriate *flirting* have nothing to do with that, I guess?" I roll my eyes so hard, that I'm sure they'll get stuck at the top of my head and get an inside look at my brain. Honestly, I love Carl with all my heart, but sometimes he can be a real ass and a childish one at that. Just then, there is a knock on the door. Greg and Elijah are back. Looking at my watch, I jump up. Damn it; I have to hurry so I won't be late. Placing a kiss on Carl's cheek, I mumble a hasty goodbye and run for my car.

◊◊◊

Racing into handover like a bat out of hell, I throw myself on a chair. Sarah giving me the stink eye doesn't make me feel any better. I'll have to deal with that later. Being thoroughly filled in about all the weekend drama with the kids, I'm about to get up when the manager walks in.

"We have a problem. A big one." I look at him, stunned. What on earth can be so wrong that he comes in this early on a Monday morning? "We just had an inspection, and not only has one of our bathrooms been condemned, but they revoked our transport permit as the minibus lift failed inspection. We have enough money to fix either the shower or the minibus. So, for now, I'll have to put the shower first. Until we save the money to either fix or replace the Minibus, there will be only taxi or public transport travel to urgent appointments. I'm sorry, guys." We all stare at him in shock, and murmurs break out across the room as he walks out the door.

"That is just not possible!" Sarah throws into the room. "Can you imagine what would happen if we used the bus with the kids? Imagine Franklin; he wouldn't be able to, and neither would most of the others!" She's heated up now and on a roll. "Something has to be done!" she fumes.

"But what? Unless you have a hundred grand to spare, lying around in your underwear drawer that you could donate, it ain't gonna happen, Sarah," James throws at her. He works shifts on the other floor.

"Bake sale?" Gina's sarcasm has no bounds today.

"We should all think about it. Maybe we could do something community orientated with the kids that are not as bad? Raise community awareness about who we are and what we do?" I throw in quietly.

"Not bad," Gina pipes up.

"We should all come up with some names of kids that could participate and ways we can raise awareness of our program here, not to mention the impact we have on the kids who are enrolled. I volunteer to coordinate. I'll leave a box on each floor and put your ideas on paper. I'll collect them at the end of the week, and James can help me sort through them. That okay, James?"

"Sure, I'm on board with this. Why not? We have never done anything like this, and as we are not fully state-funded, I think it's about time we did some fundraising."

That seems settled then. It appears we have all been volunteered to fundraise by the self-appointed committee. I grin to myself. It's great to see that everyone is so invested in this place and the children under our care. Pride for the place I work for and all of us working here floods me. We try to do our best.

"I'm still pissed at you," Sarah hisses at me as we walk out of the staff room and onto the floor.

"I know, Sarah, I know. I'm so sorry." Tears are burning in my eyes, and I know she can see them. "Please, Sarah, let me explain. You are my best friend, and I love you. I would never intentionally do anything to upset or hurt you and Leo, and I cannot tell you enough how sorry I am." She looks at me, doubt in her eyes.

"Let's get on with work, and we'll talk during the afternoon break."

Sarah's face conveys how conflicted she is her anger warring with her loyalty and curiosity. She *knows* I would never do anything dangerous or anything that would affect her and Leo.

The afternoon drags. I've had a thought, so I text Jamie.

Me: Hey, bro, can I pick your brains on something?

Jamie: I hate it when you call me bro.

Me: Rather I'd call you stink face? :)

Jamie: You're evil. That only happened once, and I was a kid! Stop bringing it up! : (

Me: Okay, Jamie, brother dear. I'll let bygones be bygones (for now) ;)

Jamie: What do you want, anyway? I thought you were at work.

Me: I'm just taking a quick five-minute break. Are you still wanting to raise the club profile? Like doing stuff for charity?

Jamie: Haven't had time to think about it for the last week or two, club business, but yes, of course we are. Why are you asking?

Me: The home has a problem raising money for minibus repairs. I wonder if the club could help with fundraising.

Jamie: Not a bad idea. I'll bring it to the table at church this week. Let you know after.

Me: KK, no problem, STYL xxx

Jamie: Laters, sis xxx

As I shove my cell into my pocket, Sarah comes in with two cups of coffee. I breathe a sigh of relief. At least she seems to be willing to listen. She places a cup in front of me and sits opposite the small table.

"Go on then, let's hear your pathetic excuses." Sarcasm is an art form for Sarah. She has been fighting for herself and Leo for so long, that she becomes a lioness where Leo is concerned and has no qualms about fighting like one for him. She shows no mercy where he's concerned, and I have often pitied those who went up against that fantastic duo. Now I'm the one on the receiving end of her ire.

I take a deep breath, collecting my thoughts, not sure where to start.

"Sarah, look, I'm so sorry," I repeat myself. "It was a bad day. I went to Ally's and had a panic attack. It took some time to settle, then I went to see Carl and overheard things I shouldn't have. I'm sorry, I cannot tell you the details. Carl made me promise to keep it to myself. But I can tell you he's in trouble. He's like my brother from another mother. I was shocked and unsettled, and I ran out on him screaming. Then went back and made up with him. Unfortunately, I took my time with it. That's what made me late. I'm so sorry. I'll tell you exactly what happened when Carl is ready to tell people, but it is his story to tell, not mine. Please understand that I can't tell you any more now. You're my best girlfriend, Sarah. I love you, and I love Leo, you know that. I look at Leo as my nephew. I'd never do *anything* to put him in a difficult position, nor would I knowingly upset or hurt you. I'm so grateful that you're my friend," I blubber, tears running freely down my face. She and Ally are the only people I can trust. I cannot lose Sarah. I just can't. I know I'm getting too emotional and can feel panic rising.

Grounding myself, I look around the room and concentrate on five items I can see, taking deep breaths, then five things I can hear, taking deep breaths, and when I've calmed a little, Sarah speaks. She knows the signs of my panic attacks only too well and helped me learn grounding techniques in the first place. So, she knows what I'm doing.

"Okay, it sounds a bit strange that you can't give me details, but I know how close you are to Carl, and I know how you get with your temper, so I believe you had to go back and make up with him. I will accept that you cannot give me details for now, and I know you'd never hurt either of us. But I have to ask, do you have the faintest idea how much trouble your being late caused? My mother was furious. Leo was in a corner rocking when I got there and was beside himself. It took over an hour to get him out of his catatonic state.

"My mother's language left *nothing* to the imagination, and I doubt that she will *ever* look after Leo again. Nor would I let her. Leo used her living room as a toilet, pooping on the floor. He's not done anything like that in years, so it shows how distressed he was at the time. I don't know what happened while he was there, but I wouldn't want to put him through that again. So, you owe me, sister. You will be on babysitting duty until you're old and gray, and you better move into a bigger place, or convert Nathan's bedroom into one for Leo, because you will be his caregiver overnight. Do you get me?" Her serious eyes hold mine.

"I get you, Sarah. I'm so sorry. I feel awful that Leo had to go through all that." Tears continue to burn at the back of my eyes.

"Now then, wipe your snotty nose and, for God's sake, stop blubbering. You look like a mess." Grinning, Sarah hands me some tissues. They're crumpled and have probably been used to spit wash Leo's face, but at this precise moment, I don't care. I take the tissues, stand up and hug my best friend tight. I know I'm forgiven. "Love you, Ash, even though you're a pain in my ass," she tells me as she hugs me.

"Love you too, Sarah and Leo," I return, squeezing her hard.

"You can start showing that by not squeezing me to death," Sarah coughs out, and I immediately let her go. I'm so relieved. "Back to work now, bitch," Sarah orders, pointing her finger at me. "Your break was over thirty minutes ago, and I almost missed mine. Now, go away and do something productive, snotty nose." She laughs and wags her finger at me.

The next few hours fly by, and all is good in the land of Sarah and Ashley. I grab her arm as we walk out of the building after our shifts. I almost forgot!

126

"Sarah, Dougal asked me for your phone number. I told him I wouldn't give it out unless you say it's okay. He mentioned something about club business, so I have no idea what he wants. Club business means it's something he can't tell me anything about and will only speak to club members and people it directly concerns. The club likes to keep nonmembers out of their business. It gives plausible deniability," I explain. Sarah looks at me with eyes as big as saucers.

"What the heck can he want? I don't know about any club business or want to. Though I have to say, he's hot." She winks at me. "So, yes, by all means, give him my number. He's quite the specimen. I could see myself having Dougal therapy while you spend the night with Leo." I gasp in mock outrage.

"You wouldn't." Sarah laughs at my performance and giggles.

"Oh, but yes, I so would. He's hot, and I need fun and lubrication of my shriveled and dried up lady parts." I shudder in mock disgust.

"Stop! Stop! Hell to the no, I don't want to hear this! Lalalalalalala!" I stick my fingers in my ears, walking away from her. I can hear her laughter ringing through the parking lot. That's way too much information. Just no . . . way too much information was definitely overshared. I quickly unlock my car while Sarah is still bent over laughing, hands on her thighs. Is that a tear she has in her eye? Time to get out of here and go home. I open my phone and send Dougal the number. Let them sort it out.

-15- VEGAS

Dougal winces as he walks into the clubhouse and sees my face from where I'm sitting at the bar.

"You run into a door face-first?" I knew it was coming after the way Raven rearranged my face. It taught me a valuable lesson. To stay away from Ashley, no matter how much I want her or how much she calls to me. I nod to Dougal, put down the cold pack, throw the bloodied cloth in the bin and make my way to the door. In no mood to talk to anyone, I cock my leg over the old girl and start her up, her deep rumble comforting me. Not that I need comforting, but it has that effect on me every time. She vibrates through my bones and feels like she's part of me. The only thing better is feeling Ashley's hot body up close against me.

Where the hell did that come from? I can't even think about that! She's just another girl, family at that. It's not as if I've suddenly developed feelings for her. I'm a hit it and quit it guy. It's time to revisit Violet's. At least, that's what I convince myself I should do. I shake my head as my gate comes into view. I must have been on autopilot, as I can't remember even leaving the clubhouse. Not good, Vegas, not good. I roll into the garage. Once inside, I make my way straight to the kitchen. My jumbo-sized fridge contains not a lot of food, but plenty of beer, so I

128

can anesthetize myself. I open the freezer side and get a pack of peas out. I hate peas, and wild horses couldn't make me eat that shit, but they make a great ice pack.

I call Sparks and let him know I won't be in today. I need to get myself sorted out and my head on straight. Rummaging through my kitchen drawers, I find what I need—Tylenol and ibuprofen. I take both and lie on the sofa with an ice pack on my face, trying not to think. When I wake up, it's getting dark. I must have needed that. The swelling looks a bit better, but my eye remains almost closed. I'm pissed at myself. How could I have been so stupid and let things get *this* out of hand? I shove myself up, make my way into the hall, enter the gym, and kick the door shut with force. The next few hours I spend working out, as hard as my face will let me. I run on the treadmill, row across the Atlantic and back until the rower creaks, then move over to the punching bag hanging in the corner and let all my frustration out. The bag swings wildly as I hammer into it, punch after punch. I imagine Rusty's face when I hit it and try my hardest to make it look like ground beef! It makes me feel a little better. He's a cunt, and I hate the bastard.

◊◊◊

The next day, I arrive at the garage to find everyone staring at me. By then, the word is out that Raven has rearranged my face and why. Nothing I can do about it. Brothers gossip, and sometimes they're worse than women. Ratchet walks up to me and slaps my back.

"Stupid, bro, but brave. I hope it was worth it." He smirks at me, and I nod at him, going to my space to arrange my tools and get on with the day. I swear, anyone else comments, and I'll wrap the rather large torque wrench I'm holding around their head.

Luckily, everyone else gives me a wide berth. My shitty mood radiates from me, and I don't need any of these dickheads' advice. I know I fucked up.

129

I finish my first repair, a cylinder head gasket on a small Jap 'bike'. No idea who's it is. I just fix the damn things. Probably belongs to a chick. Has to, because it's bright yellow, and I bet she has a yellow Power Ranger suit to go with it.

My stomach growls in protest by the time lunchtime comes around. I hear snickering behind Sparks and me saying, "This should be interesting." I turn around and groan. Ashley just walked in, carrying three pizza boxes, a six-pack, and a box of doughnuts. As much as I hate to admit it, she catches my eye, and her eyebrows go straight up to her hairline, causing her to nearly drop the pizza boxes. She catches herself quickly and turns to Sparks and Halfpint.

"Thanks for fixing my car, guys. I know you won't take money, so I thought I'd bring you lunch. Three large meateaters, fully loaded, garlic bread, Bud, and doughnuts. If you don't want them, just say the word, and I'll take it to work with me." She smiles, mischief on her beautiful face. I smack myself on the head—mentally, not physically because that would make me look stupid.

I see her leaning into Sparks and whispering, and I see Sparks look at me, then at her, giving her a nod. She places the pizzas on the workbench, and like hyenas, everyone descends. Ashley storms out of the garage, slamming her car door and revving the shit out of her engine. I'm not sure what pissed her off, but man, that door slam sounded mad. I feel just a little bit sorry for her car. I quietly get my share of pizza and doughnuts, then get back to work, keeping my head down. Even this shitstorm will pass, eventually.

After a long day, I get home and put my feet on the table. I grab a beer from the fridge and sit in to watch some TV. As I switch it on, Sons of Anarchy is mid-episode. The series drives me insane. It's responsible for many Jax Teller wannabes and gives real MCs a bad name. If it were at least a tiny bit realistic, I wouldn't mind. But it's not. It's a fantasy of what people like to think MCs are about and bears minimal resemblance to the real thing.

Unable to stare at Jax's white sneakers any longer, I switch to the sports channel and watch a rerun of the weekend's football game. During my second beer, my phone dings. I can't be bothered, and am sure if it's anything urgent, whoever it is will call. The dinging continues a few times. Then blessed silence. An hour later, the group text message tone goes off. I open that one without looking at the other ones.

Ferret: Church, Sunday as usual. All members required, no excuses.

Ferret: Emergency meeting for all who received this message. Tomorrow, 6:00 p.m. No excuses are acceptable.

I groan. What the hell is up now? Lately, there isn't a week without emergency meetings or shit going sideways. That's it. I've had enough for the day, and I take my ass to bed. Shrugging off my cut, I hang it over the back of the chair in the bedroom, then take my gun out of my shoulder holster and put it on the bedside table. No matter where I am, I carry. Call it an insurance policy, but my gun always rests next to my phone.

I make my way into my bathroom and turn on the shower. Man, it feels good to wash off the dirt from the day. I let the hot spray soothe my aching body and relax, thinking about today and how Ashley made a hasty exit. She probably realizes by now that I'm not worth shit, but I can't get her soulful green eyes out of my mind. And I can literally taste her and feel her lips on mine. That was the hottest kiss ever.

My dick agrees and makes his agreement known. *Traitor!* I close my eyes and imagine Ashley's hands on my skin, her lips on me, and her tongue chasing mine. I can feel her erect nipples grazing my chest. My hand grabs my cock and gives it a few hard pulls. I grunt as I feel her hand pushing mine away. She looks up at me with those eyes I could lose myself in and drops to her knees.

She strokes my cock, keeping her eyes on me, before licking from root to tip, her other hand massaging my balls. I won't last if she carries on like this. She slowly and gently licks the pre-cum drops off the head of my dick, pushing me close to the edge instantly. This is torture, and I struggle to restrain myself, to not fuck her mouth with all I have. I dig my hand into her hair and pull her toward me. She willingly follows and wraps her lips around me. Tight. I drop my head to the wall of the shower and groan. Oh yes, just like that.

She picks up her tempo, and my hips involuntarily push forward to the rhythm she's setting. I feel myself hitting the back of her throat, but she doesn't gag. Instead, she changes the angle slightly and swallows around me until I see stars. I can feel the tingle at the base of my spine, and my balls draw tight. I push in one last time and release with a roar, planting myself in the back of her throat as she swallows all of me. Every . . . last . . . drop. What a beautiful sight.

I slowly open my eyes, look down at my hand, and am disgusted with myself. If Raven knew I just jacked off to fantasies of his little sister, he would shoot me. I wash away the evidence of my guilty pleasure, turn on the cold tap, and let the icy water run off me until I feel breathless. Wrapping a towel around my waist, I brush my teeth, switch off the lights, and make my way to my bed. I drop the towel and climb in, my cock still at half-mast, but I push any other thoughts of the minx who occupies my thoughts out of my mind. Not sure what kinda spell she weaved on me, but it has to stop.

I pick up my phone to set my alarm and see the message icon blinking. I open the app and look at the messages I ignored earlier. Damn it to hell!

7:00 p.m. Ash: Did Raven do that to you? Don't bother denying it. I know it was him!

Damn, I'll kill Sparks tomorrow. Fucking blabbermouth has been running his mouth.

7:05 p.m. Ash: I will kill his sorry ass! I know he thinks he needs to protect me, but I can look after myself. It's not as if we bumped uglies in the middle of the bar. It was just a kiss! I'm pissed. I can make my own decisions, and you should not bear the brunt of it! If he has something to say, he can say to my face!

A small smile plays on my lips. She has fire, that is for sure! Misguided ideas, but fire.

7:15 p.m. Ash: You can ignore me as much as you want, Vegas, but I will see Raven right the fuck now and will rip him a new asshole! This is not right! Not happening. He will not make my decisions. Neither do you BTW. No one controls or railroads me! You can both think again.

7:20 p.m. Ash: I'm at the clubhouse now, God help him. You're such a coward. You could at least reply! Fuck you, Vegas, just fuck you!

I slowly release the breath I'd been holding. What the hell is she talking about? Not sure what she had for lunch, but it must have contained anger pills. She sure isn't thinking rationally. I sit up with a start. *Fuck!* She's at the clubhouse, or at least was a couple of hours ago, and is giving Raven a piece of her mind. *Fuck, fuck, fuck!* He's gonna be consumed with rage. I hope this isn't what the emergency meeting is about. Is he going to take my patch? Panic rises in the back of my throat. The club is all I have now. They're my family, not by blood but family nonetheless. I don't know what I'd do without the club and don't even wanna contemplate that. I'll grovel if I have to and take shit duty forever, but I can't lose my patch. Nothing and no one is worth that.

Me: Hey, sorry I didn't reply, was watching football and missed your messages. Yes, Raven punched me, but I deserved it. We both knew he would hate it, yet I kissed you anyway. You were drunk and I took advantage of you. I'm sorry. That cannot and will not happen again. Don't give him a hard time. He did what any good big brother would do. He protects his little sister from the big bad wolf. You know what I'm like, no good for you. No good for any woman unless she has a strong constitution. Sorry, princess, it will not happen again.

I wait for a moment and see three dots appearing on my screen, showing that she's writing. Then they stop and disappear, reappear again, then disappear. When they reappear, it ends with the dinging of my phone.

Ash: You are such a dickhead, Vegas, and a coward. I will not be dictated to. I thought what we had was worth something, but I was very much mistaken! But don't worry, I won't accost you again, tipsy or sober. Guaranteed!

My big stick definitely prodded the hornet's nest. I sigh, close my screen, put the phone on charge, and try to catch some sleep.

-16- ASH

Shock and fury run through me when I spot Vegas. Unbelievable! Vegas's beautiful face!

I can hardly make out his eyes, and it's a struggle not to gasp in shock. He hasn't spotted me yet,

but I can hear the guys murmuring and staring at me. As Vegas turns around, I nearly drop the

pizza boxes. *Fuck my life!* Sparks is coming toward me to take the pizzas, and I lean toward him.

"Is that Raven's handiwork? What the fuck did Karen tell him?" Sparks looks from me to

Vegas, then turns to me with an apologetic look in his eyes, aware of my fake crush but not

knowing that it's become very real. He nods and has the decency to avoid my eyes. I'm furious.

The anger is rushing hot through my veins and leaves me struggling to remain composed. Taking

a deep breath, I look at Vegas and the others, silently seething. I paste a smile on my face.

"Thanks for having my car fixed, guys. I know you won't take money, so I thought I'd

provide you with lunch. Three large meateaters, fully loaded, garlic bread, Bud and doughnuts. If

you don't want them, just say the word, and I'll take it to work with me." My voice sounds

lighthearted, but my anger is vibrating through me. This is not over, by no stretch of the

imagination, and Raven is not going to get away with this. And yes, it's Raven, not Jamie,

because the brother who loves me would not be such an asshole. The club President, however, that's a different story. The pizzas are taken out of my hands. I leave, stomping over to my car and slamming the door shut. I'm so pissed off right now that I can't see straight.

I texted Vegas several times. Bloody coward, he's ignoring me, but it's no less than I expected. He loves the club. It's his family, and he'll do as he's told: leave me alone. I know Jamie too well for his own good.

I will not let him get away with controlling who I can see, kiss, or anything else I can think of in any way, shape, or form. If he thinks he can dictate to me, he has another thing coming. He wants to play? Bring it on! I can play with the best of the boys.

Luckily, it's a short shift today. Sarah catches me in the linen room and shuts the door.

"What has crawled up your ass and died today?"

"Nothing," I reply, slamming the freshly folded sheets into their place on the shelves. I pick up a towel and vigorously shake it out before folding it.

"Ash, I hate to tell you this, but the towel is already dead. You don't have to kill it before folding it," Sarah tells me with drawn-up eyebrows. I huff and carry on accosting the towels. She leans in and takes the towel out of my hand. "Sit!" she orders, pointing to a stool. I do as I'm told but fidget. It's impossible to sit still. I'm so enraged and resentful. "Now, spill. I cannot watch another towel get tortured,"

"So, after we fought, I may have gone to Stormy's and gotten a tad drunk," I start. "While drunk, I may have taken a liking to Vegas," I swallow and hunch my shoulders in embarrassment.

"Interesting," Sarah replies with a knowing smirk. "Continue." I shoot her a squinty glare.

"So, we may have had a moment, or several moments, ending in the hottest, most toe-curling kiss ever. It was so scorching hot, and it made the paint on the walls melt."

I can't help it. Grinning from ear to ear, I relive the moment for a second or two until Sarah rips me out of my moon-eyed stare.

"What took you so long? It's clear you have the hots for him, and the way he looks at you, and more importantly, the death stares he sends everyone else who shows the slightest interest in you, clearly, he wants you. What's so terrible about that?" She looks at me with questions in her eyes.

I blow out a breath, my voice instantly hardening. "Raven."

Her confused look tells me I'm going to have to elaborate.

"Raven knows about it. The bitch, Karen, who manages Stormy's, couldn't wait to tell him. So, he punched Vegas, and not just once either. Vegas has obviously been told to stay away from the *princess*. Well, I'll tell you what Raven can do with his princess, or rather what his princess will do to him. She'll take her size six spikey-heeled boots and bury them in his ass. That's what the princess will do. How dare he try to order who I can and can't see, kiss, fuck, or do whatever else I want to do with? I'm a grown woman, not a child. And God help me, he will get what's coming to him," I rant to Sarah, who looks at me with enormous eyes. I've never been one to get angry, and certainly not yell. I've always been the quiet one, getting on with my life, but enough is enough.

"He owes me, and he owes me big. All these years, I've picked up the pieces for the club and raised Nathan. I deserve better than this. I was forced to make my own decisions from an early age, and I'll continue to do so. What a prick! It's not as if I'm an untouched virgin, either. The time for protecting my virtue has long gone. Fair enough, so I haven't got lots of ever-changing boyfriends, but that doesn't mean I'm an innocent. I worked at Violet's. I know what the world is about. And though I asked for my membership to be kept private, I have one and use it from time to time. However, that's no one's business but mine. Not even Sarah knows about that. I don't like to sit in a glasshouse for all to see, nor do I leave my laundry out for others to inspect! I like my privacy, so shoot me!" Sarah's eyes bulge out of her head in surprise, and for once, she's stunned into silence. It takes her a moment to process my ravings.

She clears her throat noisily. "Oh my god, Ash, what an asshole! And you have a membership at Violet's?" her eyebrows have reached her hairline with a look of pure disbelief. "Which you kept from me?" Well, shit, I must have said the last bit out loud. I cringe. My secret is out, and despite knowing it will be safe with Sarah, I know she will want to know all, and I don't want to tell.

It's my private life, which for this very reason is why I keep it private. What happens at Violet's stays at Violet's. Time to change the subject.

"Has Dougal called you? I gave him your number." Sarah puts her hands on her hips.

"Oh no, missy, you're not getting away that easy. You are not off the hook, not even a little!" I sigh in defeat, but tell her.

"Look, I know you have questions and lots of them. I promise I will answer, but not here. I'll need something stronger and a comfortable seat for that conversation." I try to placate her. To my surprise, she replies.

"That's fair enough. I agree this is not the time or the place for more revelations about the sex dungeon," she snorts.

"As far as your dickweed of a brother is concerned, let him have it, sister. His delusions about you being too little to take care of yourself need to be dealt with before they get out of hand. You are your own person and one of the strongest women I've ever come across. Do you need backup? Just shout, and I'll bring a baseball bat to beat some sense into him. Club Prez or not!" Sarah is ferocious with her protectiveness and her unwavering support of me. She's the best friend any woman can have, and that realization puts a smile on my face.

"Thanks, Sarah. I'll find him tonight after work, rip his arm off, and beat him to death with the soggy end. If that doesn't help, he'll find himself with a freshly ripped, oversized new asshole!"

"Woo-hoo! You go, girl. I might just come along and cheerlead!" Sarah is chortling. "And if it goes too far, just call, and I'll help you bury the body." I know she's only half-joking.

"The thing is, Sarah, I like Vegas. I really like him. Like a lot. It has been the hardest thing to admit to myself, and I'm still struggling with that revelation a little myself. I can't help how I feel though, how he makes me feel. I'm well aware that we wouldn't fall under your ordinary relationship category, but I'd like to see where this could go." Exhaustion overcomes me, as well as a healthy dose of sadness. I'm starting to fall for that beautiful man and have no idea how to get him to give us a shot.

◊◊◊

I nod at the prospect at the gate, who lets me pass without stopping. My fury has not subsided, not even a tiny bit. I'm revved and ready to go. Watch out brother. Princess is about to smack you out of your arrogance and overprotectiveness! I send Vegas another text, letting him know exactly what I think. He can fuck off. If he's too much of a yellow belly coward to decide I'm worth standing up for, he can go fuck himself!

139

I take a deep breath, get out of the car, and storm straight into the clubhouse. Dougal is at the bar, chatting with Pennywise and Mom, who winces when she sees my face. My pissed off features give me away.

"Raven?" my voice is hard as steel. Dougal and Penny look up in surprise and toward the office.

"He's in a meeting." Penny throws in.

"Watch and see if I give a shit!" I hiss at him. He raises his hands in a placating gesture as I stomp past him, heading toward the office door.

"Ash, I wouldn't do that if I were you," Dougal shouts after me. I spin around, my eyes giving him the death ray.

"Mind your own fucking business, Dougal. Your opinion is neither required nor wanted and certainly not going to stop me!" He shrugs his shoulders as if to say, *'Have it your way, your funeral,'* and turns back to his beer. I don't knock but shove the door open with force. It bangs against the wall and slams closed behind me. I look at Slender and Ferret and hiss.

"Get the fuck out!" Looking at Raven and receiving his nod, they'll get up.

"We'll finish this later," he tells them. I don't even wait until they have left the room properly.

"How fucking dare you!" a few decibels above yelling. "How fucking dare you meddle with my life! You're my brother, so you get a free pass on lots of things, but not this time. And before you start, don't tell me to calm down. Let me tell you; I'm way beyond that." I'm sure if my eyes could shoot sparks, he would catch fire and incinerate with the god damn desk he's still sitting behind.

"Ashley, what's the matter? Why are you so—"

"Shut up! Just shut up!" I screech at him. "Don't pretend that you don't know why I'm here! I'm not stupid, so don't insult both of our intelligence. Not that I believe you have any of that left at all, you damn asshole." My voice is glacial. His audacity amazes me, so much like our father. No more!

"Did you think, in your misguided notion of having to protect me, that I'd appreciate your meddling? My dear brother, the time to protect me was when I was ten, not twenty-six. If I want to kiss Vegas, I damn well will. Hell, if I want to have sex with him on top of that bitch's bar, I damn well will. With or without your approval." I can see him change color from red to white to red, a bit like a failed traffic light. Do I care? No, I don't. It's time to stand up and be counted.

"Jamie, I love you, but you have gone too far this time. Have you ever thought that I might like Vegas? In all your actions, did you *once* try to think about *me* instead of yourself? I hate to tell you this, but you're getting more and more like our father the older you get. When I needed you to protect me, you weren't there—before and after Mom died. You hid behind our father for years, and although you made a valiant effort to change things, you're now acting just as autocratic and selfish as he did. Yes, you turned the club legit, but that's where it ends.

"I know you have to be strong and can't show weakness with the men, but Jamie, let me ask you, is it worth it? Carry on the way you're going, and I'm gone. I love you, Jamie, but this has to stop. Where were you when I needed you, Jamie? Where . . . were . . . you? I'm a grown-ass woman, and I know my mind. I like Vegas, have for years, but I never acted on it. What gives you the right to use your fists on him? If you must know, *I* kissed *him*! Not the other way around! I was a little tipsy but not inebriated. He wasn't taking advantage of me. If anything, I took advantage of Vegas. So, what now? You gonna rearrange my face as well?"

141

Panting after my outburst, out of breath, I can feel tears stinging in the back of my eyes. I wipe my hand over my face, swallowing hard to keep them back. No way will I give him the satisfaction of seeing me lose it.

Jamie slumps into his chair, closing his eyes. His face looks pained, whether from the assault of my voice on his ears or whether anything I said sunk in; who knows?

"Ashley," he groans, "you and Vegas can't happen. Ever. He's a great brother, and under normal circumstances, I would be happy for you two to get together. I've known for a while that he was looking at you differently than other women. But it can't happen. He's no good for you," Jamie says calmly.

"And who makes you judge and jury about who or what is good for me or isn't?" I shoot at him, my temper still flaring.

"Ashley, listen to me," he starts. "I don't know how to tell you this except straight. He's not an easy man and has certain interests and tastes. He might hurt you."

"Oh, how valiant of you," I scoff. "I take it you're talking about him being a Dom and his membership and visits to Violets?" Jamie looks at me, stunned by the bombshell I just dropped. See how he likes the detonation! "I have a membership to Violet's and know very well his appetites, having seen him in action plenty of times when I worked there behind the bar."

I can see Jamie visibly flinch as though I slapped him hard. "See, you think you know me, brother of mine, but realistically, you only see what you want to see. You don't really know me. You never talk to me long enough to find out anything about me and my life other than the superficial stuff. To you ,I'm the club princess. But let me tell you, I'm no princess, club or otherwise. I lost my virginity when I was twenty and have been active since. I know what I want, what I like, and what I need. And your interference is not it!" I pace in front of his desk, adrenalin stopping me from being still.

"Ashley, I'm sorry. Please sit down, and let's talk about this. All of this." Raven says quietly. I don't think I've ever seen my brother subdued. There's a first for everything.

Jamie sits back and scrubs his hand through his long black hair. If it weren't so serious, it'd be funny. He looks like he's been dragged through a hedge backward, not just once but several times. He looks tired and much older than he is.

"Ashley, I don't know what to say. You are my little sister. Wherever I can, I want to protect you. I'm sorry I did not see that you've grown up over the years. I worry about you and don't want to see you hurt. I'd have to kill whoever hurts you. I made sure the men knew you were out of bounds. Now, I see I should have spoken to you. Taken time with you. It kills me to see you so upset and to hear the bitterness in your voice. It reminds me so much of Mom," His voice is breaking, and he clears his throat.

"I've been so busy with the club. I forgot you needed me too. I left you all those years to deal with Nathan on your own. It was completely unfair and a real dick move. You had so much to deal with. I tried to make your life easier, and instead that backfired spectacularly. I'm so sorry. Without realizing, I let you down." He looks me in the eye for the first time.

"I hate to find out that you worked at Violet's. I did not know things were *that* bad, Ash, why didn't you come to me and ask me for more money? You know I would have given it to you."

"Jamie, that is exactly the point. You never bothered asking what we needed or wanted. Just for your information, I didn't work at Violet's because I was desperate for money. I did it because it paid well, and I was curious about what goes on there. It turns out it is a place that

143

suits me, where I fit in. No one made me sign up for a membership. I did that on my own. And before you ask, no, I have never been involved with Vegas at Violets or any other place. I avoided him for years." I can't help but notice the relief on Raven's face.

"Raven, I know you love me and want what's best for me, but you must trust that I know what is best for me. I promise, if I need your protection, I'll come and ask for it." I try to put all the sincerity of my words into the look I give him.

Raven sighs. "Okay, Ash, understand that it's difficult for me and will take time to adjust, but I'll try to trust you. I won't stand in your way if you want to be with Vegas. I can't guarantee I won't hate the thought, but I'll get used to it."

Inwardly, I high-five myself and want to do a victory dance. "Thanks, Jamie." I stand, walk around the desk, wrap my arms around him from behind, and kiss his head. "I'm not saying we'll be an item. Let me live my own life, that's all I'm saying. This is hard for you, I know. Just let things happen in their own way." I can feel him nod. He turns his chair and drags me down into the chair with him. We are both exhausted and just seek comfort in each other for a moment.

"You need to get yourself a good woman," I half groan, half laugh. He hugs me tight, and a deep chuckle escapes him.

"No way, sis. The woman who can put up with me hasn't been born yet."

"Maybe I could set you up?" I tease. He looks at me as though I have lost my mind.

"No, just no, sis! That is a firm no, by the way. Or a *no way in hell* type of no, just to make it crystal clear." I laugh as I get off his lap.

I look at him more seriously and tell him, "Watch your back, Jamie. At the bar, I overheard Karen telling the others how Rusty is talking about you." I hold my hand up and stop him as he starts to reply. "I know he's your VP, and I know you trust him, but just be careful.

144

What he did to Sarah was awful, and I'd like to rip his balls off for that alone. Just be careful, okay?" He gives me a strange look and nods.

"Thanks, sis, I will. Always. Love ya, now get out of here so I can carry on with my meeting if you haven't scared Slender and Ferret senseless," he grumbles. I throw a grin, finger wave over my shoulder, and make my way out the door. It is late by the time I get home and check my phone. I see Vegas's message, and anger is sparked again.

I type a quick reply, throw my phone on the kitchen counter, run myself a bath, and relax before bed. My adrenalin is still running high.

-17- VEGAS

I rolled into the parking lot ten minutes before the meeting. I'd be lying if I said I wasn't a tad concerned about this. Is Raven going to want my patch? I can't do anything but head into the lion's den. As I stroll into church, a few others are already there—Slender, Pennywise, Dougal, Raven, Spen, and, to my astonishment, Neil. This is no ordinary church meeting. Non-members are a big no-no at church. Not even prospects are allowed unless they're being voted in, and even then, they're only allowed in at the end to receive their patch. No one is sitting in any order, apart from Raven, who is in his usual spot, and Spen, who has a laptop and is using the projector.

"This is a meeting to discuss the bar. Over the last few days, some worrying issues have come to light, so we replaced Karen as manager, and I appointed Neil in her place. All access to the books and finances was taken away from her. She can stay on behind the bar, and I allowed her to pick up shifts since her wages are now considerably reduced and she has bills to pay. I know I got reports from all of you, but Neil spoke to me yesterday in detail, and the outcome was worrying. I asked Spen to look at the bar's books and update us on how things are. Spen, you have the floor." Raven sits and lets Spen take over.

146

"Okay, so the bar used to be a great little earner, always packed with a lot of returning customers. The books show a solid profit until about six or seven months ago. Then suddenly, they started decreasing. First, I thought it was seasonal, as alcohol sales vary a bit with the season, especially around here. Tourist trade and all that. Fair enough, it's not huge, but it could have an impact.

"In the last quarter, the revenue has been down dramatically. The beer orders have been reduced too. So, on paper, it looked as if it tallied. I compared the bank deposits to invoices, and it looked good. Then, I dug a little deeper with Neil's help. He found some old cash register receipts and bank deposit slips. Going back a year, they matched. Going back six months ago, they were also accurate. However, in the last three months, we know of at least one month that doesn't reconcile.

"The other cash register printouts have vanished. As you can see from the Sunday cash-out total, each week's take was over a thousand dollars, but we only deposited just over seven hundred into the bank. We know that happened four weeks in a row, so we know of at least a thousand dollars that have gone missing in a month. The question is, where has it gone, and who has it? Karen signed the deposit slips, but as Penny, Dougal, and Vegas said, she insists she didn't do the banking." Spen shifts in his seat, visibly uncomfortable as he looks around.

I had expected many things for tonight, but this was not one of them. I'm just as stunned and silent as the rest of my brothers. We conduct club business with loyalty, respect, and honor. None of the brothers would dream of stealing from the club. That would have severe consequences for anyone. And by that, I don't mean we'd call the cops.

Neil clears his throat. Then he looks at Raven and Spen. "May I?" he asks. They both give him a nod. "I've only been at the bar for a few days, but I can tell you that it will go under the way it currently is. The clientele is sketchy, to say the least. We're attracting riff-raff, and the returning customers are lacking. I stopped the watering down of the beer immediately. The lines will be cleaned and flushed; until that happens, only bottled beer goes on sale. That, however, has a further impact.

"From what I can see just in the past few days, the trust in the bar is gone, and its reputation is in the shitter. I've had words with Karen, just like you did, and she insists she hasn't done the banking. I'm not accusing anyone at this point, as there's no evidence, but is it possible to find out who did the banking?" He looks directly at Raven, Spen, and Slender. Slender opens his phone.

"Ferret, get your ass in here. You're needed." He hangs up and tells the table, "He'll be here in a few moments." Ferret lives on the property in one of the cabins, with one room as his living area and another fully tricked out with all of his IT equipment. While waiting for Ferret, Dougal gets up.

"I need a beer. Anyone else?" We all take him up on his offer, and he trundles off into the bar, returning with a bucket full of ice and bottles. "Figured we could probably use more than one," he grumbles and shoves a cold one toward each of us. Just at that moment, Ferret enters, tablet in hand. He picks a long neck out of the bucket and takes a seat.

"What's going on that you need me right this second?" he asks suspiciously.

"The bar," Raven replies, and by his tone, everyone is aware of the gravity of the situation. Slender looks at Ferret.

"Hey, man, we have a problem. Money has gone missing between the cash register totals and deposits. Karen signed the banking slips, but she's adamant she's not the one taking it to the bank." Ferret raises his brow in disbelief.

"Then who is? The fairies?"

"Hardly," replies Slender, "but the who is what we need you to dig into. Do you think you can find out who did the banking? And who has the money stashed?"

"It'll take a while, but I'm sure I can get to the bottom of this." Ferret nods to Raven and Slender. "Do we have a suspect? Other than Karen?"

"No," Raven answers quickly before we can throw speculations around the table. Neil is right—there's no evidence, and we can't go accusing people without evidence. And we can't dish out retribution.

"Okay, do you need me for anything else? Or can I go back to the pussy in my bed now?" Ferret asks with a rather smug smile.

"Nope, that's it. Go back to what you were doing and don't do anything I wouldn't," Raven goads him.

"Ah, that leaves me a wide variety of options then." Ferret laughs and walks out the door.

"Any suggestions about what to do with the bar? If it's not profitable, it'll cut club funds deep. I'm open to *any* suggestions." Raven looks around at all of us before Neil raises his hand.

"We're not in school, man; just say what you want to say," Slender encourages him.

"My suggestion would be to close it down." A lot of murmuring breaks out all around. Neil raises his voice. "Hear me out. I'm not talking about closing for good. I'm talking about closing to remodel and rebrand. Distance ourselves from the poor image the bar has obtained and attract a different clientele, one that will spend money. Lots of money." Everyone quiets down and starts to listen now. We're all ears.

"Do you think you could buy the warehouse behind the bar?" Neil looks at Spen and Raven.

149

"The club has enough money to do that," Spen says as he looks over the treasury reports. "Let me hear what you're thinking, Neil," Raven interjects.

"Right, if we could buy the warehouse behind the bar, we could break through and turn it into one big property. Rip everything out of the old place, completely refurbish, install a large stage, poles, mirrors, etc., and make it a posh strip club. Offering a membership would guarantee returning customers and include a public space for those who don't have a membership. I'm not talking whorehouse—I'm talking classy strip joint with dancers, a couple of private rooms for lap dances, a couple of rooms for bachelorette or bachelor parties, and a once-a-month ladies' night with male dancers." Laughter breaks out around the table. Ladies' night with male dancers? Now, that is some funny shit.

"I managed one of those clubs in Minneapolis, and it made a fortune. Especially ladies' night. The climate is changing, boys, and women like to look too and stick dollars into thongs." Neil winks.

"I like that idea," Raven agrees. Yeah, he would because he has no old lady who'd go to those nights to see strange dick. Not that I have an old lady, either, but if I did, I'd hate her looking at someone else's man-meat. My thoughts drift from the table to a beautiful dark-haired woman with piercing green eyes holding me captive. *Where the hell did that come from?* I shake the thought away.

"Okay, Neil, can you create a provisional business model structure plan? Help Spen work out a business plan to show us on Sunday?" Raven questions. "We have to take it to vote, but it sounds like a great idea."

Neil agrees. "Sure, it'll be thrown together, nothing exact or fancy. Not a lot of time 'til then, so a rough draft."

150

"That's okay. Dumb it down for us as much as you can, so even our stupid asses can get the drift," Slender jokes.

"Okay then, anyone else have anything to say on bar matters? No? Let's all get home then," Raven orders. I stand with the rest of the guys.

"Not you, Vegas. Sit," he barks. Oh great, here we go. He waits for the room to empty before he pierces his gaze on me. "I had a visitor last night, and she was pissed. Extremely pissed. In fact, she ripped me a new one," Raven states, keeping his eyes steady on mine. "She made me realize I can be a real asshole sometimes and sometimes act like my dad. Not what I had in mind for myself, admittedly." He sighs, then pulls out a bottle of Maker's Mark and two glasses from under the table. He pours us both a generous helping.

"She told me she waitressed at Violet's and knows about you and your . . . shall we call it . . . appetites. She also told me you didn't start this, that she did. Be that as it may, she firmly put me in my place. She seems to like you, and, as she correctly stated, she's twenty-six, not ten. She's a grown woman and makes her own choices. I'm not apologizing for beating you, Vegas. As far as I'm concerned, she was off-limits, and you went against that." He pauses to look at me. "However, since she likes you and made it clear that her life is her decision, I won't stand in the way should anything develop between you two. However, I'm warning you, Vegas. I will make good on my promise. Hurt her, and I will bury you," he finishes with a glare that could make grown men piss themselves.

"Wouldn't have it any other way, Prez," I answer and tip back my shot of whiskey. It burns all the way down but calms my nerves at the same time. Raven gets up and walks out of church without looking back. It's obvious I'm dismissed.

◊◊◊

151

I can't believe she did that. I'm useless talking about feelings, but right now, I'm angry as fuck that she stood up for me when I didn't and equally very proud of her for speaking up for herself and taking Raven on. But why would she do that? It's not as though we're an item.

I try to make sense of it but can't quite get my head around it. Raven said she likes me, but what does that actually mean? I don't completely repulse her? This shit is confusing and is not easing my already pissy mood. I'm restless and pacing.

Before I can change my mind, I get on my bike and start riding aimlessly. It usually clears my head. Except this time, it's not working. My head is throbbing with a mother of a headache, my brain is working overtime, and looking back at the meeting, I try to work out why the shithead Rusty wasn't there. Never occurred to me to ask, but now I wonder.

Without planning to, I find myself outside Ashley's house. The lights are on upstairs, so she's awake. I get off and stand against my bike, watching her window. With every breath, I get more agitated.

What was she thinking? Did she think I couldn't fight my own battles? I imagine her in Raven's office, tearing him a new asshole, and can't help but smirk. She's quite something. My dick agrees. She seems fragile at times, but God, that woman has a backbone made of steel. I need to readjust myself since just the thought makes me hard. Like a creeper, I sit here thinking and watching her window. She just opened the curtain and is looking straight at me, which has me sitting up straight.

Damnit, my stealth technique is lacking. Like a puppet on a string, I push off my bike and make my way to the front door, which is open. She must have opened it. *What the fuck?* I make my way up the stairs, taking two at once. She's standing at the top of the stairs, smiling at me.

"What took you so long?" she teases. "Knew you'd turn up, Vegas. We need to talk. Even if you can't or won't admit it, there is some crazy chemistry between us. Tell me you don't feel it," she states, looking me straight in the eye.

Before I can control myself, I've kicked the door shut, ran up the stairs, pushed her into the room, and shoved her against the wall. My dick is as hard as iron, and my mouth descends on hers in half a second. It's not a gentle kiss like you see in movies. I punish her. My lips crash against hers again and again with brutal force, and my tongue pushes into her mouth. I'm in total control.

She makes a sound deep in her throat that drives me insane. My dick is throbbing, and I cannot possibly get any harder. I pull her closer, if that's possible, and let her feel what she's doing to me. Her hand is in my hair, pulling me in, while her mouth is dueling with mine, fighting for control. One hand leaves my hair and runs over the front of my jeans, finding my hard cock and rubbing it through the material of my jeans. If she keeps it up, I'll make a mess like a teenager who just got his first hand job. I have to stop this now, but when I pull my head back, her eyes are on fire, and she's panting. I take a deep, calming breath.

"What did you do? What do you want from me, Ash? I'm no good for you, and you know it," I hiss at her. "I'm not your knight in shining armor, princess. I'm a black-hearted, harsh man who likes it rough, definitely not prince material."

I flinch when she lifts her hand and slaps me hard. Lucky for her, I don't hit women in anger, but I *do* grab her hands and pin them to the wall.

"You asshole," she spits out. "I know exactly who and what you are. I make my own decisions about what my so-called knight looks like, and I don't give a shit about how bad you

153

think you are for me. Have you ever considered that you may not be the only one with darkness in them? Have you?" She pants at me, fury flashing in her eyes as she shoots daggers at me.

"Princess, I'll give you one chance, and one chance only, to step away. I have a few years on you, and you know about my needs. You're hotter than the equator, and I can only fight my wanting in your pussy for so long. This is your one and only chance to step away. You don't step away right the fuck now; I will fuck you until you scream. I'll fuck you harder than you have ever been fucked before. I don't do vanilla, you know that, so you know what you're getting into. I'm giving you this chance to change your mind and walk away. Make your decision, but be certain you can handle what I'll dish out. And make no mistake, if you stay, we will be exclusive from this moment on. I want to see a test that you're clean, and I'll provide you with the same. I expect you to go on birth control because a child is not what I want or need right now. I'll be in control, and you'll be mine to do with as I please."

She stares at me with unreadable eyes and opens her mouth.

"I don't do submissive contracts. I'm not a full-on sub. Just fair to let you know. Domination inside the bedroom only, outside the bedroom, my life my rules. Condoms until we both have our test results. Now, fuck me already."

That was all I needed to unleash the animal.

-18- ASH

I hoped he would come, that he wouldn't let my silent challenge stand unanswered. By taking on Jamie, Vegas would interpret my action as a challenge to his manhood. I'd been waiting all evening with the front door unlocked. When I finally hear his bike pull in, I lose my nerve for a moment, especially when I look out the window and find him sitting there, staring at me from a distance. My heart is thumping in my chest, half excited, half in fear that if my plan backfires, he'd hate me, and talking this out would no longer be possible. Once I saw him move, I knew it was game on.

Challenging him, I ask, "What took you so long?" Fire explodes in his eyes, a feverish need burning in them as he grabs my arms and pushes me inside and against the wall. His lips crashing onto mine is a brutal assault on my senses, driving me crazy with need. I'm instantly wet, the heat traveling through my body from head to toe. His tongue demands entrance into my mouth, and I can't hold back a groan of pleasure when it invades me.

His smell, taste, heat, it's all fast overwhelming me. My knees threaten to give way under his onslaught. His erection throbs against me through his jeans, and I can't help myself. I move my hand from his hair to his boner and stroke it over his jeans. Every move I make, it pulses again in my hand.

He douses my passion when he lifts his head with an ice bucket of words.

"What did you do? What do you want from me, Ash? I'm no good for you, and you know it," he hisses at me.

Letting him finish his tidy little speech without thinking, I slap him hard. The fucking nerve of this guy!

"You asshole." I'm furious, and he's genuinely clueless. "I know exactly who and what you are. I make my own decisions about what my so-called knight looks like, and I don't give a shit about how bad you think you are for me. Have you ever considered that you may not be the only one with darkness in them? Have you?" I pant like a marathon runner, my anger taking my breath away as my eyes lock on his.

"Princess, I'll give you one chance, and one chance only, to step away. I have a few years on you, and you know about my needs. You're hotter than the equator, and I can only fight wanting in your pussy for so long. You don't step away right the fuck now, I will fuck you until you scream. I'll fuck you harder than you have ever been fucked before. I don't do vanilla, you know that, so you know what you're getting into. I'm giving you this one chance to change your mind and walk away. Make your decision, but be certain you can handle what I'll dish out. And make no mistake, if you stay, we will be exclusive from this moment on. I want to see a test that you're clean, and I'll provide you with the same. I expect you to go on birth control because a child is not what I want or need right now. I'll be in control, and you'll be mine to do with as I please."

Game on. Time for me to show that I made my choice before I realized there was a choice. I stare him down.

"I don't do submissive contracts. I'm not a full-on sub. Just fair to let you know. Domination inside the bedroom only, outside the bedroom, my life my rules. Condoms until we both have our test results. Now, fuck me already."

As I finish my little speech, quite proud of myself, he pulls me toward him with a grunt and punishes me with a hotter than hell kiss. My legs instantly turn into jelly: this man and his magic mouth. I want to feel that mouth all over my body in other places. I need him to take charge but lose control at the same time. My panties are soaked, and I can't wait to feel his cock deep inside me. I moan as his kiss heats me to an unbearable temperature. My body feels as though it's on fire, and only he can douse the flames.

He puts his hands under my ass and lifts me. I automatically wrap my legs around his hips, and now, I can feel his denim-clad cock teasing and applying pressure where I need it most. Pushing back, I rub myself over his bulge. I need friction to get some relief, as the need drives me insane. I dimly notice that we're moving and am only partially aware that he has carried me over to the bed. He throws me onto the bed making me catch my breath as I land, while he stares at me from the foot end.

"Off," he commands, nodding at my clothes. I stand next to the bed and slowly take off my jeans, socks, and emerald green lacy panties, then I pull my t-shirt over my head and undo my matching bra, letting it fall to the floor. My nipples are hard and tight, so hard they hurt.

I need his hands and mouth on me, but I know I need to take what he's giving me for now. Swallowing hard, I feel my wetness making its way down between my thighs. I clench my thighs together to put pressure on my throbbing clit. Vegas smirks, clearly sensing my need and discomfort.

"I can smell you from here, princess. Are you wet for me?" I can't get out any words, so I just nod. "How wet? Show me," he commands. I slowly run my hands down my body, one hand tweaking my stiff, aching nipple while the other delves between my saturated folds. I bring my fingers up to show they're glistening with my excitement.

"Now, lick them clean, princess." I comply instantly and suck my wet fingers into my mouth, tasting myself. A moan escapes me as I continue to twist my nipples. "Enough," he thunders at me, his eyes full of heat. "Put your hands by your sides, no more touching. I'm the only one who touches that body," he growls.

Vegas slowly steps toward me, taking off his jeans and shirt. I marvel at his body, so cut and muscled. I'm sure a male body shouldn't be described as beautiful, but his rough, Viking-like beauty takes my breath away. All I can do is stare and hope that I get to trace my tongue over every inch of him.

"Like what you see, do you?" he teases me. Again, I can only nod. My eyes rest on his many tattoos, all of which I want to trace and get to know every inch of his incredible body. As my eyes travel down, I draw in a deep breath. His boxers are not hiding a thing, and I can see his massive erection tracing through.

Definitely not average-sized. I should be worried about his size, but I instinctively lick my lips. I've never wanted to wrap my lips around a cock so much in my entire life. I can feel my saliva running wild in my mouth. The need to taste and feel him is overwhelming, and I shift on my feet. He smirks at me and shakes his head, tutting.

"Bit impatient, are we?" His voice is drenched in his desire and need. "On the bed," he commands.

I lie down in the center of the bed, watching him. My breath comes in panting bursts. I've never been so turned on in all my life. He slowly removes his boxers as I watch, as my brain struggles to reconcile what my eyes are seeing.

He's huge, hard, and standing to attention. I watch his hand go to his cock, giving himself a few hard strokes. Instinctively, I open my legs so he can see my heat and wetness. My folds are soaked. My hand moves down my body on autopilot, and I can't take much more. My clit needs some relief.

"Touch yourself, and not only will I spank you, but I won't let you come for hours," Vegas threatens, his eyes locking on mine. Sighing, I put my hands onto the sheets and grab hold. "Good girl," Vegas rumbles. He kneels between my legs and runs his hands slowly up and down, caressing my calves and knees, then running slowly and tantalizingly over my thighs from the outside to the inside. It's driving me crazy, and I shift on the bed, needing more.

"Keep still," he demands. I do my best to comply, my fingers clenching the sheets hard. Leaning over me, his body brushes mine, making my need flare to unbearable proportions. His lips crash down on mine in a searing, demanding kiss. It rips a moan from me, which only makes him kiss me harder. He nips my lower lip before his tongue invades my mouth and the taste of him devastates me. I'm like an addict going cold turkey, shivering uncontrollably. My skin is racing with goosebumps, and I can't contain my moans. I turn my head and whimper,

"Please, Vegas."

"Please what, princess?" He looks down at me.

"Please, Vegas, I need to feel you."

"Feel me where? Tell me what you want, what you need," he demands.

159

"I need you inside me, Vegas. I'm going out of my mind. I need you to make me come on your cock," I gasp, holding his eyes.

"All in good time." He smirks at me. "I'm going to savor this princess, and you'll be patient, or I won't allow you your release."

I groan at his statement. I've seen him operate and know he will make good on his threat if I don't comply. He sits up and places his mouth over one of my erect nipples. All the air whooshes out of my lungs, and a loud groan escapes me. At last, some relief for my needy buds. He lavishes attention on both, nipping, sucking, and biting, with an edge of pain. The pain mixes with pleasure, and heat floods my body.

"Oh, princess, you like that, huh?" He smiles.

"Yes" is all I can breathe out. "Please, Vegas, more."

He obliges me this time and continues to lick and suck, covering my breasts with small hickeys. My brain can't keep up with all the different sensations. My hips lift off the bed automatically. I can't do a thing about it. I feel myself being flipped and turned onto my hands and knees. No sooner have I got all limbs on the sheet than a sharp smack lands on my ass cheek. I whimper at the pain. His hands gently rub my cheek, massaging, and the pain turns into crazy pleasure. He repeats the same treatment with the other side and then alternates until I'm mindless with pleasure. I don't notice that I'm dripping onto the sheets nor that he has changed position behind me. All I can do is feel. Feel his fingers tracing my folds, teasing, the roughness of his skin assaulting my softness in stark contrast. His fingers enter me, first one, then another, stretching me, and I let out a muffled scream of relief.

"Oh yes, baby, you will scream. First, you'll come on my hand, then in my mouth, and you will scream my name when you do it." His husky voice is thick with desire. "And only then will I fuck you. Hard, fast, and until you pass out," he threatens, but I take it as a promise. His fingers pump into me, hard and fast, and I can feel a tingle start all the way down in my toes, moving up, and my belly tightens. I'm so close to going over the edge.

"Come for me," he commands, changes the angle, and rubs over my most sensitive spot. Most men need a compass and map drawn to find the g spot, not Vegas. I scream as I fall over the edge, contracting around him again and again. I can feel a rush of moisture leaving me and coating him.

Without realizing his fingers have left me, I'm still in the throes of my orgasm when I feel his tongue lapping at me, and I groan. It's too much. My senses are overpowered and hypersensitive. I can't breathe. His tongue enters me and rides out the contractions and quivers.

"So delicious. You taste as good as I thought you would." I hear him groan before he grabs my hips and flips me onto my back. My hands clench the sheets as his tongue licks through my folds, from top to bottom, like a man in the desert, not wanting to miss a drop of moisture.

I throw my head from side to side, panting. He's taking me right back onto the precipice. I wouldn't have believed my body was capable of feeling this much pleasure, but he's proving me wrong. He teases me until I can't take anymore. Then, his lips latch onto my clit, and he sucks and licks as though this was the most intimate French kiss.

"Vegas!" I scream his name as I come hard for a second time. My universe explodes, and I see stars.

"There she is," he murmurs when I start to come down. He's smiling down at me, his lips finding mine, and I can taste myself on him. It is so damn hot. He kneels between my legs, nudging at my entrance. I notice the empty condom wrapper on the end edge of the bed. I hadn't even noticed him sheathing himself. Instinctively, I wrap my thighs around him and open to him.

161

With his eyes dark and heated on mine, capturing me completely, he enters me in one swift stroke until he hits the end of me. I gasp. He's so huge, it feels uncomfortable to have him buried to the hilt. He pulls back slightly, and holds himself there, giving me time to adjust to his size.

"Jesus, you're tight," he grinds out behind gritted teeth. I nudge him as I need him to move. He nods and pulls out almost all the way, then slams back in with such force, that it moves me up the bed.

"Oh. my god," I pant out. "Oh my god, so good." He smirks.

"Not quite God but close enough." As he slams inside me repeatedly, I can't suppress my giggle. "Think this is funny, do you?" He looks at me seriously, amusement dancing in his eyes. "I'll show you funny."

He picks up speed and fucks me harder until coherent thoughts leave me entirely. He angles me up, so he enters me even deeper, and his huge cock massages my sensitive spot with every thrust. His pubic bone rubs on my clit as he swirls his pelvis at the end of each thrust.

"Baby, come for me. I won't last much longer," he whispers in my ear and nips the side of my neck. That is all it takes for my orgasm to crash into me. I can feel him thrust hard several times, then root inside me. I feel him pulsing as he releases into the condom. My brain implodes, and my vision dims with the force of my orgasm.

I eventually come around and feel something warm and gentle between my legs. I raise my eyes to Vegas's in question. He has a warm washcloth in his hand and gently cleans me. I try to open my mouth, but he shushes me. This is not the time for words. His gentle care of me fills my eyes with tears. He smiles, throws the cloth in the hamper, climbs back onto the bed, wraps me tightly into his arms, and pulls the blankets over us. As I'm dozing off, I hear him whisper, "You are mine. I can't ever let you go."

Despite my heart beating like a machine gun, I pretend to be sleeping and keep my breathing steady. Is this what I wanted? To be his?

-19- VEGAS

Calming my tired body, I wrap Ashley in my arms. She's just about asleep. This was Earth-shattering sex. And to me, it meant more than just a fuck. I'm hooked. I keep telling myself to take it easy, as this is a dangerous path, but my mouth opens anyway.

"You're mine. I can't ever let you go," I whisper into her hair and stiffen. Oh shit, I'm in deep trouble. I didn't mean to say that. Her breathing is even, so I hope she's asleep and didn't hear my words. I've wanted Ashley for a long time. When I saw her behind the bar in Violets two years ago, it hit me like a thunderbolt. I've been fighting my attraction to her since then, and I'm tired of fighting.

I'm not a cuddler. I'm a kinky pig, but right now, I feel at peace with Ashley in my arms, just feeling her warmth and steady breathing. While I hold her, nothing can touch either of us. My brain is tired, and my body aches, so I adjust my position and feel her ass pushing into me. A small smile plays around my lips. I never thought something so simple could make me feel so good.

◊◊◊

I wake feeling disorientated. There is heat in my back, my god, it's like a furnace! I try to shake myself awake fully. As I open my eyes, I realize I'm not in my bed. Suddenly last night comes rushing back in. I roll onto my back with my arm over my face and take a deep breath. When I turn my head, I see Ashley. She looks peaceful, with a slight smile playing on her face. She scoots closer to me and throws her arm over my chest. I thought this would be awkward, but she feels so natural next to me, as though it's where she belongs.

Letting her warmth seep through my body and soul, a feeling of deep peace settles over me. Peace, I haven't known in a long time. Too long, I realize now. I also realize that I don't want to let her go, which is worrying. I'm not looking for an old lady. It is the farthest thing from my mind. However, my body appears to feel different, and my dick seems to agree.

I carefully remove her arm and slide out of bed. Putting my boxers and jeans on, I make my way to the kitchen and find all the makings for coffee. My stomach rumbles, so I forage for breakfast items. Not much there, but enough for pancakes and bacon, so I set to work. It feels weird to stand here in her kitchen, very domesticated and strange, because I don't feel like getting the hell out for once. My phone shows it's five-thirty, so if Ashley has an early start, I make my way back into the bedroom while the pancakes are resting and the bacon is under the grill.

"Morning, princess." I lean over her and place a kiss on her cheek. She starts to move and groans.

"What time is it? And what smells so good? Coffee . . . I need coffee." I put the cup I filled for her on the bedside table and smirk. Not a morning person then.

"What time do you need to get up, princess? What shift are you on? It's just half-past five." I wait for her reply.

165

"It's my day off today," she groans.

"I gotta get going soon, head home, shower, change, and get to work," I tell her, "but I made breakfast. Pancakes and bacon, all ready. Want me to bring you some?"

"No thanks, Vegas. I'm awake now. I'll get up and come into the kitchen to join you." She smiles at me. That smile hits me right in my gut, and my protective instincts crash right through me. I turn on my heel, return to the kitchen, set the table, and bring the bacon and pancakes over. I load my plate and spread plenty of maple syrup over my bacon. Heart attack on a plate, just the way I like it—my mouth waters.

"Wow, that smells soooo gooood." Ashley moans, and that little sound makes my cock hard as steel. She loads her plate and digs in. "Mmm, so good." She moans again.

"Glad you're enjoying it," I say between gritted teeth. My cock is threatening to burst out of my jeans.

She looks at me, her eyes grazing over my shirtless torso, inspecting my many tattoos. They're all meaningful to me, like the storybook of my life.

"Your artwork is amazing," she says, reaching out and running her finger over my right bicep. She stops and traces the tree of life placed there, then she looks at me and asks, "Who's Elvira?" I guess it's only fair to ask about another woman's name on my arm.

"She was my grandmother, princess. She brought me up for most of my life. It's a long story, and I don't have time to tell it all right now." She nods at me, unperturbed.

"Okay, maybe you can tell me about her sometime. I know little to nothing about your life," she tells me, and I sit looking at her, stunned.

She didn't push nor snipe, just accepted my answer for what it was. The truth. That was easier than I thought.

"Sure, princess, I'll tell you about her when we have more time." Pushing my chair back, I walk into the bedroom, leaving Ash at the table. Pulling on my t-shirt and cut, I pull my boots on, which are still where I chucked them off last night. I rejoin Ashley, bend down, and kiss her hair. "Gotta run, princess," I tell her. "Have a great day off. I'll text you later."

She peers at me with a strange look in her eye but says, "Bye, Vegas, have a good day too." Her attention goes back to her breakfast, and she doesn't look up at me when I open the door and leave. I'm not sure why, but I feel guilty for leaving her there. My head is fucked. If I *had* any feelings, I'd say I'm utterly conflicted, but since I don't do feelings, I won't.

I get on my bike and join the traffic, making my way home in no time. After a shower, a change of clothes, and another large coffee, I head to the workshop and start my day.

By lunchtime, I feel like a bear with a sore head. My mood is glacial, and I grunt or bark at everyone. What a shitty day. Suddenly, my overall is grabbed, and I'm dragged from behind. I'm just about to swing for whoever it is when I hear Sparks' voice.

"Easy, tiger, if you need to go a couple of rounds to settle your damn mood, then so be it, but I'd rather not and just drag you out for lunch instead." His words instantly deflate me. Having been an ass all morning, I think I needed a change of scenery.

"Let go, dick, or I'll have your hands," I growl at Sparks, earning me a snicker.

"Promises, promises. It would give me time off to spend and molest my old lady, so go ahead, see if I care." He chuckles. In the changing room, I peel out of my overalls and follow Sparks to the bikes.

Predictably, we end up at Ally's. We order, and I look out the window while waiting for grub to arrive. Sparks clears his throat.

167

"What's up with you, man? You're not yourself today, and I'm getting fed up with being growled at. I'm here for you, man, so talk to me." I look at him over the rim of my coffee mug.

"What is this, a sisterly heart to heart?" I mock.

"For fuck's sake, Vegas, drop it. You've been a pain in the ass all morning, and either you talk, or I'll wrap any tool I can get my hands on around your head." Sparks is pissed. That doesn't happen often, and I sigh.

"Is this about Ashley?" he inquires.

"Wow, you guys been spying on me?" I grouse.

"No, man, but you have been looking at her in a certain way for months. Then there are the rearranged facial features by Raven. I can count. One plus one makes two if you'll excuse the pun." Sparks looks straight at me. "Are you gonna claim her?"

"Fuck no." I nearly jump out of my seat. "I don't want an old lady. I'm not the type to be tied down."

"Calm the fuck down and sit down," Sparks growls at me. My voice had risen without me realizing it.

"Are you just stupid? Or can you not see what's right in front of you? Meeting Ally was the best thing that ever happened to me. Do I look pussy whipped to you? Or under stress and hating my life?" he continues. "Let me tell you something, asshole. Ashley is an amazing woman. Not only has she mooned over you for a while, but she deals with her shit. And she sure had plenty of it to deal with. And you are a grade-A fool."

That made me sit up straight. "What shit?" I ask tightly.

"Can't tell you, Bro, Ally would have my balls. I'm not supposed to know, only overheard bits the other day by accident. Can't let on bro, sorry. How about you just fucking ask her if you want to know so bad?" he grates back at me.

"You are one lucky asshole to have her crushing on you, don't fuck it up. Raven will calm down, but you fucking hurt her, and he will kill you. I'm also sure a few of us would help him bury your body." Suddenly my appetite is gone. I take out my phone.

Vegas: Hey princess, how is your day? Sorry I ran out this morning. Had to get ready for work. A few minutes pass, and have me drumming my fingers on the table.

Ashley: Hey you, my day is going great. Thank you. Just on my way to see Carl. What are you up to?

Vegas: Just having lunch at Ally's with Sparks. Want to come over to my place tonight? I'll put some steaks on the grill.

Ashley: Can I bring anything?

Vegas: No, princess, I got it. Salad and baked potato, okay with you?

Ashley: Sure, no problems.

Vegas: wear appropriate bike clothes, we'll go for a ride after dinner.

Ashley: What time?

Vegas: Seven-thirty okay for you?

Ashley: See you then. Text me the address. STYL

Sparks looks interrogatingly at me.

"Are you gonna get your head out of your ass and act like a human being, or dare I say, man, for once?" He quips. I nod at him.

"I'll get to the bottom of this," I tell him.

"You better, and man, if Ally weren't joined to my hip, I'd so make a go of getting Ashley," he smirks, "And I know I'm not the only one," He chuckles when I growl at him. Actually, growl.

"Keep your hands to yourself, or you'll lose them. Ashley is mine! Put the word out!" Sparks laughs, pointing his finger at me.

"Make sure you let her know, else Flakey might get in there," he bends over, laughing. Just then, both of our cells ding. I open mine and find a group text. They have declared Saturday a bar day for all members. I groan. Oh great, just what I want.

◊◊◊

I struggle to keep my mind on work for the rest of the afternoon. My thoughts go to Flakey. It's my turn to sit with him next week if he's still in. Ashley spends a lot of time with him. I heard the prospects talking about her turning up at all hours, sending them for breaks, and spending time with Flakey. They also mentioned how close they seem. I know they are close, but now it bothers me. Do I have to step in? I sigh in relief when it is time to put the tools down for the day.

A smile is plastered on my face on the ride home. I take the long way round. The feeling of six hundred solid pounds of steel between my legs, growling, and the wind in my face blows out my bad mood. I *love* the smell of the countryside, wooded areas, and fields, and feeling the temperature changes when riding. It makes me feel connected and whole.

I turn into the garage, walk into the house, open the freezer, and get some steaks. I find some baking potatoes in the fridge and shove them into the oven. Next, I make the salad and put it back into the fridge. I go to the gym and run on the treadmill for a few miles. After lifting some weights, my body feels pleasantly tired, and I escape into the shower.

My hair still wet, I take the steaks out onto the back porch, where I start the grill. I check my phone, having texted her the address earlier with directions, but no reply. It is quarter past seven, so it is safe to start dinner. The potatoes are almost done when I look up. My phone notifies me that the security camera is activated. I can see her car coming down the drive and push the button for the gate before she can stop and ring the intercom. Walking back inside, I open the door, watching her pull up in front of the garage. She gets out, and the surprised look on her face makes me chuckle. Never fails to amuse me to see other people's reactions to my pad, not that many have seen it. I walk toward her, pull her to me, and hold her close.

"Hey, you're early" I smile down at her, placing a kiss on top of her head. Her smile is blinding and makes my heart miss a beat.

"Yup thought I'd surprise you and see if I can help." She wraps her arms around my middle and squeezes.

"No princess, nothing left to do. I've just put the steaks on the grill. Let's get inside." I lead the way inside the house, set the alarm, and watch her taking it all in.

"Wow, this place is amazing, Vegas!" she breathes. I laugh.

"It's alright," I smirk.

We walk through to the kitchen, and she sits at the kitchen island. "How do you like your steak?" I ask.

"Medium rare, please." A girl after my own heart. I can't stand to ruin a good steak by turning it into well-done shoe leather.

I walk out on the deck, check and turn the steaks. When I get back inside, I see she has been making herself useful. Ashley has taken the potatoes out of the oven and he table has been set. The salad and condiments are also out.

"Thanks princess, way to make me feel inept," I tease her.

"Nonsense," comes her immediate reply. "You've been at work and did all the cooking. Giving you a hand is the least I can do." I bring in the steaks, we load our plates, and eat in peaceful silence.

"That was great, Vegas. I didn't know you were such a skilled cook." she grins at me, leaning back, rubbing her stomach. "I couldn't eat another crumb." I grab a beer out of the fridge and offer her one. She shakes her head, so I pass her a bottle of water.

"I'll give you five minutes, then we'll go for a ride," I throw over my shoulder as I close the fridge door. Grabbing her hand without waiting for a reply, I pull her up and walk her out onto the back porch. Ashley looks around.

"Wow, is this all yours?" She points at the wooded area behind the house.

"Sure is, princess. I like my privacy. My home is my refuge. Very few people know where it is or what it is like. You are one of the chosen few."

I capture her eyes with mine and don't miss the slight widening in surprise. She turns, steps up to me, and puts her arm around my waist. I rest my chin on the top of her head and just enjoy the moment.

"Thank you," she says quietly. "For inviting me here and showing me all this. I appreciate it." I pull her closer and kiss the top of her head. Her shampoo smells of some exotic fruit, and her perfume is intoxicating. I inhale deep.

"Are you sniffing me?" She laughs.

172

"I am, princess. You smell so damn delicious," I grumble, knowing I've been caught.

I reach down and slap her fantastic ass in her tight jeans. "Come on, let's go." I step away and walk inside. She follows, closing the patio doors.

"Meet you at the garage," she throws back at me as she makes her way out the front door.

I hurry to disable the alarm, but it's too late, making a hell of a racket. "Oops!" She grins at me while walking to her car and swaying her ass. As much as my dick appreciates the view, riding with a hard-on is uncomfortable. *Down, boy!*

-20- ASH

I giggle at myself, feeling his eyes on me. I know they are glued to my ass, which I sway a little more than usual. It is fun teasing him. My doubts and bad mood left me as soon as he came out to greet me. His place is amazing, with tight as hell security. I spotted the cameras at the turn of his drive. I don't blame him. Privacy is scarce nowadays.

Opening the trunk of my car, I get my biker boots, leather jacket, and helmet out. I perch on the driver's seat, tug my boots on, fasten the clasps and zips. Unworn for years, but they still fit and feel so comfortable. I throw my jacket on, pull my soft leather gloves out of the helmet, and walk toward the garage. I bought the helmet new today. It is full faced—I value my jaw and teeth, thank you very much—a dark burgundy metallic red with blacked-out mirror visor. It looks badass, if I *do* say so myself.

The garage door rattles open, and Vegas rides the Rocker out. Looking at him steals my breath away. Devastatingly handsome, wrap-around glasses hiding his piercing gray eyes. I walk around the bike, lower the passenger pegs, and put my helmet and gloves on. I swing my leg over the bike, which is already rumbling and vibrating. Adjust my position, scoot closer to Vegas, clamp my thighs around his hips, and wrap my arms around him. This feels amazing. He

174

pushes a button on the bars. The garage door creaks as it shuts, and the gate opens as we ride toward it. So cool! I smile and relax. I trust him to keep us safe. He's a very experienced rider.

We hit the highway and head north toward Rice Lake. After a little while, we stop to fuel up. Half an hour later, we are at the shore of Rice Lake. The ride has flown by. I wait for his signal and get off. Taking a deep breath of the fragrant woodland air, I take off my helmet and run my hands through my hair. I hand my lid and gloves to Vegas, who locks everything in his saddlebags. He holds out his hand. I grab it, and we start walking.

He looks at me and asks, "Princess, I meant to ask, how's Flakey doing? I know you see him regularly and send the prospects for meals. I haven't had time to catch up with him. Things have been crazy the last few days."

I can feel the blood draining from my face, and take a deep breath. I need to sit down before my legs go out from under me.

"Ashley, are you alright? What's the matter? Here, sit down. I'll run back and get you some water." I hear Vegas's concerned voice like it's coming through a long tunnel.

◊◊◊

Five hours ago . . .

"Hey, honey!" I smile brightly at Carl and wink at Dawg sitting on a chair next to him.

"Time for me to go. I'll leave you two lovebirds to it. Dougal will be here later tonight, Flakester, to be your night guard. You've worn the prospects out." Dawg laughs, and Carl waves him off.

"Fuck off already. Your ass stinks, and I can't stand any more of your nasty curry farts, you smelly bastard!"

"Tell Dougal to bring a card game, burgers, and beer," he shouts after Dawg.

I watch the door close, and Carl instantly sags back into his pillows. His face was pale and dull, his eyes tired. I sit on the side of his bed.

"You got the results, I take it?" I ask. My heart is hammering in my chest, and a feeling of doom settles over me. Carl looks at me, and I can see him fighting tears.

"Yes, Ash, the results came back. It's advanced acute myeloid leukemia. The biopsy results were not good, and my blood tests weren't encouraging either. They are discussing treatment tomorrow, but it isn't looking hopeful. Ashley, I don't know what to do." A sob escapes him, and I instinctively wrap him in my arms and hold him close. I snuggle up to him on the bed, stroke his hair, and try to comfort him as best as possible while my heart breaks for him, me, and the club. I hit the call button for the nurse.

"Carl, can I speak to the doctors and the nurse, please?" I ask him, and he nods, unable to speak. He's seriously unglued and distraught.

The door opens, and Chloe walks in, a smile that doesn't reach her eyes plastered on her face.

"Hey, what do you need?" She takes one look at Carl and takes a step toward him. I hold up my hand and send her a pleading look. She nods at me.

"Chloe, could I talk to you about Carl's condition?" I ask.

Chloe looks at Carl and asks, "Is that okay, Carl? Can I share information with Ashley? If you agree, I put it in the notes and mark her and Raven as your official next of kin, so you don't have to answer this question every time." Carl turns his head away but nods.

I follow Chloe out of the room and into the private family consult room, where she offers me a cup of coffee.

"I think I could do with something stronger right now." I sigh. She grabs hold of my hand and smiles at me, sadness written all over her face.

"I take it he told you about his results," she says. I can only nod with tears in my eyes. She stands and hugs me tight while my eyes fill with tears. She gently rubs my back to comfort me. After a while, I can sit up straighter.

"Give me the truth, Chloe. How bad is it?" I ask, not sure whether I want to hear the answer.

She sighs and looks me straight in the eye. "It's bad, Ashley. His results are one of the worst I've seen. The doctors are discussing chemotherapy but also a palliative approach. The chances are, he won't make it through the full chemo cycle. I'm so sorry. We'll know more tomorrow when the doctors discuss it with the other teams." Tears are now flowing freely, both from Chloe and myself.

"Is there anything we can do? Can we help in any way?" I snivel, and Chloe wipes her eyes and blows her nose.

"Not at the moment, Ashley, but I promise to let you know if there is. The only thing you could do is try to persuade him to tell his family. He told me he has no blood relatives, that the club is his only family?" I nod at Chloe. "Try to persuade him to let them know, Ashley, so he isn't alone in dealing with this," she pleads with me.

"I'll try Chloe, but he's a stubborn ass sometimes," I choke out.

"You're telling me," she teases through tears.

"Chloe, please look after him. He's my brother, not by blood but by choice. I love him as though he were, though," I plead with Chloe. She nods at me, grabs my hand, and squeezes it tight.

177

"He's a great guy, and I would do anything for him, Ashley. I'm so impressed by how the club looks after him. We all are. There's hardly a day where he's on his own. He needs that support right now." I nod and stand. Chloe is good people. I hug her and open the door.

"Thank you, Chloe, for everything."

I stand outside in the hall, trying hard to regain my composure, struggling to comprehend what I just heard. Carl is one of the nicest people I know. How can this happen to him? Where is the fairness in all of this? Breathing deeply, I steel myself. I can't crumble now.

I need to be strong for Carl. He'll need my support.

I walk back in and find Carl staring out the window, not turning toward me as I enter. His shoulders are hunched, and he looks defeated.

My heart aches unbearably, seeing him like this. I can see his shoulders shake, knowing instinctively that he's in tears. I so want to make everything better for him, do the fighting for him, but I can't. All I can do is be there for him and lend him my strength. I sit on the edge of his bed, not saying a word, just putting my hand on his shoulder to transfuse him with some of my strength and willpower. I'll fight for my friend, no matter what.

"Ash, please leave. I don't want you to see me like this, and I need to get my head around this bombshell that just dropped into my lap." Carl's broken, rough voice reaches me. He hasn't turned around to face me. My heart is breaking for him, and I have to hold back my tears, struggling to stay in control.

"Okay, honey, I'll leave for now. But I will be back tomorrow, the day after, and every day after that. You will get through this. I will be by your side every step of the way. Promise you will call if you need me, even if just to talk things through. And please, please, tell Raven so he *can support you. The club can support you. They're your brothers, your family. We love you and want to be here for you. They want to be here for you."* I sigh, sensing him fighting for control.

"I'm going now, honey, but please think about what I said." Bending down, I kiss his tear-stained cheek and squeeze his bicep. My legs feel as though they are loaded with lead, as does my heart. I slowly walk out of the door and out of the building.

◇◇◇

"Here, baby, drink." I can hear Vegas's voice through the dull roar of the blood in my ears. Mechanically, I grab the bottle he's holding and put it to my lips. After a few small sips, I feel sick, turn around and vomit up what I have just taken in.

"Ashley, what the fuck? What's wrong? Are you sick? You're scaring me here. Talk to me! What's wrong?" Vegas's voice is full of concern and worry.

I can't help it. The tears I've held back all afternoon run down my face, and I sob uncontrollably. Vegas's strong arms lift me, then gently lower me on his lap as he sits on the ground and rocks me while I cry. I can't stop and am hiccupping with the force of my anguish and anger. Why him? Life had dealt him such a crap hand as it was. He doesn't deserve this.

"Shh, darlin', shh, I'm here. Everything will be okay." I hear Vegas's tender voice trying to calm and soothe me, but I bury my head in his shoulder and cry harder.

I have no idea how long we sat on the ground here—Vegas is still rocking me, but it must have been a while. Darkness is closing in, and the moon and stars are coming out. Somehow, that soothes my aching soul a little. I lift my head and look into Vegas's deep eyes. His tone is gentle when he speaks.

"Ashley, do you feel better now? What brought this on? You scared me, darlin'. I hate to see you hurting and not being able to do something about it. Will you please tell me what's going on?" he asks.

My insides are warring. I promised Carl I wouldn't tell, but this is too big for me alone to carry. Vegas cares, that much is clear. I can see it in his eyes and feel it in the way he holds and supports me here. He hands me a packet of tissues. I look up at him and give him a slight nod. After I've blown my nose and dried my tears, I shuffle around in his lap to find a comfortable position, needing to feel surrounded by his warmth, protected and safe, without looking at him directly.

"I'll tell you, Vegas, but please don't be mad at me." I can feel him stiffen but take a deep breath.

"It's Flakey . . . Carl. He's one of my best friends, like a brother to me. I love him dearly, and before you jump to conclusions, it's not like that. As a brother only." I can feel him relax slightly. His hand rubs up and down my arm, comforting me. "I went to see him earlier. It was awful, Vegas. He got the biopsy results, and the doctors say he has advanced acute myeloid leukemia."

Vegas takes a deep breath, his body tightening, his arms holding me tighter. "I realize this isn't good, Ashley, but what does it mean?" Vegas asks quietly. I lean my head on his shoulder and look up at the sky.

"It's an aggressive form of blood cancer Vegas. I spoke to his nurse. Carl gave his permission, and both Raven and I are named next of kin for him. His chances are not good. They are discussing treatment tomorrow. I've tried to keep his secret for almost a week now, and I just can't any longer. Please don't be mad. I knew before the biopsy that this was likely the cause of his problems, but he made me swear to keep it a secret. I wasn't even allowed to tell Raven." I can hear Vegas draw in a shocked breath. "It broke him, Vegas, seriously broke him. This hit him like a sledgehammer. He made me leave, and was in tears when I did," I stutter.

"I'm scared Vegas, for him, for me, just scared out of my mind. I can't lose my friend!" I cry out. All my anguish in those words. My fear, my grief, my sadness, desperation. I've thrown all those built-up, pent-up feelings into my words and, with that, into Vegas's lap.

Unable to look him in the eye, I know he will be at least disappointed, if not mad, that I kept such a big secret. From him, from the club.

Vegas sits stock still. I try to move away a little, get a little distance between us. "Don't do that," he scolds me. He has every right to.

"I'm sorry, I shouldn't have kept it to myself," I whisper, feeling desolate.

"Ashley, I'm not talking about that. I'm talking about you pulling back. Creating distance." he scolds. "Turn around and look at me," he orders. I comply.

"Listen to me and listen good. Am I disappointed? Yeah, I sure as shit am. Disappointed that he felt he couldn't talk to me. Am I mad at you? I sure am. Mad that you didn't trust me enough to know I'd get it, be there for you, catch you when you fall, and keep your confidence. Ashley, don't keep serious shit like that from me. Ever," he grouses.

I nod, my eyes held captive by his, seeing pain, guilt, and a mix of emotion in them. His eyes tell more than words could.

"I've been asking myself for a long time whether I missed something or let my brother down. He hasn't seemed like himself for a while now, but we all dismissed it because he can be a little flaky. Then we blamed it on Karen and the work at the bar. Now, I wish I'd dragged his sorry ass to the doctor and made him have a check-up." He sighs.

181

"I'm so sorry, Ashley. I know you two are close, and I'll keep your secret for now. But not forever. The club needs to know. See if you can persuade him to speak to Raven. I won't let on to Flakey that I know either. Unless, of course, he tells me himself. Now come here, let me hold you." He draws me closer and gently places his lips on mine. It is the sweetest kiss I've ever had. I feel so damn protected and safe.

After a few moments, Vegas moves me off him and gets up, holding his hand out. I grasp him, and he pulls me to my feet. "Time to head back," he murmurs. I keep my hand in his as we slowly make our way back to the bike. Throughout the ride, my mind is racing and I can't escape my thoughts. My mind will not switch off, and my thoughts keep returning to Carl and his pain. With that, my anxiety rises, minute by minute. I'm antsy and struggle to sit still. As we pull into the garage, I know what I need to do.

I take my helmet off, shrug out of my gloves, handing both to him, and then follow him into the house. Just inside the door, I stop and look at him. It's now or never. He looks at me questioningly, and I take a deep breath.

"Vegas, please, I need you to take me out of my head." I nervously shift from one foot to the other. I just can't seem to keep my anxiety from taking physical form. "I can hardly breathe. My anxiety is sky high, and my head and heart just hurt. Please, Vegas," I beg.

He stands there for a few long moments, just looking at me. "Ashley, are you sure about what you're asking me for here?" he narrows his eyes at me.

"Yes, I am, Vegas. I'm not asking. I'm begging. Please make me feel better. Take me out of my head." The tears return to the back of my eyes, and I watch his internal debate mirrored on his expressive face. I know when he resigns and steels himself. I let out a slow, long breath I didn't realize I was holding, sending up a quick prayer. I got a taste of his softer side, but I need the other Vegas right now.

-21- VEGAS

I try to hide my shock as best as I can. I know damn well what she means when she asks me to take her out of her head. So far, I've been able to hold myself back, to keep the dark beast inside of me under control. But now, she's poking the bear, and the bear is ready not just to growl but roar at the challenge. The beast is chomping at the bit, but will I be able to maintain control? To not lose myself to the darkness.

Her emotions and anxiety are vibrating through her. She's clinging onto the ledge by her fingertips. She's been through so much the last few days and is coming up short, dealing with everything threatening to overwhelm her. I know I have to help her before she loses her grip completely.

"Are you absolutely certain? Once we go down that road, there's no turning back. I don't want to hurt you, Ashley, neither physically nor emotionally, so I gotta ask, are you one hundred percent sure?" I capture her eyes, needing to know, to see her reaction.

"Please, Vegas, help me. I have a membership to Violets, so I know what I'm asking."

Her broken voice reaches me, and my eyebrows rise nearly to my hairline. Membership to

Violets? That I didn't expect. The beast in me growls louder and is thumping its chest inside me.

So, I comply, though I'm sure regrets will haunt me later.

"I'll help you, darlin', but—and this is a big but—we do this in neutral territory. I'll take

you to Violet's, and we'll get a private room. You will address me as 'Sir,' and you'll have and

will use a safe word if needed, Ashley. I'm dead serious about this. I don't want to hurt you.

We're doing this on my terms or not at all." My voice is hard.

I need her to agree and see just how serious I am. I watch her expressive face and hold

her eyes with mine. She nods. "Words, Ashley, use your words." I need to hear her answer to

judge her emotions and understanding.

"Okay, Vegas, I agree. To Violets, a private room, safe word, and everything else. I have

hard limits. I won't be gagged or have a riding crop used on me," she tells me. Her voice is clear,

and her eyes hold mine.

"That's okay. I repeat, " no gags, no crop whipping," and she nods. I let out a sigh,

looking at my boots and then up at her again. "And, honey, stop calling me Vegas. When it's you

and me, it's Vince or Sir. Okay?" I grab her face in my hands and pull her into a gentle, tender

kiss. She leans her head on my shoulder, nods, and lets her body melt against mine. So much

trust, so much acceptance, I can feel it as a powerful tug all the way to my soul. This is

dangerous territory. Feelings are awakening, and alarmingly, it feels like I could fall for her. I've

got to shut that shit down.

We walk back to the bike, her hand in mine, and I don't want to let go. We gear up and

ride back into town, taking the exit that leads us directly to Violets. After crossing the parking

185

lot, we sign-in. Ashley has her own locker here, so she goes to change while I book the room and make sure it has everything needed. After changing myself, I wait for her outside the locker rooms. My clothing now only consists of my jeans and a pair of shoes I always keep in my locker. My cut covers my otherwise naked torso.

A few moments later, Ashley steps out, and my heart stops for a few beats before it starts up again. She's in a black, tightly laced corset that pushes her breasts up and makes them look amazing. She wears a short, tight, patent leather skirt and sky-high heels with a silver anklet. The shoes make her legs look twice as long, and I'm instantly hard. I want to rip her clothes off and fuck her into the next millennium, but I know I can't. I *must* stay in control. She avoids looking into my eyes and keeps her head bowed.

"Are you ready, Ashley?" I ask her, my tone stern. She bites her lip, which is so damn sexy, and I'm immediately fighting for control here.

"Yes, Sir," she answers quietly.

I praise her. "Good girl."

She follows me to the room I selected, and as I open the door, she drops to the mat, waiting on her knees, her hands on her thighs and her head bowed. She's the picture of submission, making my hard-as-iron dick jump in my pants, forcing me to undo the top button.

After divesting myself of my shoes and cut, I open drawers and remove whatever I need. She obviously has some experience, so I won't have to explain too much. I light a few candles around the room to give it indirect soft light and then turn to her. "Your safe word is canyon," I tell her.

She nods and repeats, "Canyon. I'll use my safe word if I have to." I nod.

"Stand and walk to me," I order. Ashley complies beautifully. My hands are shaking as I turn her around, remove her skirt, unlace her corset, and drop it to the floor. I lead her over to the cross, place her in position, and shackle her arms and legs in place. A tremor goes through her body. I look her in the eye and repeat, "Canyon. Use it." She nods again. "Words, Ashley," I bellow at her. She flinches, but her eyes shine with excitement and heat.

"Yes, Sir, I understand." I nod and place a blindfold on her, tying it off tight, taking away her vision. She shivers as I run my hands over her body in long, slow strokes until she's almost vibrating with need, and I can smell her arousal. I stop and just watch her quietly. Her chest rises and falls rapidly, and her nipples are pebbled up to hard, tight nubs. I want to draw them into my mouth, but they'll have to wait.

Grabbing a soft suede flogger, I raise my hand and let the tails land on her breast. Not so hard it would hurt, but hard enough she can feel it as more than a gentle caress. She lets out a hiss and throws her head back, exposing her neck to me. My flogger hand takes this as an invitation, and the next strip lands there, drawing the tails down over her breast. Her skin is flushing, making me increase the intensity to harder flogs all over her body, front and back. Her arousal is visibly leaking down her thighs, and I want to lick it off her so badly. But she's not ready for me yet. Changing the aim of the flogger, I place a hit on her clit, and she groans deep in her throat. After repeating this move a few times, she's shaking.

I walk toward her and close my lips around her left nipple, biting it with my teeth. She moans and shivers, and I repeat the same treatment to her right nipple. They're so sensitive, and she's so responsive to me. I turn and grab my next item from the drawer next to us. Sucking her nipple into my mouth hard until her legs shake. I lap the nub with my tongue and fasten a nipple clamp I warmed up in my hand. Then, I repeat the same procedure with her other nipple.

A track of tears formed on her cheeks. I've only inflicted minimal amounts of pain, so I know it's not caused by that. I thread a chain through the clamps, keeping them connected, and hang a small weight from it.

Her reaction is instant. She throws her head back further and lets out a loud moan and sigh. She's the most beautiful thing I have ever seen. Her skin is flushed and sensitive, and she's in the moment with me. I feel ten feet tall to elicit those reactions from her. It often takes a long time to build that kind of trust necessary, but Ashley shows me she trusts me at every turn.

I change to a different flogger, a leather one this time, increasing the intensity. I cover her breasts, her ass, all of her body, and beautiful rosy stripes are forming all over her delectable skin. My cock is ready to burst out of my jeans. I have to undo the remaining buttons.

Ash is moving around in her shackles. Unable to keep still, her moans echo through the room, and her moisture leaves a track down the inside of her thighs. Using the magic wand, I switch the vibrations to high and hold it firmly against her needy clit. Ashley screams as she comes hard, but I keep the vibration up and rhythmically pull on the weight of her nipple clamps. It doesn't take long until she explodes again, the moisture gushing down her legs with the intensity of that orgasm.

I remove her from her shackles and blindfold, and she blinks a few times. Her voice is hoarse from screaming when she looks at me and says, "Thank you, Sir."

I smile at her deviously and lead her to the leather covered bench. "Lie down," I command, my voice harsh. She complies instantly. I tie her wrists with rope and then tie her ankles to her hips with intricate shibari knots. She's now splayed out before me, her breathing coming in pants. I move slowly through the room, making sure she can see me at all times. Her pupils are dilated, and her eyes are glassy. I pull her to the edge of the bench so that her heels are just touching it. She's soaked, and her bare lips and mound are glistening. I grab a candle and start dropping wax. First on the taut muscles of her belly. She hisses. I drip a path down her right thigh and shin, then back up the other leg. Last, I drip some large patches on her nipples and the clamps while pulling on the weight, which has her moaning loudly. I can see her getting wetter.

Taking an ice cube out of the ice tray, I graze it over the hardening wax. I touch her lips with it, and she sucks on it. Unable to help myself, I trace my warm tongue over her cold lips, eliciting a deep moan. Running another ice cube down her stomach and over her pubic bone has her panting harder with need. I press the ice cube onto her sensitive, hard clit, then place my mouth over it and suck hard. She screams my name, and I'll forgive it as it nearly makes me come in my pants.

Inserting my finger deep into her drenched pussy, I can feel her tightening around me. I continue to tease her with my tongue and slowly enter another finger. Then another, taking my time moving in and out of her, bringing her to the edge and then back off. She's crying in frustration; she wants to come so bad.

"You do not come without my command," I tell her harshly. "You can't handle it? Use your safe word. Do you need to use it?" Her voice is unsteady when she answers.

"No, Sir, I don't. I'm fine." She knows I asked to make sure she's okay.

I flip her over onto her front, placing her knees on the bench. I take another length of rope and tie a more intricate pattern, testing that the bindings are not too tight but will hold. Her arms are now tied to her feet behind her back. I add a few more safety knots and connect the bindings to a frame, which I have lowered from the ceiling. I check everything again for the last time before I hoist the frame up and watch her body lose connection with the bench.

Her body stills, and she completely relaxes. Ashley likes this. There is no way to be certain, but I was hoping she would. I stand behind her and lick her folds from top to bottom and back again. I grab her knees and lightly swing her back and forth into my mouth, entering my tongue into her, licking, and sucking. Her moisture is perfect for lubricating my finger as I start massaging her puckered hole. Her whole body tenses, and I know she's getting closer and closer to the edge. Her moans and chants are ceaseless.

"Please, please, please . . ." Her cries show the intensity of her need. I smile.

"Please, what, Ashley?" I ask.

"Please, Sir, let me come, Sir. Please, Sir, more, Sir . . ."

"You come when I tell you to and not before that," I order. I can hardly contain my dick anymore; it's *that* hard and painful. Grabbing a condom, I rip it open, let my protesting cock out, and sheathe myself. I capture more moisture from her folds and rub her puckered rear entry. Slowly, I insert my fingertip and move it around, stroking her hole. I bring her toward me and, in one long thrust, pull her over my cock while my finger pushes deep into her ass. As she starts to spasm, I stop all movement, making her cry out in frustration. I start moving inside her again when she starts to relax a bit.

My woman is so beautiful, suspended in the air, the dark rope a beautiful contrast to her pale skin. I never thought I could come from just looking at her and dominating her, but right now, that is a distinct possibility. My balls and the bottom of my spine tingle, and my cock is painfully hard. I move again, swinging her onto my cock hard and sinking my finger all the way into her ass.

I withhold her orgasm three times, and she gets wetter and more desperate each time.

I'd fuck her harder, but I won't last like this. My balls are already drawing up tight, and I can't stop my own explosion.

"Don't come," I grate out at her and push myself deeper into her, swirling my finger in her ass as I come hard . . . so hard, I see stars, and my vision blackens around the edges. I keep pushing into her through my orgasm and can feel her fluttering around me. I command her, "Come now," as I slap the globe of her ass cheek hard. She screams my name as she comes and comes, squirting all over my cock. She sobs at the intensity of her orgasm, and I wait. Once she goes limp, I lower her back onto the bench. She's out in subspace. I remove all the knots and rope, remove her nipple clamps, and wrap her in a blanket, then carry her to the sofa in the room. I sit her on my lap, hold her tight, and rock her, massaging her limbs as I gently remove the wax from her body.

"Ashley, honey, come back. Open your eyes for me, sweetheart." She slowly opens her eyes and looks at me, her pupils still dilated, and her face is radiating peace. She burrows her head into me, leaning into me more. I'll give her a few more minutes before I start the aftercare.

I gently lay her on the sofa and start unwrapping the blanket. She groans in protest, which has me smiling. I rub ointment all over the front of her body, massaging her gently—her legs, arms, chest. I then nudge her over and repeat the same treatment on her back. Legs, arms, paying special attention to the globes of her ass, which are a lovely shade of pink right now. I grab a bottle of water and sit her up. She takes the bottle and drinks it down.

"How are you feeling?" I ask her.

"Hmm," she mumbles with a smile. There's no way she'll be able to ride, so I make a call for a prospect to pick up my bike and take it to the clubhouse. I get dressed, collect Ashley's clothes, then call for a taxi. I carry her to the locker room and help her change back into her clothes. I don't bother with my t-shirt, just change from my shoes to my boots, carry her to the waiting taxi and give the driver my address. I hold Ashley tight the entire way home. She was fantastic today, and seeing her like this melts my cold, frozen heart a little more.

-22- ASH

A groan escapes as I slowly open my eyes with the sunlight dappling my face. Delicious soreness in my muscles reminds me of what happened last night. I bolt upright in bed and look around. Strange room, strange bed. Vegas's cut hung up neatly over the back of the chair in the corner, and my confusion and anxiety are lowered considerably.

The room is decorated in warm browns and gold tones, not a typical masculine room. A huge bed sits at one end of the room, with two bedside tables. All the furniture is made from tulip wood. How do I know? Call me a wood fiend. It's what I would have bought but way out of my price range. Come to think of it, everything here screams class and expensive.

I swing my aching legs out of bed, notice I'm naked, and search for my clothes. Since I can't find them, I walk over to the dresser, open it, and grab a pair of Vegas's boxers and one of his T-shirts, which drowns me. I inhale deeply—it smells of Vegas, all male with a sandalwood note. The place is quiet, so I decide to explore. There's a door on an inside wall opposite the window, and I open it to find the most luxurious ensuite bathroom I have ever seen.

A long double sink bench with a full-length mirror sits to one side. A large walk-in, hotel-style rainfall shower with multiple shower heads sits opposite it. At the other end, a large picture window looks out over trees. Underneath sits a huge claw-foot bathtub with spa functions

193

and integrated LED lighting. My eyes nearly pop out of my head. I can't help myself and turn on the water. Even the temperature regulation is digital.

A slow smile creeps over my face. I'm excited, like a sixteen-year-old schoolgirl before her first date. As the tub fills, I spot some relaxing bath salts, which I add as I continue to fiddle with the controls and switch on the jets. Stepping into the deep tub, I slowly lower myself and turn off the water when it's high enough to cover my boobs. I lay back, close my eyes, and relax. A deep chuckle pulls me from my pleasant doze. Vegas stands by the door, arms crossed over his chest, grinning at me.

"I see you found the bathroom," he teases me, his gray eyes lit by a smile.

I look into his eyes, and my heart pitter patters. He's a stunning specimen, standing there leaning against the door frame, his torso on full display, biceps bulging, every muscle defined, and a happy trail leading down to the delicious V of his body, disappearing inside his jeans with the top button undone. I instinctively lick my lips. Wouldn't I just love to trace each and every muscle and tattoo with my tongue right about now? He looks delicious.

"Like what you see, princess?" he asks. Like? Not quite. Mesmerized and getting needy for it is more like it.

"I like very much, not that I can see a lot." I wink at him, watching with heat coursing through me as he moves away from the door and walks over to me, my fire and need reflected in his eyes. His hand unbuttons his jeans, and he removes them; I notice he didn't bother with boxers this morning, his erection standing tall and proud.

I crook my finger at him, beckoning him closer. He steps toward me. I can't help myself and rise onto my knees. I lean forward and swipe my tongue over the glistening head of his hard cock. He tastes amazing. I love his salty, musky taste. Grabbing him at the root, I gently start

194

stroking him. He throws his head back and groans. I swirl my tongue around and around his head, let it travel down his shaft, tracing the bulging veins. My other hand wraps around his balls and squeezes gently.

He looks down at me; his eyes are burning darker with need. I wrap my lips around him and slowly take more and more of him into my mouth, laving him on the way down and up again. My tongue plays with his shaft, caressing him, my pace slow, unhurried. After a minute or two, I increase the pressure of my lips and begin sucking harder while my tongue traces his head and licks pre cum from his slit. I can feel his hands going into my hair and holding my head but am impressed that he's not started pushing forward. I smile to myself and continue torturing him. Rolling his sensitive balls in my hand, I can feel them starting to tighten. I look up at him and find his eyes fixed on me.

I hold his eyes and increase pressure and speed. A deep growl vibrates through him, and he takes control. He pushes forward, forcing me to take more of him into my mouth. He's huge, and there is no way I can take all of him. One of my hands still gripping him firmly at the root, moving up and down in time with my mouth. I'm so horny right now, I could just jump him, but he's in control now. He pushes in hard and hits the back of my throat, making me gag a little. I change my angle slightly, and at his next push forward, I'm ready for him. He reaches the back of my throat, and I push a little more and swallow around him. Feeling him deep in my throat turns me on even more. He growls, and the sound rumbles deep in his chest.

"You're killing me here, princess." He groans, and I hum in agreement while he's deep inside my throat, making him hiss and moan.

"Oh, yeah, just like that, princess." He moans, head thrown back, sinews and tendons standing out on his neck, lost in pleasure.

I'm squeezing my thighs together to get some friction on my clit, where I need it now. This is not for me, though—this is for him. His strokes come faster now, and every time he pushes deep, I swallow around him and hum. I can feel his balls drawing up and know he's close.

"Princess, fair warning, I won't last much longer, so if you don't want me filling your mouth, you need to move." He moans again, and I take that as a challenge and double my efforts. His hands tighten in my hair as every muscle in his body goes solid.

"Fuck yes," he hisses, filling my mouth with stream after stream of delicious cum. I swallow it all and continue lapping him until he softens. Removing my mouth, I kiss the tip of his cock and smile brightly at Vegas, whose head is thrown back and his eyes still closed.

He opens his eyes and looks down at me. "Minx," he teases me, a smile playing around his lips. "Scoot up," he says, gesturing at me to move to the middle of the tub. He gets in behind me and pulls me back to his front. The jets still running and the water temperature cozy and warm, I relax against him, my head on his chest, his arms around my middle, his chin on my head. I feel so safe, so sheltered in his arms; I can't help but snuggle into him. I feel his arms tightening around me.

We sit in silence, enjoying each other and the skin-to-skin contact. A deep peace creeps through my bones. This is where I want to be, with this man. My heart beats wildly as the realization hits. I have fallen deep and hard for this biker! Something I never wanted, but it happened anyway. Everything feels so damn right, so I soak up his presence and revel in the moment.

After we're both wrinkly, he empties the tub, lifts me out, wraps me into a huge towel, slings a smaller one around his hips, and carries me back into the bedroom. Not a word is

196

spoken. He dries my body and lays me down on the bed. His steel-gray eyes locked onto mine, and a serious but soft look crosses his face. He crawls over me and rests himself between my legs, his elbows and arms by my head. Then, he lowers his lips to mine in a searing kiss. The gentleness of it and the emotion it communicates is overwhelming. All I can do is cling to him and return the kiss with equal tenderness and fervor.

All coherent thought leaves me as he makes slow, gentle, tender love to me. It's intense, and my orgasm brings tears to my eyes when I finally come. Long, slow intense waves roll over me, and I can feel Vegas deep inside me, feel his orgasm deep in my soul. We haven't used a condom, but hell, I don't care right now. I remember my check-up paperwork, which I have in my handbag and was going to give him last night. I know I'm clean.

He rolls to his side, taking me with him, and I snuggle close and enjoy the calm that has settled over me. I must have fallen asleep again because the next thing I know, I'm being woken by the sun sitting high. A cup of coffee sits on the bedside table while Vegas sits on the edge of the bed, smiling at me. I sit up, grab the coffee, and grin at him.

"Thanks, Vince, I needed that. Sorry I drifted off again," I apologize.

"You looked so peaceful. I left you alone for an extra couple of hours. Your clothes are laundered and dry. I figured you might appreciate clean underwear." He winks at me. How very domesticated.

At the end of the bed, I spot my clothes and boots. I still can't remember getting back last night, but I do remember him helping me get changed and carrying me out to the taxi. I can recall getting undressed and feeling the soft mattress under me, but that is about it. His gaze on me makes me shiver.

"What time is it?" I ask.

197

"Almost noon, darlin'," he answers. "You got plans? I need to go to the clubhouse in a bit to pick the bike up and wondered if you'd give me a lift?" he asks, and I nod. It's the least I can do. "How are you feeling" is his next question, referring to last night.

"I feel great, Vince. Thank you for last night. I really needed you." He nods in understanding.

"You don't have to thank me, darlin', never for that. I'm glad I could help. I'll always help you, Ashley, no matter what. And not just by taking you out of your head. I'll always protect you and help you. You're mine, and I look after what's mine," he declares.

Wow, that was a statement! I should be angry about being treated as property, but I can't find it in me. In my mind, I'm his, and he's mine. Hence, I just nod and quietly reply.

"I'm yours," I nod, "for however long you want me to be."

"I'm going to claim you, Ashley. As soon as I'm back at church." It's not a question, but a statement, and his eyes are firmly locked on mine. The gravity of the situation hits me. I never wanted to be an old lady, never wanted a biker or club life. Yet here's Vegas, making me reconsider my life choices.

"I won't wear a property patch," I tell him seriously. He nods, understanding my hesitance. It won't be a problem if we're not going to any functions or meetings outside of our area.

He sighs and says, "There's a club night out on Saturday at Stormy's. Since I guess the other old ladies will be there, would you like to come?" He looks at me questioningly.

"Can I bring Sarah?" I ask, smirking, and he groans.

"Only if you keep her off the tequila," he teases. I take out my phone and text Sarah.

"What time?" I ask.

"About eight-thirty," he replies. "Tell her to find her own way. You'll be riding with me," he orders, making me smirk. I'll let him believe he's in charge for now.

We get dressed, have a late breakfast, and take his truck to the clubhouse. Elijah waves at me as I drive Vegas's truck through the gate and throws me a winking smirk. He's funny and makes me giggle. I hear Vegas growl, and I giggle even more. As if I'd even look at Elijah.

"Hey, Vince, I'm off today, so I'll just take your truck back to your place, pick up my car, and go to the hospital."

I'm surprised when he replies firmly, "Don't bother getting your car, just take my truck to the hospital. Spare keys for the house are in the glove box, and that button on the dash there," he points, "is the garage opener. The gate opens automatically." I send him a questioning look. "Make yourself at home, princess. I'll be back after work, about seven. I'll bring dinner," he states, but I shake my head.

"No way. If I'm at your house, I'll cook. Dinner will be ready at seven-thirty," I announce. Did I just insist on cooking at his place while waiting for him to return from work? I must admit, I'm a little shocked at myself. He opens his door and gets out, with me following suit, and as I walk around to the driver's side, he catches me, pulls me into his arms, and kisses me soundly. I can hear Eli hollering and Dougal whistling and clapping. When he lets me go, I turn in their direction and take a bow, much to Vegas's amusement. I get in the truck and get the hell out of Dodge before more embarrassment comes my way.

◊◊◊

I'm halfway into town when my phone rings. It's a number I don't recognize, so I ignore it. When it starts ringing again, I pull over, turn off the engine, and answer.

"Hello, Ashley speaking."

"Sorry, Ashley, it's Chloe. Can you come to the hospital? Carl has taken a turn for the worse. It's not looking good." My hearing dims as blood roars through my veins with rising emotions.

"Please, call my brother," I almost whisper.

"I've done that, and he's on his way, but Carl is asking for you."

I take a deep breath, anxiety restricting my chest.

"I'll be there in fifteen minutes. I'm already on my way," I tell her.

"See you when you get here," she says, ending the phone call. My hands shake as I text Vegas to tell him what's happening.

Once I get to Carl's corridor, I go straight to the nurses' station, where Chloe is waiting for me. She takes me into a small room and sits down with me. I'm vibrating with angst. She takes my hand and squeezes it.

"Ashley, things are not looking good. Carl is in surgery. He was vomiting blood and bleeding from his nose. His blood isn't clotting at all now, and we had to stop the bleeding. The hematologist said he'll need a bone marrow transplant."

"Has he got any close blood relatives? Siblings, parents? They usually have the best chances for a match." She looks at me, question in her eyes. I shake my head.

"His parents died years ago, and there aren't any siblings. Just us," I snivel, tears running down my face. There's a knock on the door, and they usher Jamie into the room.

He looks at me, wraps me in his arms, and holds me tight. "What's going on?" he asks. I can't answer for crying, so Chloe repeats everything she just told me. "Is there any way we can help?" he asks, and she regards him thoughtfully.

"Maybe there is something. Could you arrange for a donor drive in town? We need to get as many people to donate bone marrow as possible. Initially, it involves a blood test to look for matches."

"The hospital is part of the National Marrow Donor Program, and we have a center, right here, where you can register."

Jamie nods at Chloe. "I'll go register right now and give a blood sample. Club members will arrive soon. Could you direct them straight to the center to register and give samples? I'll send a text telling them what is happening." Jamie states decisively, and Chloe nods at him.

"I've already registered, so have most of the staff on the ward. Carl is very popular with the nurses. We'll all give blood samples over the next few days. We'll try our hardest to find a match." Chloe's reply is emotional, her eyes full of unshed tears. I admire her. She's so strong and has so much empathy and patience. She's a lovely person, and I don't miss how she measures Jamie up when he isn't looking. If the occasion weren't so somber, I'd giggle.

I hear Jamie talking with Chloe, but I don't take in their conversation. I'm in a daze, not knowing what the hell to do.

As though Chloe can read my mind, she says, "Ashley, he'll be in surgery for a while, so why don't you go down to the cafeteria, and I'll phone you as soon as I know something." I look at Jamie. I know he doesn't have the answer, but I need his reassurance.

"Come on, sis, let's go and grab a coffee before the club arrives." He gently grabs my hand and leads me from the room, nodding gratefully at Chloe.

-23- VEGAS

Ash: Just had a phone call from Nurse Chloe. Carl is worse. She wants me to hurry. Not sure when I'll be back xx

That's not what I wanted to see when I opened my phone. I know they wouldn't have called her if it wasn't serious. Not five minutes later, my phone dings again.

Prez: Everyone, close the businesses and get to the hospital. Flakey's not doing well. You're all asked to help. Meet me at the downstairs reception desk.

Holy shit, this must be serious. Everyone simultaneously drops their tools with a lot of grunts and cussing. Concerned faces everywhere, it takes a few minutes until we're on our bikes and on the way to the hospital. Several others joined us on the road, all coming from different directions. By the time we reach the parking lot, it's heaving with bikes. We make our way into the reception area and group around Raven.

Raven looks apprehensive and on edge. So many bikers in one place, and no one dares to breathe. You can hear a pin drop. Finally, Raven clears his throat.

"There is no easy way of saying this. Flakey is not good. He's been diagnosed with advanced acute myeloid leukemia, which stops his blood from clotting. He's had another big bleed, so he's in surgery now."

202

Stunned whispers are making the rounds. I knew it was bad but hadn't recognized how bad, even though Ashley told me.

"We can all try to help him," Raven continues. "He needs a bone marrow transplant. We know there's no blood family, so it is up to us to try to stand by him. There is a bone marrow donor center here in the hospital. I'm on my way there to give a blood sample to be tested. They're trying to find a suitable match for him, which is difficult. I am going to register now. Does anyone want to join me?" He looks around at every one of us. Not that it was needed, as we all nodded almost as soon as he finished his sentence.

"Lead the way, Prez," declared Clusseaud.

We all agreed and, as one, followed Raven to the registration office. We sit, fill in what seems like never-ending forms, and finally, one after the other, are called to give a small blood sample. Raven goes first, and everyone else follows when called. As I come out and join Raven, I can't help myself, and I have to ask.

"Where's Rusty? I haven't seen him in a bit." I try to sound concerned, but I guess I haven't quite hit the right tone since Raven looks at me quizzically.

"He's taken two weeks off. He had to look after Ellie. She got herself into a little situation. He'll join us at the Slayers rally."

Oh, how convenient, is my first and only thought. I know better than to voice it, though. Instead, I ask, "Is Ellie okay? Do we need to help get her out of trouble? She always was such a great girl. Shame she left."

Raven nods and sighs. "I don't think it's that bad, I offered, but Rusty is convinced he can handle it on his own. Whether or not she lives here, she's part of our family. I worry about her sometimes." Raven sounds uneasy.

203

"Brother, I'm sure if she needs us, she'll reach out," I try to reassure him. "I'll ask Ash if she has heard anything from Ellie lately. I know those two were as thick as thieves."

"Talking about Ashley, brother, I will remind you again. I will bury you in a hole so deep, no one will ever find you if you hurt my sister," He hisses at me.

"Whoa, calm down, man! We have talked and sorted shit out. We are together, and I will claim her at the table on Sunday. I'd never hurt her knowingly. Sure, I will fuck up once in a while, but I'd never knowingly hurt her," I promise Raven, and I hope my voice reflects my sincerity.

"I can't say I'm happy about this Vegas. I'd be lying if I did, but I will try to get used to the new situation for Ashley's sake. It'll take time for me not to want to rip your fucking head off, so tread carefully, brother," he warns me, and I nod at him. I get it. If it were my sister, I would react the same.

"She's in the cafeteria," he grouses. "Best go take care of her, don't ya think? I'll wait for the others, and we'll meet you there." I nod at his request, turn and make my way into the cafeteria.

I see her sitting at a table by the window, her shoulders slumped, and hopelessness is cast like a mask over her beautiful face. My chest aches to see her like that. My strong warrior princess looks so fragile; I want to scoop her up in my arms and be her knight in black shining armor. I've never seen her look so defeated before. I quietly make my way to her table, sit beside her, and wrap her in my arms.

"Hey, princess," I whisper in her ear, and she melts against me. I can see how hard she's fighting her tears.

204

"Let it out, baby, just let it out. I'm here. I'll keep you safe." That's when the first sob breaks free. She buries her face into my cut, grabbing it with both hands, clinging to me like a monkey, bawling her eyes out, and all I can do is let her know I'm here for her, strong for her, and comfort her. My hand rubs her back and strokes her hair. I move my chair back, and she climbs into my lap, clinging to me for dear life.

Slowly, her sobs become quieter and are interspersed with hiccups. When she sits up a little, I hand her some napkins, which Raven quietly put on our table before he walked away to sit with the brothers, giving us some space. I look at her red, swollen face, and my heart breaks for my woman. I wish I could take her pain away, but I know that's impossible. Instead, I hold her close, kiss her hair, and let her know I'm here for her. It is all the reassurance I can give her right now.

"Hey, babe, I know you're upset, but I need to ask you something. Well, several things, actually. Are you still in touch with Ellie?" Ashley looks up at me with her tear-stained face and nods.

"Yes, Vince, why do you ask?" she inquires between hiccups.

"I'm sorry, sweetheart, I don't mean to pry. I just wondered if you could call her and make sure she's okay. Maybe let her know about Flakey as well. I'm sure she'd want to know."

"Oh my god, yes, of course, I had completely forgotten she knows him as well as I do. I need to get some fresh air and collect my thoughts. I'll go outside for a bit and call her from there. Don't wanna sound like a complete mess when I do. Then I'll also register for the donor search and get my blood taken." She went from blubbering to insisting in under ten seconds. My warrior princess is getting her composure and shows her steel backbone. No one could be prouder of her than I'm right now. Letting her out of my lap, I watch her stride with determination toward the cafeteria doors, nodding at the rest of the brothers on her way.

I meander over to the brothers. Raven is pointedly ignoring me, so I sit down with Pennywise.

"Pen, a word later, please?" I quietly ask him.

He looks at me, surprised, but nods. I'm surprised myself. I've had concerns for a long time but never voiced them, so why now? An hour later, we still haven't heard any news about Flakey. Raven calls the nurse, who tells him the operation is nearly over. She'll call him as soon as Flakey is back on the floor. Sparks called Ally, who is now sitting with us, and Dawg picked up Caroline. Debbie has made her way to the hospital, and Ashley must have called Sarah because she's sitting by Dougal. All the old ladies and Sarah have registered and given blood samples. Sarah phoned work, and all of her and Ashley's co-workers will turn up over the next couple of days to get tested. It looks like the ball is rolling.

Raven approaches our table. "I called the Slayers and let them know what's going on with Flakey. Most of them have known him for years and asked how they could help. They'll all get tested at their end too, and have a collection for Flakey at the rally. They asked if we would like to man a stall for Flakey? You know, telling people about bone marrow donations and having registration forms there for people to fill out if interested. I said yes, but I'm not sure how that would work?"

Ferret looks at him and suggests, "Why not ask his nurse, the one who seems invested and explains everything to you and Ashley? She might be able to help. And we could raise some money for the hospital cancer unit at the poker run after the Slayers rally."

"Great idea, Ferret, thanks. I'll ask Chloe and put the fundraiser on the agenda for Sunday." Raven looks relieved to have gotten so many offers to help and suggestions already. Ally must have overheard because she pipes in.

"Hey, the Wild Pixies are at the rally too, camped next to you hoodlums. We'll man the stand for you and charm the pants off the peeps. You'll have lots of registrations," she half teases, but her eyes show she's genuine and eager to help. She's a diamond.

"Woman, your wily charms are just for me, remember that," jokes Sparks good-naturedly. He knows she loves him truly, madly, deeply. After all, she's been putting up with him for nearly ten years. I see Dawg with pen and paper, jotting things down to put on the agenda, taking notes of offers, and compiling a planning list. Everyone is doing their bit.

I hadn't noticed Ash coming back, but suddenly, I feel her hands on my shoulder and her warmth transfusing into me.

She leans down, kisses my cheek, and whispers in my ear.

"I spoke to Ellie, babe; she's fine. She's upset about Flakey but insisted she was absolutely fine. Well, other than moaning about Rusty taking up residence and not being able to get rid of him." Ash visibly shudders.

Others notice her affectionate way of approaching me, and there are catcalls. Ashley smiles sweetly at everyone, then shoves her middle finger at them, making everyone chuckle. That's my girl.

Suddenly, Ashley's phone goes off. "Hi, Chloe," I hear her answering. "He is? Oh great! Can we come up? Yes, there are lots of people here. Okay . . . .got it; I'll let them know. See you soon, Chloe." Ash turns around and looks at everyone. "Well, he's out of surgery and back on the ward. He's exhausted and still groggy, so only two people at a time, and only five minutes each." We all walk to the elevators, taking us back up to the floor.

Chloe is waiting for us outside Flakey's room. "He asked for you, Ashley." Ash nods and lays her hand on the door handle. I grab her other hand. There is no way I will let her go in there on her own. She's been through enough. Raven approaches Chloe.

"May I have a word, please? I need to ask your advice on something."

"Sure, follow me. We'll use the family consult room again," she assures him. Before she walks away, she looks around at everyone. "Don't forget, two people at a time, five minutes only. Don't make me come in there and throw you out. And absolutely no whiskey or beer is to be smuggled in." She winks, and everyone chuckles. She seems okay and is good-looking at that. Not my type, but beautiful. She's curvy, tall—I'd guess about five-foot-eight or nine—with blonde, slightly wavey hair with red highlights. She wears her hair in a messy bun, so I can only assume it to be long. She's down to earth, open, and honest. I like her.

Ouch! Ashley slaps me around the back of the head and glares at me. Shit, she must have noticed me assessing Chloe. Damn it!

"You go, girl. Knock some sense into him," Sarah teases. I put my arm around Ash, draw her close, and kiss her temple.

Flakey is awake as we enter, but just slightly. He looks like death rolled over. White as a sheet, with dark rings under his eyes, his face looks thinner than the last time I saw him. Watching him sag in his pillows, clearly exhausted is quite a shock.

Ashley moves to his side and sits on his bed, careful not to disturb all the cables and lines attached to him.

"Hey." Flakey smiles at her then looks at me and states weakly, "I see you dragged the riff-raff in with you."

"Giving me lip already?" I banter back. "Operation must have done the trick. How are you, brother?" I ask, my tone turning more serious.

"Honestly? I feel like shit. I'm sure they let Tyson pound me while I was under."

"You in pain, man? Want me to call the nurse to get you some pain relievers?" He shakes his head at me. "No need. I have my magic box here. I push the button and get a little hit, makes me as high as a kite." He grins at me.

Ashley smiles at us, looking reassured. She looks at Flakey. "You asked for me?"

"Yes, honey, I did. I need to talk to you about some things. You know, in case I don't make it. I'll give it my all to fight this shit, but I need to be realistic here and cover all my bases." I see Ashley's eyes moisten up again, but she nods bravely.

"We're only allowed to stay five minutes. The others are outside and want to see you, too. You gave us quite a scare. Is it okay if I come back tomorrow and we talk about it all, then?" she queries softly. Flakey sighs and nods his head. He's struggling to keep awake. We say our goodbyes and leave to let the next couple of people go in. I nod at Raven and Pen. The chat with Pen can wait until tomorrow. Getting my woman home and chilled out is the number one priority right now. It was a hell of a day.

I follow her back on the bike and overtake her just before we get to my place. My bike triggers the gate and garage doors, allowing her to drive straight into the garage. She shuts off the truck, jumps out, and locks it. I meet her at the door and hold it open for her.

"Shit," she mumbles.

"What's up, princess?"

209

"Damn it, Vegas, I forgot to do the shopping. I was going to cook." I smile at her. She's cute when she's irritated with herself.

"Hey, never mind, baby, it's been one helluva day. Let's just order something in. What do you feel like? Pizza?" She smiles brightly at me, making me feel instantly lighter.

"I could eat pizza. Could I have ham and pineapple, please?" she asks innocently, and I look at her in horror.

"Pineapple? On pizza? Are you insane? Pineapple is a fruit and has no business as a pizza topping!" I shudder in disgust, making her laugh out loud.

"I beg to differ," she contradicts me. "Pineapple is one of the most delicious pizza toppings ever." Oh yuck, if that crazy woman thinks I'll kiss her after pineapple pizza, she can think again. Gross, gross, gross! I call in the order and put on some coffee while we wait. The shit in the hospital was more like dishwater than coffee. I think we could both do with a pick-me-up. We grab our cups, move to the living area, and flop onto the sofa. I switch the TV on with the volume turned low.

"What would you like to do tonight? After the pizza, obviously." I look directly at her, waiting for her to answer.

-24- ASH

I'm slouched on Vegas's sofa, considering what he asked me. If he really wants us to work, we need to talk. About him, me, us, all the stuff festering away in the background. I know as his old lady, I'll be expected to attend club functions, parties, and rallies. But I'm hesitant. Rusty isn't going to enjoy seeing me around regularly. I think I need to come clean and explain why I'll struggle with that. If we're ever going to work, honesty is the best policy and the only way to move forward. If he can't deal with my past, he isn't worth my efforts, or so I keep telling myself.

"Err . . . babe . . . would you mind if we just sat and talked?" I can hardly look at him.

"Sure," he agrees, "whatever you want to do, princess, is fine by me." He leans over and kisses me deeply. "I've waited all day to do that," he groans, and I giggle. He kissed me like a starving man even though it hadn't been that long.

At the chiming of the security system, it's clear the pizza is arriving, so Vegas lets the delivery driver in, tips him, and plonks the pizzas on the table. I swallow hard, thinking about what I must do, and instantly lose my appetite. My anxiety is running rampant.

"Babe, do you mind re-setting the alarm?" My tone demonstrates my nerves. Vegas looks at me with raised eyebrows but goes back and does as I ask. We spend the next ten minutes with Vegas eating and me nibbling on a slice of pizza. Until Vegas takes it out of my hand, takes the box and plates into the kitchen, and sits opposite me, leaning forward, elbows on his knees and looking at me intensely.

"Okay, Ashley, that's enough. You have an issue or problem or whatever, so just spit it out. We can have our dinner afterward. You clearly aren't in the mood for food, and nervousness is just radiating off you. I'm not playing silly games here. Whatever your problem is, I promise I'll listen and try not to interrupt. You're important to me, Ashley. You're as good as my old lady. Please trust that I will listen and not judge," he states, his voice soothing and calming.

I look into his eyes and see nothing but curiosity and concern. Taking a deep breath, I know it is now or never, but I'm also painfully aware that this will have serious consequences. I'm not sure if I can stop Vegas from doing what he'll feel he ought to. His hand is grabbing hold of my restless one, and his thumb is soothingly stroking the back of my hand.

"It all started many years ago," I begin. "It was during the worst times of the club, the most violent and heinous times. Stone was in charge, and Raven was a pretty blinded member at the time. I was the club princess and expected to toe the line at every turn, told what to do, what to think, and how to act. I was young, and my mother was still alive but drinking heavily, so I was often left with Nathan alone.

"She was drunk about every night, and if there was going to be a warm dinner, I cooked it. I was ten years old, and Nathan was only three. I can't remember my mom ever not drinking, but Raven said she only started this downward spiral after I was born. So, whether it was me

212

driving her into being an alcoholic, I don't know, but I wrestled with that guilty feeling for years."

"Ashley—" Vegas interrupts, but I hold my hand up to stop him.

If I don't get it all out in one go, I won't. Seeing the disgusted look on his face when I've finished will be bad enough. I can't bear to think I could lose him through things long gone in the past, but better now than later. After a deep, shuddering breath, I continue.

"Please wait, Vince, and let me get this all out. It's difficult enough as it is." He nods, gets up, and walks out, returning a few seconds later with a glass of water and a glass of amber liquid.

"Here, drink this. It might help with the nerves." I grab the glass and tip it back in one go, feeling the warmth and sweet burn of whiskey running down my throat and into my stomach. It is comforting, like a hug. I place the water on the table and continue.

"Anyway, so times were not the easiest, and I had a lot of responsibilities before I even hit puberty. I managed as well as any ten-year-old could. One afternoon, when I got back from school and picked up Nathan from Mom, who tried to help as much as she could, I walked in and heard strange noises. As any kid would, I went to investigate, and that's when I found them. My mother and Rusty were in the kitchen, going at it.

"Mom saw me and shooed me away with her hand, so I turned and ran into my room, keeping Nathan close. What I saw frightened me. Even then, I knew the person my dad trusted should not be touching my mother. I knew Stone would go crazy if he knew. He'd likely shoot both of them."

"I sat and cowered until I heard them in the hall and the front door slam. I opened my door and ran outside while Nathan ran to our mother. No sooner had I stepped foot outside did

213

someone grab me under my arms, slapped a hand over my mouth to stop me from screaming, and dragged me behind the trees. I kicked and struggled, but Rusty was too strong for me. It was before his hip was smashed, so no struggle for him."

My voice is full of disgust and terror. The terror of a little girl manhandled and carried away by a grown man. I can feel the tears burning behind my eyes. The dam I'd been building for so long is about to burst. I fiercely blink away the tears and steel myself to tell the rest of my story. If he doesn't want me anymore after that, so be it. I'm done hiding.

I look at Vegas, and he's as stiff as a board, his posture radiating anger, shock, and disgust. Well, I can't help that. He wanted to know, so now he's going to listen to the end, whether he likes it or not. Then I'll pick myself up, walk away with dignity and cry the ocean of tears waiting to burst out at home, in my solitude. Anger flows through me. How dare he? He told me to trust him. I did, and now, he's disgusted and angry with me?

At least I see this side of him now before it's too late. I swipe the few escaping tears away with an angry arm. Let him see I'm furious with him, bitter, disillusioned. I'm strong. I *will* survive this as well. So what if I've fallen hard and fast for this beautiful man? Just goes to show that beauty is only skin deep, huh?

And, yes, I've known for a few days that I'm in love with Vegas . . . Vince . . . whatever he wants me to call him. I thought maybe he was the exception to the general mentality of club members. Club and brothers come first, then themselves, sex, and a whole lot of nothing after that. That'll teach me. I'm such an idiot.

"Don't," I bark at Vegas in the coldest voice I can manage as he tries to speak, a look of surprise on his face. See? I can do this! "He dragged me behind the trees. The house, back then, was on club property. It no longer exists, burned to the ground in retaliation, and Nathan and I were almost burned alive. Brass, Pennywise's dad, rescued us and got severely burned. They later killed him in the shootout that killed a lot of the original members and put more in prison, Stone on death row in Nebraska, as you know."

I take another deep breath, thankful that the history lesson is over. "He had me clamped tightly to his front, one hand over my mouth and the other holding his gun to my temple. I was only ten, for fuck's sake, but he made sure I understood what he expected from me." *'You breathe one word of what you've saw, and I will put a bullet in your airy-fairy head, girl! Then I'll come for your little brother! Then for Raven, he needs a smack over his puppy nose anyway!'* The memory of Rusty's threat comes to the front of my mind. "I'll never forget his manic, evil laughter . . ." I shudder, lost in my memories.

"He threatened me over the years, and as I grew older, the threats became more violent. One time, he told me he'd take me to some people he knew outside of the club and let all of them have a go at me, let them pull a train on me."

I hear Vegas gasp before he rockets off the table where he was sitting and starts pacing.

"I never told anyone. Not Raven, not Nathan, not Mom, not anybody. I'm sure he'd eventually come for me and make good on his threats if I had. He's evil, a slithering snake in the grass who bad-mouthed Raven at every turn. He knows I can't tell on him because no one would believe me. He's the VP, after all. Who would Raven believe? His sister or his VP? The club always comes before family; I know that. He used to touch me, sometimes still does when he thinks no one notices. My butt, my boobs, anything he can get away with. That's why I stayed away. I don't need his shit, Vegas, and I sure as shit don't need your disgust, anger, or pity." I look at him for the first time since I started my confession. We are eye to eye. His are blazing with fury while mine are alight with disappointment in him.

215

"Who else knows?" Vegas grates out.

"Mom knows some, as does Ally, but no one knows the entire story, just parts of it. You're the only one, and I'd appreciate if you would keep it to yourself and just let me go home. You'll never have to look at this obviously so disgusting person again," I hiss at him.

He stands stock-still as though I slapped him. In fairness, it's what I would like to do but don't have the courage to.

"Is that what you think?" Vegas bellows at me, and I flinch back from him. "That I'm disgusted and angry with you? You're talking fucking crazy. Yes, of course, I'm angry and disgusted. I want to kill someone right now, so badly," he snaps at me. "Ashley, look at me," he commands. "I'm not angry at you or disgusted with you. How could I be? You're my woman. Someone has been threatening and scaring you for years, so of course, I'm pissed. At Rusty, the club, the world, at myself for not picking up on it or being able to help you when you needed it most."

I look at him, utterly stunned. Why is he not pissed off with me? I kept this secret.

"Ashley, listen to me and listen to me good," His voice is gentle as he walks over, pulls me out of my seat, and wraps his arms around me, squeezing me so tight it is difficult to breathe.

"I'm sorry, baby, so sorry. Sorry this happened to you, sorry you felt you had no one to go to, and sorry I didn't kill the fucker. I'm sorry you're still suffering every day, and you think you can't trust the club or that the club would have your back. Ashley, the club, is your family. Whether or not you want to be, you're a part of it. We all love you. I love you. We'd do anything for you."

My eyes shoot up to his. "What?" I look at him, eyes as big as saucers.

216

"Yeah, sweetheart, I just said that I love you, and I mean it. I've been a fool not to admit it to myself sooner, but I've been in love with you since that day in Violets two years ago. I've never looked at anyone else the way I look at you." He smiles down at me.

"But—"

"No, Ashley, no ifs, no buts. This is me telling you how I feel, so don't try to question it. I love you. End of discussion," he says with finality.

I close my eyes and finally let the tears escape. "I love you too," I sob. "So much." Clinging to him for dear life, he picks me up, cradles me, and sits us down on the sofa with me in his lap, blubbering and shedding all the tears that have built up through years of anxiety. He just sits with me, holds me, and lets me get all my anguish out.

His T-shirt is thoroughly wet, my eyes swollen, and all I can do is hiccup after a long while, but my soul feels a little lighter, and I'm a lot less anxious.

"Hey, baby, feeling a little better now?" His gentle eyes look down at mine, and I nod at him. He sits me on the sofa beside him, disappears for a few minutes, returns, picks me up, and carries me to the master bathroom. The bright lights are off, and the water in the tub is running with only the soft color-changing tub lights on. He slowly starts undressing me, showing me so much care that my eyes are filling again. Leaning against him, I let his comfort seep deep into my bones. I don't notice that he's undressed. He carries me to the tub, lowers me in gently, then gets in behind me. Cradling me close, my back to his front, there is nothing sexual about this, just close comfort, relief, and peace settling over me. I'm emotionally exhausted.

We sit there, just being with each other for a long time. He washes my body with such gentle tenderness that I feel a little overwhelmed. When he's done, he lifts me out of the bath, dries himself and me off, and gently carries me to his bed.

217

"Sleep, beautiful, I'm not going anywhere," he whispers, kisses me sweetly, and as he lifts his head from mine, my eyes close, and I give in to my exhaustion.

My dreams are haunted. Rusty is coming for me. He takes and kidnaps me, and I can feel his hands on me and the gun at my head. I wake up screaming, and Vegas rushes into the room.

"Baby, are you okay?" His voice is heavy with concern.

"Sorry, I'm okay, just a bad dream."

He climbs on the bed with me and cuddles me close. "Shh, it's okay, I'm here. Nothing is going to happen to you." I let his soothing voice wash over me.

"How long have I been asleep?" I look at him questioningly.

"Two hours, princess. You needed it." A loud growl from my stomach interrupts him. I can feel myself flushing pink, and Vegas bursts into laughter. "Okay, okay," he chuckles, "I can take a hint. Come on, princess, let me feed you."

He throws me one of his T-shirts. The smell of him on his shirt is comforting and makes me smile. I follow him into the kitchen, where the pizza is still sitting. He switches on the oven and places the pizza and some garlic bread from the freezer in it. I hop off my stool and open the fridge. He has all the makings of a salad. So, I get to work cleaning and chopping everything. I look around for a bowl, and it appears right in front of me as if by magic. Vegas is smirking at me. With the salad prepared and the pizza almost ready, I wash my hands while Vegas takes out and portions the garlic bread. Just as we finish our tasks, the timer for the pizza goes off. We load our plates with salad and eat in peaceful silence.

After cleaning up our mess, we climb back into bed. Vegas pulls me into him.

"I want you to stay with me, princess," he murmurs in my ear. "No, let me finish," he insists when I'm about to protest. It's too soon for this. "I know what you're going to say—that it's too soon, that you don't want to depend on me, that you want me to have my own space—and you probably have a hundred more objections. Just let me tell you, you're it for me. As far as I'm concerned, you and I are forever. So, you staying here would just shorten the process a little. I want everything with you, Ashley. I want you with me, to build a life with you, fill your belly with our babies, and watch them grow, and eventually, I want to marry you. I want to give you the world and everything in it, to make you feel loved and strong."

He continues, "Unlike you, I had a good upbringing. The first few years weren't great, but my grandmother took me in when my mother couldn't be bothered, and she gave me all the love and security I ever could've wanted. I loved her so much. She was more of a mother to me than my real mother ever was. My grandad died in World War II and left her a fortune. He was from old money. Grandma always lived frugally, and I never realized her financial situation until after she died and left me everything.

"I gave my mother the house to shut her up and moved here. I bought this property and the one hundred fifty acres it sits on and made it my home. Very few people know where it is. It's my sanctuary and one I want to share with you. If you really feel you need your own space, I get that. We'll just have some alterations done to the house, extend it, which I was thinking of anyway, and add bedrooms for at least ten kids." I hear the laughter in his voice.

"Ten? Oh my god, I'm not a broodmare," I object laughingly.

"Details." He waves away my objection, quickly dismissing it. I turn around to face him.

"Seriously, Vince, I can't. What about the house? What about Nathan?" His steely gray eyes capture mine and the love I see in them melts my heart and my resistance.

"You could keep the house, Ashley. Rent it out for now if that would make you feel better. I can speak to Dawg. I know he and Caroline are looking for a place to settle down.

219

Nathan can stay here when he's home. This is a three-bedroom, two-bathroom house, so there's no problem there," he replies seriously, a look of concern and steeliness in his eyes.

"Okay," I answer, feeling happy for the first time in years. "Okay, yes, I'll stay with you. Under one condition . . . well, several conditions."

He smiles at me. "Let's hear them."

"No babies, not yet, and when we decide to have them, I want three, max. I'll contribute to half the bills and shopping." His brows draw together in displeasure, but I soldier on. "I'll rent my house, so I have somewhere to go in case something goes wrong, or you change your mind or something. And we'll add two extra bedrooms, one for Sarah and one for Leo." I feel a little wounded when he starts laughing.

"Oh, princess, you are precious." He chuckles. "How about this as a counteroffer? I pay the bills, and you can pay for the shopping. Anything we need for the house comes out of an account that you'll have a card for, so don't think you're paying for anything to do with the house. We can add as many bedrooms as you like, and even an annex for Sarah and Leo if you want, though somehow, I don't think they'd use it much. And how about five kids instead of ten?" He snickers.

I want to protest, but he cuts me off by placing his lips on mine, sealing them with a toe-curling, panty-wetting kiss.

A glowing red backside and four mind-melting orgasms later, I feel boneless and don't have the strength or mental capacity to object any further. I'm sure he short-circuited my brain with the last one; I feel like I am floating on a cloud. It wasn't gentle, and he was in complete control. I knew he needed that, so I submitted to him happily. I smile up at him as he's half leaning over me.

"One more condition," I get out before my eyes close. "Please, can we have a playroom?"

I don't hear his reply, just his quiet snort of amusement before I fall into a deep, dreamless sleep.

-25- VEGAS

I can hear Ashley's even breathing next to me. I worked hard to contain my fury, to be there for her, absorbing her anxiety and pain. I found some solace in the spanking I administered to her and the way I restrained her when I fucked her hard and rough, but now, the fury and hate are overwhelming. Crawling out of bed, I make a few phone calls. A short while later, bikes pull up at the gate, and I can tell it's Pennywise, followed by Slender. As I let them in, they cut their engines and roll up in front of the house, like I asked them to. I don't want them to wake Ashley.

Closing the bedroom door tight, I lead them into my man cave at the other end of the house. There sits my other huge ass TV, several game stations, and a small but perfectly equipped gym.

After back slaps and shoulder hugs from my brothers, Slender asks, "Hey, bro, what's the big emergency that you needed to drag us out in the middle of the night? This better be good, or I'll have to beat your ass for interrupting my session with Ebony." He's smirking at me.

Pennywise looks at me in silence. He knows I wouldn't have asked them to come if it wasn't important. I sigh and gesture toward the seats dotted around. This will be neither easy nor pleasant.

"Okay, boys, I've asked you to come over to let you know what Ashley disclosed earlier. I'm ready to kill, and you won't stop me. This is merely a courtesy call." My voice is hard as I push out my words, my throat thick as though coated with gravel.

I proceed to tell them everything Ashley had told me. I can see their physical demeanor and mood change from curious to furious in under twenty seconds. Slender gets up halfway through, punches my wall-mounted punching bag, and pummels my heavy boxing bag.

Pennywise is sitting stock still, cracking his knuckles one by one.

"Man, this is serious," grates Slender. "Are you absolutely certain? You know what this could mean for Rusty? It *has* to go to the table, man. As much as I'd like to shoot the fucker right the fuck now, it *has* to be voted on. You know that."

"No fucking vote needed," I bluster, "he's dead, and I'm the one to put him down. The bastard deserves a slow, agonizing death."

Pennywise nods at me. "I'm with you, brother, but Slender's right. It's gotta go to the table to be voted on, and we have to bring this to Raven. He needs to know what the hell is going on with his so-called VP. After that's done, I'll make sure you get your way after I get in a few licks of my own." He growls at me; his anger and need for violence are as palpable as mine.

"Keep Ashley with you and keep her away from the fat snake in the grass," states Slender vehemently.

"Let us deal with Raven," Penny agrees. "We have more to bring to the table regarding that fat fuck. It'll make sure he'll be out bad."

223

Extremely unhappy, I begrudgingly agree to keep an eye on Ashley, which I'd do anyway, and keep my hands off Rusty for now to let Slender and Pennywise deal with it. For now. I did not agree to not punching his lights out the next time I see him. And fuck, am I looking forward to that.

I keep myself together, nod where appropriate, and keep my thoughts to myself. I'm seething, my temper boiling with unrestraint fury.

It's been a long time since I've gotten my hands dirty with wet work, but I guarantee it won't be a hardship this time.

Re-arming the alarm after my club brothers leave, I quietly sneak into the bedroom, stand at the edge of the bed, and watch Ashley sleep, tired out from multiple orgasms, which hopefully quietened her head a little. I took control and demanded her submission. But not to the point I really needed.

I wouldn't have been in complete control had I let things go further than a spanking and restraining tonight. Not even fucking her mouth roughly could settle me tonight. I sit in the chair by the end of the bed, remembering spilling my guts and telling her I love her. I never thought that'd be something I'd do. Nevertheless, it is true, and I was a fool not to realize it sooner. I look at this strong woman in front of me with nothing but pride and admiration.

She carried this secret around with her for sixteen years. Fuck, she's my hero. How could anyone ever think she's weak? How hadn't I seen what was going on? I noticed that she shrunk into herself whenever Rusty was around and how she avoided him like the plague. I suspected something wasn't right, but I never followed up on it. I blame myself, in part, for not having been there when she needed me, for keeping away from her. No more. No longer is this incredible woman living in fear. My nerves are frayed, and I don't think I'll get much sleep, but I

"Well roared, lioness," I tease her, drawing her into my arms. She shrugs her shoulders and grins.

"I protect what's mine."

"Good to know." I chuckle at her, throw my arm over her shoulder, and pull her to my side. She turns and grabs her drink, winks at me, then kisses my cheek and makes her way back to the old ladies' table. I can hear Karen hiss and grumble but don't catch what she said. I give Neil a nod, and he rolls his eyes at Karen behind her back. He leans over to me.

"Time to get rid of her, I think." I have to agree. Karen's getting way too big for her britches and is developing a five-foot-two short person's syndrome, with a big mouth and nothing to back it up. She's like an annoying fly—you can swat all you like, but you just can't get rid of the pesky thing.

I stand with my brothers as Raven bellows out for silence. "Silence, assholes! This is supposed to be a meeting." He smirks. "The reason I asked you here tonight is to announce the closure of Stormy's. We decided that we are going to refurbish the club. We've bought the warehouse behind the bar and will turn it into a high-end strip club." Whistles and hoots sound from everywhere, locals and club brothers alike.

"Renovations will take roughly three months, and we plan to open in four, with new bar staff, dancers, and a free round on the house." The crowd cheers. "We'll make further announcements soon, so keep your eyes and ears open. Neil will manage the place, so any ideas for bar or club names bring to him or me, and we'll vote on it," Raven finishes. I knew what was going to happen, but the rest of the brothers are stunned. A roar of whistles, clapping, and foot stamping goes around the bar.

When the bar returns to the usual clatter, Raven turns to Karen. "Unfortunately, the new staff will not include you. After tonight, you're history. No one treats my family like shit and gets away with it. Count yourself lucky that you're a woman." Karen looks at Raven in absolute shock.

She pales and splutters. "But Raven—"

He interrupts her. "I don't want to hear it. You're out the door after tonight and banned from being employed by the Stormy Souls MC in any further capacity." I watch Dawg scratching things down on a piece of paper.

"Got it, Prez. I'll write it into the official notes in church tomorrow," he throws in with a satisfied smile.

The next thing I register is Sarah shouting, running toward me. "Vegas, get your ass over here; something is wrong with Ashley," she yells, and everyone turns toward the old ladies' table, where I see Ashley slumped over and Ally shouting at her.

"Ash? Ash, what's wrong? Ashley!" She slaps Ashley hard as I run over to the table, followed by Raven and the brothers.

Fuck, what's going on? I pick a limp Ashley up and cradle her. She's breathing but out cold.

"Shit! Someone call 9-1-1! She's unconscious!" I hear the icy panic in my voice, watching as Slender and Penny empty the bar. Neil has disappeared, and so has Karen, probably sent home. Raven kneels next to me, holding Ashley's hand, fear for his sister written on his face. He looks as though he's aged twenty years in thirty seconds.

The ambulance arrives and takes Ashley from me. I don't want to let her go, but Penny and Slender restrain me. "You need to let her go so they can work on her." Their stern faces tell me they'll do more than physically restrain me if I get in the way of the EMTs.

As she's loaded into the ambulance, connected to IV lines and monitors, one of the technicians asks, "Who is going with her?" I step forward, as does Raven.

"I'm her brother," he says, and I counter like a petulant child.

"She's my fiancée."

Slender and Penny hold Raven back. He wants to plant his fist in my face, but I don't care. Jumping into the back of the ambulance, I cling to Ashley's hand the whole way to the hospital.

-26- VEGAS

My heart is pounding when we arrive at the hospital, despite the EMTs assuring me Ashley's condition isn't life threatening. They rush her into the emergency department, and I stay by her side. They check her vitals, take blood samples, and order scans and x-rays, and I'm ushered outside to wait as they take her away. When I step out, I find myself grabbed and thrown against the wall, staring into Raven's blazing eyes.

"How fucking dare you," he bellows at me. His arm pulls back, but the punch isn't forthcoming. Slender has grabbed Raven's arm while Pennywise pulls me out of his grip.

"You need to calm the fuck down, Prez. This ain't his fault. It's more important to find out what is going on with your sister than caving his head in." Slender is trying to calm Raven, who finally nods, rage shooting from his eyes like fireworks, all pointing in my direction. *What the fuck?* He knew I was claiming her at the table tomorrow. Chloe steps out from behind the nurses' station.

232

"Chloe, what are you doing here?" I ask. She doesn't normally work in this area of the hospital.

"I swapped a shift, and I would strongly suggest you both keep your tempers in check, or else I'll have both of you removed by security." She stands directly in front of Raven, looking him dead in the eye.

"I don't care what childish little thing you've got going on here, but if you *must* beat the shit out of each other, do it outside. Ashley would be so proud of you." Her well-aimed sarcasm shakes Raven out of his haze, and he deflates and nods sheepishly at Chloe.

"Fine, I'll keep myself under control," he promises her as he glowers at me.

"Go sit down. I'll try to find out what I can," she replies. Slender grabs Raven and leads him to a seat. Pennywise stays with me.

"What the fuck happened?" he asks. I lower my head into my hands and run my fingers through my now wild hair.

"I've no idea, Pen, no idea at all. One moment, she was fine, and the next, she wasn't." My voice is breaking. "The EMT said she's stable, and whatever is wrong isn't life threatening, but it scared the shit out of me. What the hell could've happened for her to pass out like that?"

Pen looks at me and shrugs his shoulders. "No clue, man, but I'm gonna clue Raven in." I nod, watch him turn, and move toward Slender and Raven, who is still glowering at me.

A few minutes later, Chloe reappears. "The scan came back normal, as did the x-ray. They're doing toxicology blood tests. Is there any chance her drink could have been spiked?"

I jump out of my seat. "Hell no," I shout. "There's no chance. I watched her all night." Raven makes his way over.

"What was that?" he inquires, shooting visual daggers at me.

233

Chloe repeats her question. "I just asked if it was possible that her drink was spiked."

At that precise moment, Neil comes running into the area, panting. He overheard the last sentence.

"No," Raven says at the same time Neil blurts out, "Yes."

My eyes shoot to Neil in complete shock and disbelief. He holds out a bag with pills.

"I found these in one of the employees' bags and asked questions. This is what someone spiked her drink with."

Raven's mouth drops open, then closes tight. I can hear his teeth grinding and his face a mask of pure fury. Chloe takes the bag from Neil and asks, "Do you know how many she had?"

Neil nods. "The staff member admitted to putting two in her Coke."

Chloe hurries into the emergency room, bag in hand. Neil leans against the wall, catching his breath. Raven grabs him and pulls him up and close to his face.

"Who?" he demands. Just that one word makes us all flinch. Neil holds his hands up as if to placate Raven, still trying to catch his breath. In the meantime, Ashley's phone rings. I forgot that I'd shoved it in my pocket when the EMTs arrived.

I glance at the caller display and freeze. I let it go to voicemail, but within seconds, it rings again, Rusty's name lighting up the display for the second time. What does that asshole want? A few seconds later, the phone bleeps with a voicemail alert. I return my focus to the conversation in front of me.

"I noticed Karen went on a prolonged break, yet again, and started looking for her," he explained. "She was in the staff room, by her locker, changed and ready to hightail it out of there. I grabbed her, dragged her into the office, and locked the door so she couldn't just bolt. When I returned to the bar, Dawg and Caroline told me Ash had collapsed and was being taken to hospital. I put two and two together, and it seems I can add to four accurately." He takes a breath before continuing.

"Karen had been cagey these last few days. I heard her grumbling something about '*the last laugh*' when Ashley put her in her place tonight. I unlocked the door and caught her trying to smash the tiny window. Not that her ass would have fit through it. Anyway, once I had her tied to a chair, and yes, I tied her up, she started spilling." We stare at Neil in disbelief. We forgot he used to be an MC member before his club dissolved.

"She's had a thing for Vegas for years and knew she couldn't take Ashley. Vegas and Ashley made it very clear that her advances were not wanted."

Neil gulps down another deep breath. I'm trying to keep my rage under control while Slender and Pennywise listen in stunned silence. I can see Raven's fists twitching, a sure indication that he is incandescent with rage right now.

After a moment, Neil continues. "I searched her purse and found the bag with pills. Not my first rodeo. She broke down crying when confronted with the pills, knowing her number was up, and admitted to spiking Ashley's coke. She kept apologizing, but I know you'd want to deal with her yourself." He nods at Raven.

"Where is the bitch?" Raven snarls, making even me flinch.

"I kept her tied to the chair in the office, locked both the office and the bar, and came straight here," Neil replies. Raven nods at him.

"Thanks, Neil. The club owes you big time. You have done the right thing, protecting our family. I class you as one of ours too, patch or no patch." He steps toward Neil, hugs, and back slaps him. "I cannot thank you enough, brother!" As Neil just nods at him, Raven turns to Pennywise.

235

"Grab one of the prospects and transfer our guest from the bar to the dugout. That should be the perfect accommodation." I've never seen Raven ask for a woman to be detained in the dugout. The dugout is a WWII bunker we found when we built the clubhouse, and we use it to deal with the club's enemies. It is mainly Pennywise's domain. There are several cells and a larger *'communal area'* with several of Pennywise's toys and instruments.

There are rails on the walls and a ceiling with a trolley system that can be lowered and raised to whatever height is needed. I hope Karen doesn't have to find out what we use those for. She'd be better off having a bullet put in her head.

Raven and I jump as Chloe returns. "She's had charcoal, and her stomach's pumped, but some of the drug was already in her system." She tells us. "We will admit her and monitor her until she wakes up. You can both wait with her. Here is the floor she will be on and room number." She passes Raven a piece of paper.

We relay the message to the other brothers, who one by one leave the hospital. Ally and Sparks are last to leave. Ally hugs both Raven and me.

"She'll be okay. She's tough. Please call me if she or you need anything." I nod at her and walk toward the elevator with Raven. We don't speak. Once on the right floor, we find the correct room. It is tough to see Ashley like this. Pale and not responding.

I lean over and kiss her gently, but she does not respond. Can't respond because some bitch felt the need to roofie her. My anger churns in my stomach. Raven claps me on the shoulder. I look up.

"Sorry brother, I shouldn't have lost my head as I did. It's clear to see how serious you are about my sister. I feel like shit. I should have been able to protect her. And in our bar!" he says with venom in his voice.

I nod. "Join the Club Prez, join the club. I was right there and didn't notice a thing. When I get my hands on her, I'll strangle the fucking bitch myself!" I hiss.

"Don't worry; she'll get what's coming to her, Vegas. I can promise you that much. I'm going to leave you with Ashley, and I'm gonna go entertain our *guest of honor* instead," he states with a spine-chilling note to his voice. I nod at him and watch him leave.

◊◊◊

A groan wakes me. I sit up and look straight into two beautiful green eyes. Ashley, thank God, she's awake.

"Where am I?" she asks groggily.

"You are in the hospital, baby. You collapsed at Stormy's. Do you remember anything? You scared the shit out of all of us," I add. She looks at me, confusion showing in her eyes. She winces and holds her head. I ring the bell for the nurse. Chloe came in last night and explained that severe headaches are common after waking up.

The nurse comes in, checks her over, and brings her some pain relievers. Shortly after, the door opens, and the doctor comes in, accompanied by Raven, who looks like he hasn't slept a wink.

The doc explains he wants to keep Ashley until tonight to monitor her. Ashley, by this time, has fallen back asleep, groggy from the pain relievers.

"She'll be fine," the doctor promises. "You should both go home and get some rest. She'll be released around five this afternoon, all being well."

"I'll be here to pick her up," I answer before Raven can open his mouth. He and the doctor nod at me, and reluctantly, I leave Ashley to sleep.

Raven brought the club SUV since one of the prospects at the bar picked my bike up last night. We place our cuts on the backseat and get in.

We don't speak on the way to the clubhouse. As we walk in, everyone is here, all asking after Ashley, and all are angry about what happened to her. News has a habit of spreading like wildfire. It's not that we're gossips, but it's difficult to keep such emotional things under wraps. And the fact that we are hosting a guest in the dugout was difficult to keep quiet amongst the brothers.

"I've asked Neil to attend part of the meeting," Raven discloses quietly, and I nod. Best the brothers hear it straight from the horse's mouth. Just then, Ashley's phone rings again. Shit, I forgot to give it back to her before leaving. I answer it.

"Hello?"

"Er . . . is this Ashley's phone?" a female voice stutters on the other end.

"Yes, it is. This is Vegas, her old man," I tell the woman.

"Oh . . . right. This is Ellie, Rusty's sister. She called me the day before yesterday." I perk up, more alert than ever.

"Oh, hey, Ellie. Yeah, she said she spoke to you. I'm sorry, Ashley is in the hospital. She had a little incident yesterday evening, but she's okay and will be home this evening. Do you want to call back later to speak to her?" There's a long silence when I can just hear Ellie's breathing.

Then, "Oh my god. Oh my god, is she okay? I wish I'd called last night to check on her." She sounds shocked and rattled, which makes me suspicious.

"Why is that, Ellie?" I question her. I hear a male voice in the background.

"Who are you calling, bitch?" Rusty's ugly words are loud and clear.

238

"Just a friend. Yes, dear, I'll call you back later. Got to get dinner finished," she chirps into the phone and hangs up. That was too weird for my liking. I move over to Slender and tell him about Rusty's calls last night, and Ellie's just now. I see him walking over to Ferret and whispering to him.

Ferret walks to me and asks, "Can you let me have the phone? I'll trace the call, see where they came from."

I feel a little guilty for not telling Ashley about this, but hand the phone over, anyway. This is all too weird. He pockets it, and we all make our way into church and settle in our places. The only empty chair is Rusty's. Raven opens the meeting. "Brothers, there's good news and bad news. Good news first." He nods at me, and I stand.

"I'm claiming Ashley and need your approval."

When I look around at the brothers, everyone is cheering, whistling, and hollering. 'Another one bites the dust" comes as a chorus from the top right corner of the table. After the hollering stops, the vote starts. There are no objections, so Spen is told to order Ashley's property cut. Then, the meeting proceeds with business matters, as usual.

As Spen begins to discuss the bar, all eyes are on him. He explains what transpired at the last meeting and about considering turning the bar into a high-end strip club. He hands out copies of Neil's simplified business plan and projections. We glance it over, and on paper, it looks like it could be a nice little earner.

Raven adds, "I know I announced this yesterday in the bar, but I had my reason for doing so. Nothing will go ahead without being voted on." He looks everyone straight in the eyes. I wonder what his reasons were, but don't question it. He's never steered us wrong yet.

The project passes the vote unanimously and is recorded. Spen is tasked with getting the ball rolling on purchasing the warehouse behind the bar, and Zippy raises his hand.

"Raven, I'm wondering, if we're buying the warehouse, could I have a small portion of it for the tattoo studio? I'm all set with equipment, and it wouldn't cost much to do if we're already having building work done. It'd save on rent since the club won't have to pay rent and utilities on another building," he suggests. Again, it's put to a vote and passes unanimously. Zippy promises to have a plan drawn up and given to Spen and Dawg next week.

Raven looks at Slender and nods. Slender gets up and walks out. "I've asked Neil to attend for this part of the meeting, as I'm sure you'll all want to know what happened last night. I'll let him catch you up. As far as I'm concerned, he's family, patch or no patch," he declares to cut off any objections. Not that there are any. Neil is very popular with the brothers.

Neil enters with Slender and sits at the opposite end of the table where the brothers have made space for him.

"First, the bad news. Okay, Neil, let them have it." He stands and explains as he did to us what he found last night. The brothers are getting restless. Disbelief and anger rolls around the room.

Raven pipes up. "Now, Neil has ensured that Karen is our guest in the dugout, so we all owe him a big thank you for reacting as fast as he did and for protecting one of ours." All heads nod toward Neil.

"Thanks, Neil, that's all," Raven decrees. Knowing the protocol, Neil leaves and closes the door behind him. Then, pandemonium breaks loose.

"Settle down," Raven yells over the many irate voices. Calm returns to the table, but it's tense and uptight. "Now, I know we don't generally hurt women, but in this case, I think a lesson needs to be taught." He nods at Slender and Pennywise.

Pennywise gets up. "We don't have to seriously hurt her to give her a lesson in manners and appropriate behavior." He smirks at us. "Do you trust me? Do you trust me to do my job as Enforcer?" He looks around at the brothers, and everyone nods tersely at him.

"We want to watch," Dawg states, and Ratchet and Sparks nod in agreement.

Raven looks at Pennywise and agrees. Everyone moves from the room, following the officers to the dugout.

As we open the door, the stench of excrement hits us. She's been down here for almost twenty-four hours with just a bottle of water and no access to a toilet. In single file, we make our way down the narrow stairs, and at the bottom, Raven flicks a switch causing the fluorescent lights to flare to life. There, in the corner of a cell, is Karen. Her eyes blink, not used to the light and swollen from crying; she's still tied to her chair. Slender and Pennywise open her cell and carry her, chair and all, into the larger room.

First, Pennywise demonstrative holds his nose. "You need a shower," he proclaims coldly, grabs a long, large hose, and turns on the tab. Ice cold water hits Karen with high pressure. Her chair topples over, and she sputters and screams to no avail. After Pen shuts off the hose, Slender steps behind Karen and lifts her chair into an upright position. She's shaking, whether from cold or fear; no one cares.

Pennywise's eyes bore into hers. Emotionless, his voice is hard. "So, you thought you could drug one of ours, put her into hospital and get away with it?"

He's in his element. Karen is sobbing in her chair, snot running down her face.

"Now, what shall we do to you today to make sure you understand you're in trouble? I could break every one of your fingers to teach you not to touch drugs or spike drinks. Or I could mix you up a nice cocktail you wouldn't wake up from and throw you in a deep ditch where no one would find you," he bellows in her face.

Karen is trying to scramble away, but the chair prevents that.

He casually walks over to his tool bench and picks up a cutthroat razor that glints in the fluorescent light. "Or I could just cut your throat and be done with you."

He puts his hand on his chin as though pondering the thought. Karen's incomprehensibly muttering and crying. The putrid stench of urine lets us know she's pissed herself in fear.

Pennywise turns to me and orders, "Hold her." I step forward. "Hold her head still, so I can make the least messy cut," he tells me in a stone-cold voice while winking at me. Karen is now screaming and begging for her life. I hold her head tight, not knowing whether I'll be splattered in her blood in the next few seconds.

Pen grabs her by the hair and roars at her. "Shut the fuck up and take what's coming to you, or else I'll kill you slowly and painfully." Karen's mouth closes, and she's whimpering continuously. Pen pulls her head right back and brings the blade forward. *Fuck, scalping is a messy business*, I think to myself, then breathe a sigh of relief when he shaves off a handful of her long hair and drops it at her feet.

She screams out, "No, please! No, don't kill me! Please!" Unimpressed and unwavering, Pennywise continues with a deliberate, uneven, and uncomfortable head shave until she's bald. He's left not a single strand of her long hair on her head.

"Oohs," and cringes go around the room. She wasn't a picture of beauty before, and sure as shit isn't now. By this time, she's a mumbling mess when Slender steps in front of her.

242

"We gave you your marching orders last night. Despite that, you thought you could harm one of us. This is your last and only warning. I catch you anywhere near any of the Stormy Souls properties; I'll cut your throat instead of your hair." We growl in collective agreement. Raven nods at Slender, who cuts her ropes. "Prospects," Raven bellows, "escort this *lady* to the city limits. Make sure she leaves. If she doesn't, bring her back, and we'll take care of her once and for all." The prospects nod at his instructions, grab the bitch, and carry her to a waiting van.

-27- ASH

I struggle to open my eyes. The light is hurting, and a splitting headache plagues me. I ring the nurse, ask for some water, and decline the pain medication she offers. Last time it put me to sleep, and I really don't want to sleep anymore. I try to remember what happened, but it just increases the banging in my head. When the nurse returns with the water I asked for, it soothes my throat. While she's in my room, she assists me to the toilet. How embarrassing. I'm as weak as a kitten. After I'm finished, she helps me back to bed. A few moments later, she returns with a tray of food. It's three in the afternoon, and I haven't eaten since yesterday at lunchtime. We planned on grabbing something to eat on the way home. My stomach growls as I look at the sandwich, chocolate bar, and crackers on my plate, so I dive in.

The door slowly opens, and Chloe sticks her head through. "Oh, I see you're awake. I brought you a gift." She smirks and waves a coffee cup in front of me.

"Oh my god, you really are an angel." I laugh at her, cringing as the pain in my head worsens with laughter and the movement. She places the cup on my tray.

"Okay, trouble, I must go and start my shift now, I just wanted to make sure you're okay, so I can tell Carl. He's been worried sick." She states, waves, and leaves before I can even say a word.

I want to see Carl. I know he'll be worried as hell. Pressing the call bell, I ask for a Nurse to call Carl since my phone somehow disappeared. She's kind and notices that eating and drinking coffee improved my constitution. The dizziness is slowly receding and my head, although sore, is not as bad as it was.

"Would it be possible to see my friend on the cancer floor?" I ask.

After giving me a long assessing once over, she responds, "As long as you're in a wheelchair, it should be fine. Don't leave the hospital grounds, though. We need to be able to keep an eye on you. You'll need to have someone with you. Hang on a minute; I'll get you the patient's mobile." After a few moments, she walks out and returns, cordless phone in hand.

I know Carl's number by heart and dial. "Yes?" a happy female voice answers.

"Ally? What are you doing answering Carl's phone?" I question, a little puzzled. Maybe I'm not as okay as I thought yet.

"Well, it was a withheld number. It could have been anyone. What are you doing calling from this number? You should still be two floors below us," Ally sternly replies, and I sigh.

"I am, Ally, I am. Why aren't the prospects there?" I ask as I hear chattering in the background. I groan because it means it's an old ladies' visit for Carl.

"All the guys are in church. Prospects were summoned, and Sparks asked if Caroline and I could visit the Flakester to keep him company. Not exactly a hardship. We'll come down to see you once the prospects are back," Ally chirps. I hear Carl's voice in the background, loudly stating, "Please, someone help me. I'm being chatted to death."

Caroline volleys back, "Don't be such a baby. I'm here to spread happiness far and wide, even to your miserable, sourpuss ass." Caroline is in top form, sounding chipper, and her catchphrase makes me snort.

I groan as I pay for my amusement with an instant headache. "Since you're already there, could you get Caroline to get me and take me to see the Flakester?" I ask Ally.

"Are you sure you're up to that?" Ally's voice shows concern. "You frightened the living daylights out of me when you keeled over at the table. Don't ever do that again. You took at least ten years off my life!"

"I'm better now, Ally, I promise. I have no clue what happened. The last thing I remember is walking back to the table and laughing with you," I tell her, my tone serious. I hear Ally covering the speaker and mumbling to Caroline.

"Caroline just grabbed Flakester's wheelchair and is on her way to you. Don't even try to resist her; she's hell-bent on wheeling you up, and resistance is futile," Ally snorts.

"Save me from these mad bitches!" I can hear Carl beg in the background, which causes me to smile wide. My friend is up for visitors. Yay!

The door bursts open with a giggling Caroline, skidding to a stop about two inches before hitting the bed with the wheelchair. She's bouncing around like a hyperactive puppy. I can't help but feel instantly better.

"Hello, lovely lady. Your chariot awaits. I missed you." I can't help but cackle a little. She only saw me last night.

Before I can reply, she's around the wheelchair and envelopes me in the biggest Caroline bear hug known to man. For a second, her sunny disposition slips, and her tone turns serious.

"You scared me, sweetness. Don't do shit like that. I love you and need you in my life, my lovely." She squeezes me rather tight. Finally, she lets go, helps me get into the wheelchair, making sure my ass isn't showing through the gown and starts rolling me down the corridor.

I thought this would be easy, but Caroline skips to the elevator, singing entirely out of tune, "We're off to see the Wizard, the Wonderful Wizard of Oz!"

Everyone, and I mean literally, *everyone,* is staring at us. I'm so glad when the doors shut on "because, because, because, because, because" it's embarrassing that now I'm humming along with her, with a great big smile on my face.

Caroline is just like that. She's sunshine in a bottle. But God help those who get on the wrong side of her. She's a force to be reckoned with. Her mind can work in evil ways.

We arrive at Carl's room, and I lean forward to open the door. "Your audience awaits, your highness!" Caroline acts like an idiot, taking a deep bow, which has everyone chuckling. Ally is raising her brow at me as I'm still humming. Damn song, I can't get it out of my head now.

"Blame her." I point at Caroline and shrug at Ally.

"Lord have mercy, please, take me now! I cannot stand this female crazy any longer!" he raises his clasped hands skywards, imitating intense prayer. Caroline stomps over to him.

"Right, I see you need some of my special magic to sort you out, chicken!" Chicken? I cannot believe she just called a fully grown biker chicken. I try hard to subdue the laughter.

"Chicken?" Carl echoes my very thoughts.

"Chicken," Caroline confirms. "As in the cute little feathery animal." She elaborates. Ally is looking out the window, trying her best not to laugh.

"Chicken? I'm no chicken, you wicked witch! I'm a full-grown, sexy man, I'll have you know, who also happens to be incapacitated! Do you see feathers? Do You?" Carl's voice is getting louder, and his consternation shows.

247

Caroline shrugs grabs his hip and shoulder, and says, "You asked for it, my special dose of 'Caroline's Happy Medicine'. Might not make you happy, but it will me." As she speaks, she rolls Carl onto his side, with him protesting loudly, raises her hand, and smacks his ass soundly, not once but twice. By this time, Ally and I are howling like hyenas with laughter. Tears are rolling down my cheeks, partially from laughing so hard and some from my returning headache. Ally is leaning forward, slapping her knees.

"Oh my god, I can't breathe," she choke-cough-laughs. Meanwhile, Caroline is smiling down at Carl.

"Now then, biker, is that better? Feels much better now, doesn't it?" she teases Carl, whose look of sheer shock is a priceless.

"Fuck off," he grouses at Caroline.

"Now, now, language, young man, or I'll have to get the orderly to help me wash your mouth out. Wire brush and Clorox is all I need to get that mouth nice and clean." She smiles brightly at Carl, appearing enthusiastic about the idea.

Carl's eyes go wide as he sputters, "Whatever," and throws himself around in the bed to face the wall. I hear him grumble, "Abuse . . . I call abuse by three witches. The wicked one from the East, West, and South!"

When Caroline puts on her best witch voice and cackles, "Don't you forget it, biker boy," that does it. I'm almost falling out of the wheelchair, wheezing, howling, groaning in pain, and crying, laughing, and snorting all at the same time. Ally sinks to the floor.

"I think I just literally peed myself," she chokes out, which has Caroline laughing again. And when Caroline laughs, everyone laughs. Her laughter is infectious, and not just because she snort-laughs, but she really sounds like a cackling witch.

The door flies open, and Chloe runs in. "What the hell?" Looking from one to the other, her eyes rest on Carl, still showing us his backside, only half-covered by his blanket and gown from when he threw himself onto his side like a sulking child. Seeing us fighting the endless laughter, she shrugs and eagerly joins us.

"What have I missed?"

Carl groans, "I'm in hell!" This starts us all off again, and Caroline sidles up to Chloe.

"Hey, lovely lady, I don't think we've met. I'm Caroline." She stretches out her hand as if to shake Chloe's and, at the last moment, changes her mind and hugs her instead.

Chloe giggles. "Nice to meet you. I'm Chloe, the nurse in charge for today." Turning to Carl, she says, "Nice ass," then she turns and walks out of the room.

Ally and Caroline, finally calm again, look at each other and then at Carl. Ally sighs and says, "I could do with a coffee." Caroline nods, and they both look at me questioningly.

"No, thanks, I'm okay, but you go. I'll stay here like a good girl," I reply to the unspoken question.

Ally squeezes my shoulder as she walks out, and Caroline throws a "behave yourself" over her shoulder. Finally, the room is quiet. I wheel myself closer to Carl's bed. He turns toward me, and I struggle to hide the shock I'm feeling.

He's changed a lot in a couple of days. The pallor of his skin is frightening, and his eyes look more sunken. He looks as though he's lost weight, but it's difficult to tell with him being in bed and under blankets.

"How are you doing, darlin'?" I ask him softly. When he replies, I have to swallow hard to hold back tears.

"I'm not great, princess, not great. In pain most of the time and exhausted. Not been out of bed for a couple of days, and when I am, I'm so tired that it doesn't last long. Always having someone here leaves me with little to no time to think. I feel like a burden being babysat, with a lot of false hope and good spirits projected toward me.

"I'm a grown man, for fuck's sake. I know my body better than any of those quacks. The little time I *do* have to myself, I spend contemplating my life, thinking about things I should have done, could have done differently, and trying to make peace with not being able to change anything. Time is running out, Ashley; I can feel it. The pain is getting stronger every day, and it's unbearable at times, despite the medication I'm getting. I don't know how much longer I can do this."

He has tears in his eyes, and I'm lost for words, just nodding and squeezing his hand.

He's right, he knows his body better than anyone, and the change in him is severe, physically and mentally, from when I last saw him a few days ago.

"Can they not give you stronger pain relief?" I ask.

"I'm already on morphine, honey. What else could they possibly give me? I've spoken to the doctor and asked for a syringe pump to be fitted, so the medication gets to me all the time. They'll set that up this afternoon. I just cannot deal with this pain anymore," he answers, the suffering clear in his voice breaking my heart. His untouched breakfast tray remains on the table, and even the chocolate bars are intact. He's a chocoholic, so for him not to open them is a damning sign.

"I need you to listen to me, Ashley, and hear me." I've asked the doctors to complete a DNR form. I *do not* want to be resuscitated under *any circumstances*. Not the way I am now. If the situation changes, the form will be revised, but as things are now, I don't want any life-prolonging invasive treatments. I don't want to end up hooked on machines. I'd hate to wake up only to die later or become a vegetable. So, should anything go wrong, please make sure you respect my wishes and let me go," he pleads with me.

His voice breaks, and his eyes brim with tears, and so do mine. This feels like him saying goodbye, and I'm not ready to let my friend go. But equally, I respect his ability to make his own independent choices and voice his wishes. So, I nod and hope this situation will not arise. We sit quietly, holding hands, trying to collect and compose ourselves, until Chloe walks in. She looks at us and quietly hugs Carl first and then me in an unspoken understanding, empathy radiating from her.

"Carl, I'm free after my break. The doctor has just asked me to set up your twenty-four-hour syringe pump. I can do it once I'm back. Is that okay with you? Is this still what you want?" she asks, her tone conveying how seriously she takes her job and Carl's request.

"Chloe, I would be very grateful if you could do this as soon as you can. My pain is off the scale right now, and I'm struggling to cope." Carl grimaces, clearly in agony.

"Do you need me to give you a shot?" Chloe asks.

"Yes, please. Now, if you can," Carl replies between clenched teeth. Chloe nods and walks away. It hurts my heart to see Carl like this. I feel helpless, knowing there is nothing I can do to change things for him, to make things better for him. I just pray we'll find a donor in time.

Chloe returns with an injection and a second nurse. They carry a large tray with a funny, rectangular-shaped box, a large syringe, and more lines and needles.

"We got everything sorted for you," Chloe tells Carl calmly. After checking Carl's details with him, she leans over and gives him his injection. They then set up the pump, switching it on and signing Carl's charts. Chloe turns to face Carl and me and proceeds to explain.

251

"This is a syringe pump that continuously delivers your morphine and a medication to stop you from feeling sick. It takes a few hours to be fully effective. That's why I've given you the extra injection to tie you over. You won't get regular morphine as tablets anymore. The problem with them is that they start working, sort out your pain, and then as they tail off, the pain returns. With this pump, you have constant pain relief. You'll have to ask for extra if you need it, and then we can discuss it with the doctor." Carl nods in understanding, relaxing a little as his medication cuts in.

"Can he give himself extra doses?" I ask, worried he might try to do something stupid.

"No, he can't. That function is locked out, and as you can see, the pump is in a locked box. So, no one other than nurses or doctors can give extra doses," she explains.

Carl seems a bit more relaxed but looks tired. So, we sit in silence for a while. "Is there anything I can do for you? Anything at all?" I ask him. He sighs and shakes his head.

"Not at the moment, sweetheart. I'm just so tired; I really want to sleep," he answers, fatigue making his skin look gray.

"Just rest and sleep, Carl. It's okay; I don't mind. I'll wait for Ally and Caroline to return and ask them to take me back," I tell him, stroking his cheek.

"Actually, princess, there is something you could do. Speak to Raven and have him scale down the visits. It's just exhausting to have someone here all the time. I get fed up seeing the prospects' ugly mugs. Please explain to him for me, will ya?" I nod my promise.

"Sure, I'll make sure the circus leaves town, Carl. Don't worry, even if I have to post a guard outside your door, or even better, post Caroline outside your door. That would teach them, huh?" I try to joke, which earns me one of his smiles, and it reaches his eyes. Quiet returns, and he's fast asleep within minutes.

252

I can hear the girls coming down the corridor. I turn toward the opening door and hiss. "Shh," I whisper-shout at them. "Shush! He's just drifted off." Ally grabs my wheelchair and motions for Caroline to turn around. We leave the room and make our way back to mine.

They both look at me with huge eyes as we sit in my room, and I bring them up to date on the conversation and wishes Carl had voiced to me.

"I don't like this," Ally croaks, clearly affected by what I'm telling them. Caroline is serious for once.

"Hey, I watched my friend in Montana go through something similar. She knew she was dying way before anyone else did. She told the doctors, and was right, despite all the poison they pumped into her to try to cure this horrible disease. So, we can't and should not dismiss what Carl says or feels. We have to take this seriously. I'll speak to Dawg. Ally, you should talk to Sparks. They can put the word out. We'll leave Raven to you, as you'll likely see him way before us." She sighs.

The mood has turned somber. The nurse comes in and checks me over. "Looks all good. The doctor will come and see you shortly, then you'll be free to go," she chirps, annoying all of us with her jovial mood.

"Okay, my lovely, we are going and leaving you to it then. I'm sure the guys will be here soon to pick you up. Oh, and before I forget, no fancy sex acrobatics when you get home. Don't want to come and have to administer my special medicine for orgasm-imposed headaches." She wags her finger at me and grins. Though her smile is not entirely convincing.

Ally hugs me goodbye and invites Vegas and me over for dinner tomorrow evening. I wave them off and take a deep breath. The last twenty-four hours have been pure hell and a lot to take in. I still can't remember what happened last night, but more importantly, Carl's words keep repeating themselves in my mind.

-28- VEGAS

I throw the SUV into park and walk toward the hospital entrance. My mind is restless with all that happened today. The only positive thing has been claiming Ashley, making her officially my old lady. Mine. A smile sneaks across my face; the thought of her does that to me. I never imagined I'd want or need anyone the way I need her. Can't believe I fought tooth and nail against my feelings all this time, but now, I struggle to imagine my life without her. The last twenty-four hours or so have been gruesome and a little hair-raising. I look forward to seeing her beautiful, expressive face smiling at me.

She turns toward me as I open the door. She sits fully dressed on the bed, her discharge papers signed. As she spots me, she sobs and throws herself at me. *What the hell?* That was not the greeting I expected, and it pains me to see her this upset. Anger rises inside me, and I wonder who I have to kill for upsetting my girl like this. I feel protective as hell over her.

"Hey, baby, what's going on?" I ask quietly while stroking her hair. Her tear-stained green eyes look into mine, and there's a world of hurt in them.

"I've been to see Carl, but I don't want to talk about it now, honey, so take me home, please." Her broken voice reaches my ears. I'm glad she asked to be taken home because that's precisely where I'll take her.

On my way to the hospital, I stopped at her house and packed up her clothes and some personal items, which are now in the back of the SUV. She'll stay with me now, and I won't take no for an answer.

I pull her tight into my side as we walk out to the SUV. I open her door and help her inside. She looks at the back seat, full of her stuff, looks at me, and smiles the sweetest smile, making me feel ten feet tall. As I start the engine and pull out of the parking lot, I take her hand and place it on top of my thigh, holding it there. Slowly, she relaxes a little, and the tears stop falling.

We make good time on the short journey home, and as we arrive, I see bikes parked outside the house. Well, I guess the location of this place is no longer as secret as I would like. Behind us, I hear a horn beep, and as I look in the mirror, I see Ally's now bright pink hair and a big smile, with Sparks following on his bike behind her. A get-together it is.

We get out of the SUV, and everyone rushes to hug Ashley, making me growl and shoot daggers at the brothers. They hug her longer and harder to wind me up a bit more. Much as I hate it, I can't say I blame them; I'd have done the same. Raven is the first to grab Ashley, lift her in a bear hug, and swing her around.

"So glad you're okay, pumpkin," he says, relief written all over his face.

"Me too, Jamie, me too. I wish I knew what happened," Ashley states.

"I'll tell you later," I reply to the unspoken question and open the door. "Let's get you inside first," I tell her as I watch everyone grabbing boxes and bags of her stuff and following us

256

inside. We deposited all her clothes on the bed, and they put boxes with personal items in the spare bedroom. Ally has brought food, enough to feed an army, and everyone is digging in. I show the brothers my man cave, where Dougal and Dawg immediately start up the game system while Sparks and Caroline grab the other controllers and vow to kick ass.

Ally stayed in the kitchen with Raven and Sarah, who came when Dougal told her that Ashley was home. We sit around the kitchen island, Sarah and Ally cleaning up the mess from the meal and chatting quietly.

"Raven, I need to talk to you," Ashley says, looking from Ally to me, then to Raven, and back to me.

"What's up, sis?" Raven asks, sitting up straight.

"I went to see Carl today." She looks at Ally for support, and Ally smiles at her, nodding imperceptibly.

Taking a deep breath, she continues to relay the conversation she had with Carl. Now I realize why she was so upset. I walk around the island and take her in my arms, holding her tight. She leans straight into me, seeking comfort, and Raven looks stunned.

"What are you trying to tell me, sis?" he asks, shaking his head in disbelief. "I don't think I quite get it."

"He doesn't want so many visitors. He's tired, Raven, exhausted, and in a lot of pain. They set up a morphine pump for him today because of it. He feels he's not pulling through this, and although he needs support, he also needs time to process his thoughts and feelings. Times where he doesn't have to appear to be brave and strong. He believes he's dying, Raven." Ashley swallows hard and forces herself even closer to me.

257

She continues, "He asked for a 'do not resuscitate' order to be put in place and wants us all to honor that." I can see tears wetting her lashes again, and I gently stroke her arm while holding her, making sure she knows I'm here for her. This is so hard for her. I know she loves Carl dearly. Having this conversation with him and then repeating it all must take it out of her. I'm so proud of my warrior princess, and at the same time, I feel incredibly guilty for knowing I gotta heap more on her plate.

Sarah has left the kitchen with none of us noticing, and Ally is standing next to Raven with her hand on his arm.

"He needs a bit of space, Raven," she tells him in a low tone. "When we saw him, the change in him was obvious. He needs time to come to terms with his own mortality, whether or not it will hit." Ally's no-nonsense tone keeps our emotions in check.

"Okay," Raven replies, "I get it. I'll call the prospects off for now, and we'll arrange shorter visits with him as a club." I can feel Ashley relax against me.

"Thank you, Raven, he needs this," she replies quietly.

"No, thank you, Ash, for telling me and keeping me straight," he responds before walking toward the man cave.

"Be back in a second, sweetheart," I tell Ashley, who looks exhausted. "Just gotta chat with Raven real quick." She nods, and I place a kiss on top of her hair. I stride after Raven, catching him in the hallway, where he's grabbing his bike gear.

"Can you tell her what happened and why she passed out?" He raises his eyebrows in question.

"Of course, Prez. I'll do it as gently as possible. I think she's had about all she can take for now," I reply. Raven slaps my shoulder, walks out, and I close the door behind him.

With Raven's bike roaring to life, the others emerge from the man cave. Caroline and Sparks whooped Dawg and Dougal at the shooting game they were playing.

Dougal grouses. "No one likes a sore loser," Sparks says, standing there with his hand open. "Come on, pay up, boys. We won fair and square." He can't hide his triumph as both Dawg, and Dougal get out their wallets and slap fifties in his hand. He smirks and hands a fifty over to Caroline.

"I love this club. Come on, old man, take me out. I'm paying." Caroline winks and grabs Dawg's arm. He's still grumbling but follows his crazy wife outside. Ally and Sparks make their excuses and leave, too.

"Now then, big boy," Sarah challenges me, "make sure you look after my bestie here, or else I'll come and kick your balls into the middle of next year, and we wouldn't want that now, would we?" Her threatening tone scares me slightly.

I realize she'd have no problem making good on her threat. My respect for her climbs a few notches higher. She's fierce and extremely loyal to Ashley.

Walking to her, I hug her quickly, smile, and say, "Goodbye, Sarah, it was nice to see you. Come again soon." I finish with a wink.

Sarah picks up on the not-so-subtle hint, hugs Ash, and leaves. Then, we decide to sit outside by the fire pit. It is getting dark, and the quiet is blissful. I start a fire, go back inside, and grab some smores supplies. Who doesn't like smores?

The night is peaceful, and the fire keeps us warm as the stars come out. We're sat on a swing chair, snuggled up together, relaxing.

259

I know I have to burst her bubble of peace, but I'm struggling to do so. Instead, I sit with Ashley ensconced in my arms, her head on my chest, and breathe her in, enjoying the peace for now.

After making multiple s'mores, furnishing her with a glass of white wine, and grabbing a beer for myself, I look into her eyes, knowing I have to tell her.

"Ashley," I start, "I need to talk to you about something." She sits forward, arms on her knees, chin resting on her hands, and looks at me expectantly.

"Go on, what is it?" she asks. I clear my throat, feeling extremely uncomfortable. "I know my drink was spiked, Vince. The doctor told me, and Chloe confirmed."

I sigh. "Yes, honey, but that's not all."

Wanting to sit opposite her, I grab a chair and pull it over. When I tell her we found the culprit and that it was Karen who spiked her drink, her eyes grow wide in surprise, anger, and disgust.

"That bitch, I should have put her on her ass," she seethes. I'm debating whether to tell her the rest, as it's club business, and we usually don't share that with anyone, not even our old ladies, but since it affects her directly, I make an executive decision.

"We've dealt with her, Ashley. Neil found out and made sure she didn't leave the bar. The club picked her up and made her a guest of honor in the dugout." I see Ashley blanch at that. She grew up in the club and knows what we use the dugout for.

"Is she alive?" she whispers.

"Of course, she is," I reply, "but a severe lesson was taught, and we made sure she won't show her face here again. Prospects accompanied her to the city limits and let her go there, watching to make sure she left. You have nothing to fear from her now. We made sure of that," I reassure her.

She lets out a deep, relieved sigh. I know she hates some of the club's methods and the violence, although admittedly, it happens less frequently now. Sometimes, the club's gotta step up to right a wrong.

I can feel the exhaustion radiating off her; pick her up, and carry her inside. I gently place her in the shower, help her wash, shampoo, and rinse her hair, dry her, and hand her a pair of pajama shorts and one of my T-shirts. She sighs in relief as she puts them on and snuggles under the quilt. I get undressed and follow her in on my side. I'm so grateful to Sarah, who put all Ashley's clothes away, and I remind myself to thank her.

Ashley is burrowing into me. However, I have other ideas. I turn her onto her front and crouch over her, my knees on either side of her hips. I take the bottle out of the warmer next to the bed and spill the warm oil into my hands, letting it drip onto her back. Her moan of pleasure makes me instantly hard. I place my now warmed hands on her shoulder and slowly massage my way across them, paying special attention to her neck and temples. I slowly work my way down, loving the little groans and moans coming from her. My hands kneed and stroke my way down her back and sides. I can't help but tickle her a little, evoking a happy giggle from her and causing her to writhe under me as my reward. Not quite the writhing I would like, but hey, who cares? I smirk when she hisses as I hit a sensitive spot. Taking note of that for later, I move down her body, missing her glorious butt, working my way down her thighs and calves, all the way down to her toes.

"Oh wow." She sighs. "Your hands are magic." I chuckle at her words.

"Only for you, princess." I take in the sight before me, a stunning, naked beauty from the tips of her toes to the top of her head. And she's all mine. My chest swells with pride as much as my dick does with need.

"You don't have to do this, you know," she murmurs.

"I don't *have* to do *anything*, princess. I want to. I get as much pleasure out of giving you pleasure as you do receiving it," I respond to her.

Slowly, I massage my way back up her body, replenishing the warm oil and dripping blobs into the divots of her lower back. Drawing patterns with the oil on her sensitive lower back makes her moan and shift under me. I drip the warm oil onto her delicious rear end and watch as her fists clench the sheets and her head turns to the side. She arches her cheeks into my hands as I start to stroke and massage her rear. Her moans are lower and longer, and she can't keep her back from arching. I let some warm oil run between her cheeks and spread them a little to watch the oil run down her ass and to her wet entrance.

It takes all my self-control not to release my rock-hard dick and push into her. Instead, I continue my slow, teasing massage on the globes of her ass and work my way down between her cheeks, running my well-lubricated finger against her puckered hole, teasing it, while the other hand continues to massage her cheeks.

"Oh god, Vince, more," she groans, and I oblige. With the next lifting of her ass against my hand, I insert my digit into her hole, passing the tight ring and holding it there. I feel her tensing and continue to massage her cheeks. Moving between her legs, I push them open with my knees. My hand travels from her butt cheek to her folds. My fingers gently massage her wet folds around the labia, up to her hard clit, and back down past her entrance. She's panting with need now and not paying attention to my other finger. I start circling her clit with my fingers, and a deep groan leaves her throat.

"So, good! Please, don't stop." She's almost begging.

Moving my finger in and out of her tight, puckered hole while my other finger keeps rubbing her clit slowly, I continue to ratchet her up. Changing the position of my hand a little, I enter her wet entrance with two fingers while my thumb keeps teasing her clit. I can feel her tighten around my fingers.

"So close," she whimpers on a moan. I have to restrain myself and adjust my position, giving room to my throbbing cock. Pushing back into me, I push my fingers deeper inside her. When I think she's ready, I push harder into her front and insert a second finger into her tight backside, moving them back and forth, scissoring them. She whines in frustration, and I can feel her start to flutter around me. Removing my thumb from her clit, I insert a third finger deep into her entrance. She's so wet; the sheets are drenched with her juices.

My fingers fuck her ass harder. One day, it will be my cock there, and I'll own every inch of her. The thought makes my dick pulse. Her moans have turned into little cries of pleasure as she pushes back onto both my hands with abandon.

I know she's close, so I twist my fingers around, find the little rough spot inside her, and fuck my fingers as hard against it as I do inside her ass. She explodes with a scream into the pillow, and I can feel her moisture pouring over my hand.

I continue to minister to her like this until she calms before removing my fingers. She's boneless and silent; the only noise in the room is her panting. I get off the bed, walk into the bathroom, wash my hands, and wet a washcloth with warm water. I return to the bedroom and find that Ashley hasn't moved. I gently place the washcloth between her legs, clean her up,

263

throw the cloth in the open hamper, and then crawl into bed next to her, pulling her into me. I can feel her breathing deepen as my cock slowly softens, and within a few minutes, we're both asleep.

-29- ASH

The last few days with Vegas have been amazing. He's a tough nut on the outside but a marshmallow on the inside. Where I'm concerned, he's all squishy and protective. I love living with him, and all my stuff is moved in. There's evidence of me in his house, making me crazy happy.

I'm not going back to work until after the rally next week. Carl seems to be doing better and sounds more upbeat. He's had the first chemo session, and his pain is better controlled now. Overall, everything is great.

I'm in town today to get some groceries since I want to cook Vegas a special meal tonight. I'm just driving into the parking lot as my phone rings, and I let it go to voicemail. Once I'm parked, I grab it and see it was Vegas. My voicemail icon is blinking, so I dial-in.

"You have two new messages," the voicemail announces. I listen to the first message. It's from Vegas; telling me, he's going on a club run but will be back later tonight. "Love you, princess," finishes his message, making me feel all fuzzy, warm, and loved. Then, I move to the second message.

The date and time stamp are from the night Karen put me in the hospital. My blood turns to ice instantly as I hear the voice.

"Well, well, well, princess, I hear you're going to the hospital. Gotta be careful with who you piss off. You never know what might happen."

I can hear Rusty sneering. I feel sick and open the door to vomit in the parking lot. All thoughts of grocery shopping forgotten, I turn around and drive straight to the clubhouse, shaking like a leaf in a stiff breeze as I walk inside. Not knowing what to do, I go to Vegas's old room, lie on the bed, which still smells of him, and call Ally.

Within half an hour, Ally is sitting on the bed next to me, listening to the message.

"That rat bastard," she fumes. "Ashley, you have to tell Raven. This is going too far. And who would tell him? As far as I know, he's visiting Ellie."

"I can't tell my brother, Ally." I let out a deep sigh. "He'd kill him. I can't lose another member of my family," I howl, nearly hysterical.

Ally rolls her eyes hard but wraps me in a hug, comforting me. God, I must seem like an emotional wreck, but my fear of losing Raven is just too substantial. "I promise, I'll tell Vegas, though, as soon as he gets back."

I try to convince Ally to let go of my coming clean to Jamie. She looks at me critically and demands, "Either you do it, or I will. Talk to Vegas first, but you have to tell Raven. This is creepy shit, and he sounds unhinged."

Deep down, I know she's right, but it's difficult to put years of fear to the side and face your demon, even more so when your demon is usually around the corner and frequently in sight.

I drive home and nervously wait for Vegas to return, scrubbing the entire house from one end to the other to keep myself busy. Cleaning helps me stay calm.

266

It's dark by the time Vegas returns. I last checked my phone—for the millionth time—around ten p.m., but that was a while ago, so I guess it's late. I wait for him to walk in and kiss me as he usually does. But when he does, he looks at me, takes me in, and freezes.

"What's going on, princess?" His voice is full of concern.

"Listen to this," I reply and put Rusty's message on speaker. I watch Vegas's face goes grim, and his eyes grow colder and harder by the second. He immediately dials someone on his phone.

"Ferret, did you trace the phone call from Rusty? Right. Thanks, man. We just listened to a voicemail on Ashley's phone. I'll play it for you." He picks up my phone and sets the message to play again on speaker while holding the microphone end of his phone against the speaker. He picks up his phone again as I sit shivering. I can't deal with listening to this again.

"Yeah, I agree; it's time to take this to Raven. This is just too much. It sounds as if he's threatening Ashley. That shit is going to stop. Yeah, I spoke to Slender and Pen before, not about this message, though. I just got in. Okay, do what you do best, and I'll see you tomorrow." He closes his phone and looks at me.

"Ashley, you gotta tell Raven. He needs to know." His voice is stern when he speaks to me, but I shake my head. Denial is a beautiful thing, and I'd like to keep my comfort blanket a bit longer.

"Okay, let me give you some context." Vegas stands and starts pacing. "Rusty tried to call you while you were out cold in the hospital. I had your phone in my pocket and didn't answer the calls. I wish I had now. I showed the calls to Ferret on Sunday, and he traced the number. Rusty was still with Ellie. His phone pinged from a cell tower near her house." He runs his hand through his hair, showing how agitated he is.

267

"He knows you were in the hospital and why. The question is, how? The only people who knew were Karen and Neil. How would he know even before we knew? There's only one plausible answer. Karen. She must be working with him." Vegas stops pacing as he sees me blanch.

"That bitch," I blurt out. I don't think I've ever been *this* angry before. Anger is good. It trumps being an emotional wreck.

"Okay, let's call Jamie," I agree. Vegas lets out the relieved breath he was holding as he dials Raven and puts the phone on speaker.

"Vegas, what can I do for you?" My brother's growly voice comes through the speaker, and I hear a female giggling in the background. Oops, it looks like we've disturbed him.

"Raven, I need you to come over to the house. Ashley has something important she needs to tell you. Before you ask, no, it can't wait. Bring Slender and Ferret with you," Vegas tells him.

"Shit, is Ash okay?" Jamie asks. "Ebony, get dressed and get out," he orders, and the giggles stop. Vegas cringes.

"Physically, she's fine. Emotionally, not so much. Just get over here." The phone goes dead as Jamie disconnects. Vegas disarms the alarm and opens the gate.

Before long, the growl of several Harleys reaches us way before we can see the headlights. Vegas stands in the doorway, greeting his brothers and showing them into the lounge, where I sit with a glass of whiskey in my trembling hands.

"Go on, sweetheart, it'll be okay," Vegas encourages me, his inquisitive eyes never leaving mine. It takes me a moment to compose myself.

Here goes nothing. "Rusty is threatening me and has done so for years." I watch Jamie's jaw drop, and Slender looks at his hands. He obviously knew already.

268

"What are you saying, Ashley?" he asks in a stunned voice.

"It all started before Mom died. I found them, Jamie. Mom and Rusty, in bed together," I tell my brother.

Jamie jumps up and starts pacing. "What the fuck?" he roars, the fury he struggles to contain his anger.

Slender interjects. "Sit the fuck down, man, and let her finish."

I carry on and tell him everything. About the constant threats, about manhandling me as a child, about the sneering . . . about everything. Once I get to the incident at the clubhouse party, Vegas takes over and fills him in on the rest.

"You!" Jamie, apoplectic with rage, grabs hold of Vegas's cut. "You kept this from me!"

"Stop it, Jamie," I scream at my brother. "Just stop and listen to me. It wasn't his decision; it was mine. It's my life. I knew how you'd react, which is why I didn't tell you." I'm shaking with fury. "You can be such a dickhead at times. Rusty is your VP, and he was Dad's VP. Would you have even believed me?" Shock blankets his face.

"You think I would have doubted you? Jesus, Ashley, you were a kid, my little sister to protect and care for. *Of course,* I would have believed you." He lets go of Vegas and rips me from the sofa, cradling me into his arms. I can feel wetness on my cheeks and realize my brother s struggling, tears running down his face.

"Oh god, I'm so sorry, Ashley, for not noticing and not even considering something was wrong. I'm such a blind asshole and a shit brother to boot. I'll kill him."

I sigh. "And that's another reason I didn't tell you. So much blood has been spilled in the past. I cannot lose you too. The risk of you ending up in the cell next to Dad is too high. It's a price I'm not willing to pay." I look at him, my eyes brimming with unshed tears.

269

Lots of discussions follow, which I'm only listening to with half an ear. Vegas puts some food in front of me, and I eat, but I have no clue what I had. Eventually, he pulls me to his side and leads me to the bedroom.

"Get into bed, honey. You're dead on your feet," he murmurs against my hair as he gently places a kiss on top of my head. "I won't be long," he promises.

I'm restless, tossing and turning, but finally, I drift off to sleep. I half awaken when Vegas joins me in bed and snuggles into his warm body, putting my head on his chest and my arm over his abs before I drop back to sleep.

◇◇◇

"Ashley, come on, honey, wake up. We have to go." Vegas's urgent voice filters through to me. I slowly open my eyes to the bedside light turning on and Vegas standing next to the bed, fully dressed, and voices are coming from the other room. I look at my phone and see it's three-thirty a.m.

"Go where?" I ask, still half asleep.

"To the hospital," Vegas responds. I'm suddenly wide awake as ice-cold dread washes through me. Jumping out of bed, I hurry into my clothes from last night and shove my boots on while walking into the kitchen, Vegas on my heels. Discovering Jamie sitting there, head in his hands, I know immediately. He looks up at me, devastation in his eyes.

"Chloe called half an hour ago. Flakey is bleeding again and refusing to go into surgery," he chokes out. My jacket is in one hand, and Vegas's hand is in the other, holding tight as we pile into the truck. Vegas breaks every speed limit there is until we get to the hospital. Jamie,

Mom, Pen, Vegas, and I rush up to Carl's floor. Chloe is just leaving his room, and she looks at us with sorrow in her eyes.

"He's had medication to keep him calm and a lot of painkillers. Carl is adamantly refusing to go into surgery. He's asked to see you all, so go and be with him. I don't think it will be much longer." She turns and walks slowly down the corridor, her shoulders shaking, feet dragging, wiping her face.

Mom opens the door to the room, and the metallic scent of blood hits and nausea overwhelms me. I cling to Jamie and Vegas, who are keeping me between them. To see Carl is a shock. He's a waxy, sallow color. His lips are white, and his breathing is labored.

He turns his head toward us. Mom walks up to his bed, leans over him, and hugs and kisses his cheek. "What are you doing, Carl? I'm not ready to say goodbye to you yet," she tells him, her voice cracking, betraying her pain.

"I'm sorry, Mom, I don't want to either, but I have to." He closes his eyes, and tears roll down his face.

"But what about a donor? Can't you hold on for that?" Jamie steps into Carl's line of sight, looking down on him.

"No-go, brother. No match has been found, and the chemo has wiped my last reserves," Carl almost whispers, interrupted by coughing. We can see he's getting weaker by the minute. He looks around at his brothers, holds out his hands to them, and they clasp them. "It was a pleasure to ride with and know all of. I hope I'll see you on the other side. Keep the shiny side up for me." His voice is quieter, slowly failing him. The guys squeeze his hands and gently back slap him.

"Godspeed, brother. We'll see you on the other side," they murmur, their voices monotone and broken.

The men leave to get some more chairs so they can stay with us. Mom pulls up a chair to sit on his right, holding one hand, and I'm on his left, holding the other. Carl has been quiet for a few minutes. Suddenly, he turns his head toward me and murmurs, "It's time, Ashley. You promised me no interventions. Time to let me go. I love you, little sis. Always have and always will."

Tears stream down my face. "I know. I love you too, always and forever, big brother. I'll let you go when I need to, but I'm staying with you. I won't leave you alone in this." I sob, and Carl smiles at me softly. I make out a faint nod as he closes his eyes and doesn't open them again. He takes his last breath a few minutes later, with Mom and me holding his hands and stroking his hair, his brothers by his side.

-30- ASH

I can't remember how we got home or anything else about the next couple of days. Entirely numb, I hardly speak to Vegas or anyone else. Today, we're meeting to arrange Carl's funeral to be held on Thursday. We've delayed the rally until Friday and informed the Restless Slayers, who were very understanding.

The mood at the clubhouse is subdued. Everyone's minds are on Carl and his blood family, or the lack thereof.

The funeral will be simple. Spen and Dawg did most of the organizing. We'll bury Carl in the club cemetery, on club land. The local minister will hold a short service and give him a proper sendoff. We'll meet the hearse in town and ride behind it along his favorite roads. Clusseaud planned the route, and, of course, he'll have a Harley hearse. Jamie will ride Carl's bike up front.

Caroline, Ally, and I plan the wake here at the clubhouse. It's to be a celebration of his life, which is what he would have wanted. He'd want us to laugh and joke, eat, drink, and be merry. And for him, we'll try.

I went into the attic this morning and pulled out boxes of photographs. Caroline and Ally are sorting through to find some good ones of Carl that we'll have blown up and hung on the

273

walls. A Harley emblem in flowers will be placed over the coffin and the word 'Brother' spelled out in white carnations. Chloe called to ask when the funeral was, so we invited her. She was close to Carl, albeit only for a short time, but close nonetheless.

Thursday morning arrives, and we all quietly gather at the clubhouse. Vegas disappears with Spen and returns with a large box. "This is for you. I thought you might want it today." A small smile plays around his eyes as I take the box from him and open it. When I realize what's under the tissue wrapper, I burst into tears and jump into his arms. With my legs wrapped around his waist, he chuckles and sits us on a sofa. I'm trying hard not to cry because it would ruin my makeup, which I applied just for Carl.

"Thank you," I whisper in my man's ear. He holds me close, strokes my back, and then gently smacks my butt.

"Come on, get up and put it on," he tells me.

I oblige and shrug on my new cut. It has the Stormy Souls top rocker on the back, and on the front left, it has three patches. The top one reads, 'Princess,' while the second says, 'Property of Vegas'. A little lower, just above my heart, is the last patch. 'Flakey, 09/20/2021'. Tears well up, and I can't stop a few from falling as the guys stand around me, clapping and hooting. With my hand over Flakey's patch, I take a slight bow.

It's almost time to go, and the roar of bikes is getting louder. Lots of clubs are joining us today to lay Flakey to rest. Restless Slayers MC has sent condolences, flowers, and thirty of their bikes are riding through the gates. I watch as Ghoul, the VP, and Masher, the SAA, step forward, hugging and back-slapping Raven and the other officers.

We mount up and start riding, with Raven at the front on Carl's bike, Slender, and Pennywise, then the other officers and the rest of the members riding in double file formation behind Jamie. The Restless Slayers MC are also riding in formation behind us.

At every corner we pass, more bikes join us. Carl was popular with the small clubs and ordinary citizens, and the advertising for the bone marrow donor drive has touched many. By the time we get to the funeral home and meet the hearse, the line of bikers is massive. The Harley hearse takes the lead, and Jamie raises his arm, the procession waiting to follow behind him. I turn around and see hundreds of bikes behind us. People are stopping in the street, bowing their heads in respect. We ride for about an hour, slowly making our way toward the clubhouse. About a mile away, the hearse stops.

We all stop and take our helmets off. We ride the last mile without lids very slowly. At the gate, the hearse stops again. Raven stands, both feet on the floor, straddling Carl's beloved bike, and starts revving.

The roar of over a hundred Harleys thunders in respect and appreciation of our brother, Carl. He would have loved it.

After a minute, the hearse slowly rolls through the gate, and everyone follows the path to the small cemetery. All bikes are parked on both sides of the road, forming an honor guard along the path to the cemetery while the hearse waits halfway.

Dawg, Dougal, Vegas, Ferret, Jamie, and Slender step up to receive the coffin. They carry our brother to his final resting place, followed by Mom, Pennywise, me, and the rest of the club. The minister holds a short service, and we each throw some earth onto his coffin. The girls each add a flower, and the guys pour a shot of Carl's favorite liquor into the grave. One by one, in our own time, we make our way back down to the clubhouse to celebrate his life.

275

The main room and bar area have been decorated beautifully, with pictures of Carl everywhere, his smile looking at us from every angle. Around us, a lot of singing, drinking, and talking, telling stories about his life, friendships, and mishaps, but above all, about his loyalty.

I look around, smiling. I'm sure Carl is watching and raising his glass to us from Heaven. Vegas has not left my side all day, and when I look at him, it hits me just how lucky I am to have found this remarkable man I love to the moon and back.

He's my strength, my support, my confidante. The one who loves me keeps me safe and in line and makes me unbelievably happy. The emotion is almost overwhelming. I realize I want nothing more than to feel his babies growing inside me, to build a home and a family with him. He's it for me, forever.

I pull on his cut to get his attention and motion to the door. He wraps his arm around me, and we walk outside. Many people are loitering around the picnic tables, and oil drum fires are set up throughout the yard. We make our way to one of the benches, and I stand between Vegas's legs as he sits on the table.

"Are you okay, princess?" he asks softly.

"Have I told you today how much I love you?" I ask softly, leaning in and capturing his lips with mine. As I pull back, I smile up at him. "I'm fine, Vince. I was just looking at you, and a few thoughts crossed my mind."

He looks at me with soft eyes and asks, "Oh, yeah? What are they? Do I need to worry?"

I tilt my head to the side, appearing deep in thought when I reply, "Hmm, that depends, honey. What would you say if I told you I've changed my mind?" I wink at him, but he looks confused.

"About what?" he asks.

"About having ten children with you, of course," I smirk at him. The look on his face is priceless. Several emotions race over his handsome features at once—confusion, shock, understanding—and then he breaks into a blinding smile.

"Have you now?" he asks, pulling me closer. "What changed your mind?"

"I thought about Carl and how we only have one chance at life. We have to live every day as best and as hard as we can. It's not a dress rehearsal. You never know what's around the corner. I don't mind looking back, regretting some things I've done, but if Carl has taught me anything, it's not to have regrets about things I didn't do," I explain. Vegas pulls me even closer and kisses me deeply, his tongue stroking mine languidly. My panties are on fire right now. *How does he manage that with just one kiss?*

"So, princess, when do you want to start practicing?" he whispers in my ear.

"How about right now?" I respond.

A shriek escapes me as he lifts me and carries me through the clubhouse, wolf whistles following us everywhere. He opens the door to his room, then kicks it shut behind us.

Pushing me against the door, he pins me by my wrists, and I can feel his erection pressing into me. He lifts me higher, and I instinctively wrap my legs around his waist. His tongue delves into my mouth, and as I moan, I feel his dick jump in his jeans, putting pressure on my clit.

I balance myself against the door and start rubbing my wet, denim-clad heat against his hardness, chasing the friction I need from him right now. He breaks the kiss and stands back from me, eyes dark with lust.

"Off," he commands, pointing at my clothes. I jump into action and get undressed at lightning speed, toeing off my socks last and kicking them and my jeans away from me. My breasts are heaving, my nipples pebbled, and in dire need of attention. I feel the heat and wetness between my legs and rub my thighs together to give my aching clit some relief. Vegas opens his button fly and takes out his hard length, stroking it. I lick my lips, needing to taste him. Not being able to is driving me insane.

His hands reach under my butt cheeks and lift me. I automatically wrap my legs around his waist again and scream in pleasure when he shoves into me to the hilt in one big push. Whimpering, though not in pain, he reads my reaction and starts fucking me hard against the door. I don't care who hears us. I whimper, moan, mewl, and scream as much and as loud as I need to.

With each long, hard stroke, he's driving me out of my mind and even closer to the edge.

"Yes, baby, fuck me hard," I groan, and he's only too happy to oblige. The tingle of an impending orgasm starts down at my toes and begins to travel upwards.

As wave after wave of pleasure rolls through me, I scream his name and throw my head back. Suddenly, I feel myself fall and bounce on the bed. I hadn't even noticed that we had moved. He's right back inside me, taking my nipple into his mouth, teasing and sucking it, his teeth nibbling it. He bites down, and a sharp pain shoots through me, but as it ebbs away, and instead turns into deep pleasure. He repeats the same with the other nipple, switching his attention back and forth while powering into me. I feel myself building again under his passionate strokes, fucking me hard. Writhing, I fist and clench the bed sheet. I can't keep still, so I push back hard and meet him stroke for stroke.

"You're going to make me come again," I groan breathlessly.

"Come for me, princess," he commands as he clamps his teeth around my nipple. The orgasm that hits me instantly is intense. Wave after wave of ecstasy causes my whole body to spasm. Vegas grunts loudly and roots deep inside me. His hot cum releases into me, again and again, with force, and his erection jumps inside me every time my walls clench around him. It's mind blowing.

We're both trying to catch our breaths when Vegas slowly rolls to the side, taking me with him. I snuggle into him and sigh happily. "You're going to kill me one of those days." He chuckles. "Here lies Vegas, fucked to death by his old lady but died deliriously happy. That's what they'll put on my tombstone," he teases.

"You didn't complain five minutes ago," I banter right back.

◇◇◇

A few hours and several orgasms later, we make it back downstairs, where the party is in full swing. Caroline makes her way toward me, and Vegas smiles and watches her saunter over. At the last moment, she stumbles and bumps into me hard. She grabs hold of my cut and rightens herself.

"So sorry, my lovely, I gotta watch where I'm going. How are you, sweets? What a grand party we've put together. He'd love this!"

She looks at me, her eyes shining with tears, and suddenly so are mine.

"Yeah, Caroline, he'd have loved this." We hug, and she returns to Dawg, who winks at Vegas.

I notice Vegas looking at Raven over the crowd, and they nod to each other. They have finally put their issues aside, and I am happy to see them get on so well now. Raven jumps on top of the bar, and the room slowly quietens.

279

"Now that we're all finally here," he throws a knowing glance at Vegas, and cat calls break out in the room, causing my face to turn bright red with embarrassment, "we can all raise our glasses and remember our brother, Flakey, who in life as in death is unforgettable. He was the best brother anyone could wish for, and he showed strength, loyalty, and dignity right to the end. Thanks to everyone for coming from near and far to support us on this difficult day and to honor our brother. Ride free, brother. May the sun always be at your back."

Raven raises his glass, as do we all. "To Flakey," we all chant together and throw back our glasses filled with his favorite whiskey. A roar rolls through the crowd. When everyone quiets down, Raven turns to Vegas and me.

"As you all have heard by now, Vegas, the reprobate, has claimed our princess as his old lady. He wants to say a few words." I look at Raven in confusion as a quiet hush falls on the room.

Vegas stands tall next to me. "As you can see, I've managed to persuade Ashley, by the skin of my teeth, may I add," laughter erupts around the room, "to wear my cut and be my old lady, for better or for worse, and no one was more surprised than me when she actually agreed." He smiles down at me and pulls me close.

"Get a room," someone shouts from the back.

"Look in your pocket, baby." He smiles at me. I don't understand what's happening, but I push a hand into each of my cut pockets. After a moment of searching, my hand closes around something hard. I pull it out, and as I look up, I see Vegas get on one knee in front of me.

"Open your hand." One hand covers my mouth in pure shock as I open the other, finding the most beautiful diamond solitaire in my palm.

"Ashley Saunders, Princess, I love you with all my heart and want to give you the world and my babies." Snickers break out in the room, and I see Raven roll his eyes while Ally and Caroline are bouncing up and down. Vegas continues, "Will you do me the incredible honor of becoming my wife, old lady, and life partner?"

I'm overwhelmed as the tears start to fall. "Yes! Yes! A thousand times, yes," I shout as I throw myself at Vegas, the ring dropping to the floor as we do, and we lose ourselves in a soul-searing kiss. The ring lands at Ghoul's feet. The VP of the Restless Slayers bends down, picks it up, and hands it to Vegas.

"You better put that on her, bro, before she changes her mind," he says with a wink.

He laughs, and Vegas agrees as he places the ring on my left hand. Then, he pulls me close and whispers, "I'll never let you go, princess. You're mine forever."

EPILOGUE

Six months later

Standing in the bedroom of our house, it isn't easy to comprehend just how fast the last six months have flown by. We've had our trials, but overall, I'm deliriously happy to share my life with the most handsome and special man ever. I'm proud to be Vegas's old lady, and despite the rough times, I've loved every second. I tenderly stroke over my bump while trying not to well up and ruin my makeup. The door opens, and Ally steps in.

"You look beautiful," she exclaims with a big smile. Looking in the mirror, I can hardly believe what I see. A stunning bride in a beautiful, flowy white gown stares back at me. Ally nudges me and hands me a small box. I open it and find a blue garter inside. I smile and hug her tight.

"This is your something new and something blue. I'd say it'll bring you luck and fertility but I think you've already got that covered," she teases me with a grin. I place my foot on the end of the bed, and Ally helps me place the garter on my thigh.

Next is Jamie. He clears his throat and wipes a tear from his eye. "It's not too late, sis; you can still back out," he says jokingly. I shake my head at him, laughing. He steps closer and places a small box in my hand. I open it, and my mouth drops open at seeing my mother's diamond studs I thought were lost so long ago.

"Oh, Jamie, where did you find them?" I ask.

"We found them after the fire when the house was demolished. A workman handed them in. I kept them for you, knowing you'd have wanted a part of her with you," he replies, and I struggle to keep my tears in check. Behind him stands Chloe, who smiles and hugs me.

"Don't mind him; he's just a soppy big brother today." And finally, my maid of honor, Caroline, walks in with the most beautiful jewel-decorated flower veil.

"I wore this when I married Dawg. It was the best and happiest day of my life, and I've never regretted a single moment. Take this as your something borrowed, a crown fit for a princess. May it bring you as much luck and happiness as it's brought us."

I'm fanning my eyes now and can't stop the tears from falling. "No," screeches Caroline, "you'll look like a pregnant corpse bride if you cry." That has all of us burst out laughing. Catastrophe avoided.

My brother takes my hand outside the clubhouse door. The parking lot is crammed full of bikes and cars of all shapes and sizes. "Ready?" he asks. I nod and look at him. He looks so handsome in his white button-down, black jeans, boots, and cut with a white carnation sticking out of his top pocket.

He opens the door, and we step inside. I gasp. The clubhouse is unrecognizable. The old ladies decorated it beautifully with gray and white tulle covering every ceiling and flower arrangements everywhere. It's stunning. Ally, Debs, and Caroline have outdone themselves. I look at Jamie and take a deep breath.

John Legend's "*All of You*" softly sounds through the speakers, and I can hear the rustle of chairs as everyone inside the main room stands. We step forward, my hand on Jamie's arm as he leads me down the aisle toward the man I love more than life itself. I see him swallow, his eyes shining, a bright smile on his face. Jamie hands me over to Vegas and places my hand in his. He kisses me on both cheeks, then steps back, clasps Vegas's shoulder, and makes his way to his seat. Caroline walks up and takes my flowers to hold during the ceremony.

The ceremony passes in a blur, and before I know it, it's my turn to repeat after the minister. "I, Ashley Saunders, take thee, Vincent Albright, to be my lawfully wedded husband. To love and to cherish, to honor and obey, in sickness and in health, 'til death do us part. Take this ring as a token of my love and unbreakable bond." With that, I place the wedding band on his ring finger and smile up at Vegas.

Now, it's his turn. He places the wedding band on my finger and looks deep into my eyes, his blazing with pride and love as he recites his vows. Finally, we hear, "You may now kiss your bride."

He pulls me close, bends me over his arm, and kisses me senseless. When he lets me up, I'm breathless, and the room is cheering and stomping their feet.

The rest of the day flies by. We take our congratulations, enjoy a massive BBQ and buffet club style, cut the cake, and dance until the early hours. We watch our family and friends join in our celebration and love for each other. Nathan has made his way home for the wedding and is staying in his old room at the house that Dawg and Caroline bought from me. Nathan has his own room at our house, but he preferred to spend tonight at Dawgs's.

The only person missing from my big day is Sarah. Her mother died last week, and she had to attend her funeral today. I miss her dearly.

I look at Vegas, and my heart pitter-patters. He takes my breath away in his gray button-down under his cut, his white carnation in his pocket, and his new 'Vice President' patch. I'm so proud of him and proud to be with him. He deserved the recognition after the last few months, which have been difficult. Right now, though, all I want is to be alone with my new husband.

As if he can read my mind, he gets up, and we make our excuses and our exit. Instead of a proper honeymoon, we decided to lock all the doors and have a long weekend with just the two of us at the house. But tonight, we're driving to a posh local hotel to spend the night in the honeymoon suite. Tacky, I know, but worth every dollar.

We check-in and open the door with our keycard to find they've already brought our bags.

"You look stunning, wife," Vegas declares, and I smile at him.

"And you're the most handsome, hottest husband ever," I reply. He steps behind me and wraps his arms around me as we look out the window into the dark night. He cups my bump and strokes it tenderly, as he often does.

I found out I was pregnant four months ago. Counting back the days, it must have happened at the Slayers rally, but everything went crazy, so I didn't notice for a while. I blamed my missing period on the stress we'd all been under. Vegas went with me when I had my first appointment, and we saw our baby's heartbeat on the monitor. We're deliriously happy and don't want to know the sex of the baby. We'd like it to be a surprise.

Dougal and Sarah are together now, and I imagine they'll be moving in together soon. Dougal is very taken with her and would do anything for her. He gets on excellent with Leo and can better manage his autistic idiosyncrasies and special needs than Sarah. He's growing into a great father for Leo.

I lean into Vegas, resting my head against his shoulder. "Take me to bed, stud, and make me your wife," I murmur. He lifts me into his arms and smiles down at me as he places me gently onto the bed.

"Your wish is my command, princess."

THE END

Printed in Great Britain
by Amazon